ROSE OF ANZIO

Book Three ~ Desire

Alexa Kang

ISBN-10: 1535335742
ISBN-13: 9781535335744

Acknowledgements

Rose of Anzio began as a personal challenge for me, but over the course of last year, I discovered that writing a full-length novel (four novels, in fact) is a group project. Words alone cannot express my gratitude to everyone who had encouraged me and helped me bring this series to its completion. I am still amazed at the time and efforts of those who volunteered to help me make this story stronger and better.

Thanks to Anneth White, who first encouraged me to write this story and continuing to inspire me by following it faithfully throughout. Thank you to Pamela Ann Savoy, who gave me great feedback on story ideas and development along the way, and took time out of her super busy schedule to proofread my work as I wrote. My utmost gratitude to Brandon Bjorklund, a fellow writer and good friend who reached out to teach me the ropes of self-publishing, and gave me valuable advice and support throughout the process. Also, a very special thank you to Ms. CandyTerry, who gave me a huge amount of moral support, as well as the first platform for me to introduce this story.

My heartfelt thank you to both Kristen Tate, my editor, whose suggestions and insights helped me improve my story significantly. A special thank you to military historian Geoff Byers, for his tremendous help and advice on how to create and construct my battle scenes throughout the entire series, so I could keep the story as realistic as possible, and also to Aaron Sikes, my battle scenes editor, for making sure my war story stays grounded. Thanks to Stephen Reid, for making sure Tessa speaks proper British English. Thanks also to my proofreaders T.J. Moore and Patrick Cunningham, for making my story a truly polished piece of work.

Last but not least, thanks to my husband, Dan, for his unending amount of patience and support.

PART ONE

Anzio

Chapter 1

The Gustav Line.

At their base on the Anzio beachhead in a meeting with his company's officers, Anthony stared at that cursed German defense line on the map on the table. Entrenched in the Apennine Mountains between Naples and Rome, the Gustav Line had been the bane of their existence since the Allies broke out of Sicily and entered the region of Monte Cassino. He felt sorry for the Fifth Army soldiers who were still fighting there, but he was more than glad when the Third Division was directed to be part of Operation Shingle to invade Anzio.

He remembered the times in the last few months when he had to fight in the Monte Cassino region, when he began each mission climbing up those mountains. Those mountains were the number one reason why the Allies hadn't been able to push their own front forward. Not even an inch. They cut northeast to southwest across Italy and ran into the Liri Valley. The Liri Valley should have been the Allies' natural entrance to attack the German front, except it was protected by large hills.

If one could even call them hills. The first time Anthony came upon these hills, he thought they looked like nothing less than mountains. Every time they were sent out there, he would look up and wonder how they could possibly break through. On the top, the Germans were looking down, surveilling their every move and advance, ready to either pick them off one by one or shell them all at once as they attempted to mount their way up. Every mission was a death march. Every order to attack was a death sentence. They were as good as lambs offered for sacrifice at the enemy's altar. He had never felt more vulnerable.

Of course, he and everyone else followed the orders and marched forward. They had no choice. But in his mind, he wondered how they could stand a chance. The terrain had made success seem impossible. The only thing he could do was pray. Each time they went on an assault, he would look up toward the ancient abbey of Monte Cassino sitting at the top of those hills. He would tug Tessa's cross around his neck, say a prayer, and cross his heart. He did this even though it was rumored that the Germans had taken the abbey as their command outpost and the enemy might be dwelling in the heart of the temple to which he sent his prayers. Considering how things were going, he would take divine intervention from wherever it came.

As if the treacherous mountain terrain wasn't enough, the endless rain added another layer of challenge. Their armored vehicles and tanks couldn't get up the slippery mountains where the Germans waited in hiding. The rain caused constant flooding of the Rapido River, which ran east to west across the Liri Valley. The river became a natural fortress of water preventing them from getting across to the enemy. Besides all that, he was always wet. His clothes were always soaked, his foxhole always flooded, his tent always drenched.

When the rain finally stopped, snow came. Lots of snow. Sometimes, the blizzards blinded them. Other times, the snow fused with the rain, turning into sleet. A last strike against them as the freezing drops drove down like final nails in their coffins.

In only four months, he had endured enough misery to last him a lifetime.

This hopeless situation was what brought the Third Division here to Anzio, the small beach resort town thirty-five miles south of Rome and sixty miles north of the Gustav Line behind the German front. Their mission was to attack the Gustav Line from the rear and divert some of the German troops fortified in the Apennine Mountains away to the Anzio region so that the Allied divisions still fighting at Monte Cassino could finally break through.

His company had arrived at Anzio three days ago. D-day on January 22, at 0200 hours. No rest for the weary as the new year of 1944 began.

As if to reward them for all they had suffered in the last few months, their Anzio arrival had been a total success. Their amphibious landing surprised the Germans, who unbelievably put up no ground resistance. The Luftwaffe attempted a half-hearted defense from the air, but the American Navy's anti-aircraft units easily put that to an end. In less than two days, the Allied attack forces had secured the beachhead. Their reconnaissance unit even drove into Rome unopposed. Compared to how things were going back at Monte Cassino, their landing at Anzio was a walk in the park. Their next move was obvious. They should continue on and seize as many tactical positions as they could.

So why were they stalling instead of pushing ahead? Anthony could not understand. Why was Captain Harding even debating with them about this?

Along with Wesley, their company's first lieutenant, Anthony tried to make every argument he could think of to support Wesley's advice for them to advance with full force. Warren, Anthony's old University of Chicago classmate who was now an intelligence officer working with their unit, was behind them too. They wanted Harding to make the same recommendation to the command, but Harding would not take their suggestion seriously.

Wesley pointed to the area on the map where the railway connecting Rome and the south ran adjacent to Highways 6 and 7. "If we attack now, we can take over Alban Hills. We should urge regiment command to block off Highway 6." He kept his voice calm and respectful even though Harding remained noncommittal. Anthony could not help but marvel at Wesley's patience. This was the third time Wesley had made this suggestion.

Across from Wesley, Harding leaned away from the table and crossed his arms. "Command wants to consolidate the beachhead. We can't do that if we divert troops to Alban Hills."

Anthony looked at the spot marked Alban Hills on the map. The place was only twenty miles inland from their base at the Anzio beach. The area extended to Highway 6 where the railroad passed between Rome and the German front. If they seized the highway now, they could cut off the German supply line from Rome. They could expand inland to cut off Highway 7 at Valmontone and trap the German forces garrisoned in the Apennine Mountains. The Germans would then be diverted on two fronts between the Allied forces at Anzio and at Monte Cassino with their supplies cut off. If the German defenses were weakened, the Gustav Line might finally fall.

Breaking the Gustav Line. Wasn't that their ultimate goal? So why were they stalling to consolidate the beachhead?

"We need to alert regiment to what's at stake." Anthony leaned over the table toward the captain. "Alban Hills and Highway 6 are undefended. They're there for the taking now. We'll lose this chance when German reinforcements arrive."

Unconvinced, Harding shifted his body from one side to the other, then back again.

"We're running out of time, Captain."

"He's right," Warren said. He had been observing their conversation the entire time, but was mindful not to overstep his role by telling those in charge of tactical command what to do. "All our intelligence reports are showing the Krauts heading back to this area. There's a massive mobilization of troops coming in from other parts of Italy, and from France and the Baltics too." He pushed one of the reports on the table toward Harding.

Harding picked up the first few pages of the report with one hand, leaving his other arm still crossed against his chest. He scanned the first page, raising an eyebrow without any show of commitment.

"It won't be long before they arrive," Warren said. "When they do, we might not have any hope for an offensive anymore."

Harding tossed the pages down. "I hardly think we have enough troops for an all-out attack now." Ready to end the discussion, he straightened his back and stood firm. "Command said to wait for reinforcements. We wait."

Reinforcements? Anthony thought to himself. There were no real reinforcements coming. "Captain," he said, trying his best to persuade Harding without crossing him, "command barely spared enough troops to carry out the Anzio mission. The only reinforcements we have are the battalions that haven't arrived yet. If there are any reinforcements left, they'll be sent to France to support Normandy."

Harding raised his eyebrow again, more subtly this time but Anthony could see that it mattered little to the captain what he thought. Back when they were still fighting their way toward Naples, Wesley had told him that Harding had intentionally sent an inexperienced second lieutenant like Anthony to lead a dangerous attack because the replacements had little to contribute and they made good human shields for the more experienced fighters. The revelation shattered everything Anthony had thought he knew. The captain was not the benevolent leader he appeared to be when they first met.

In the months that followed, Anthony had come to realize that he, along with the rest of the infantry soldiers and noncoms under his command, were nothing more than dispensable tools for Harding. The only exception was Wesley. Wesley was a rare soldier whom everyone considered to be a perfect fighter. Harding usually gave weight to Wesley's opinions, but not always. As Wesley had said, the captain had his own agenda. What that agenda might be, Anthony could never guess. And now, he couldn't figure out why Harding was resisting their suggestions either.

"Command may have plans we don't know about yet." An odd, fervid gleam flickered in Harding's eyes. Anthony couldn't make out what it meant, but it unsettled him. "Our order is to hold," the captain said. "We'll hold. We'll secure the beachhead." He straightened up to indicate the discussion was over. "That'll be all, gentlemen." He acknowledged them and took his leave.

After he left, Anthony turned to Wesley. "That's it? There's nothing we can do?"

Wesley gave him a stern look. Anthony thought the situation had come to a dead end, but Wesley's expression loosened and he pulled a photo out of a file on the table. The photo showed a German Wehrmacht officer, an intelligent-looking man in his early thirties with a cunning demeanor.

"This is German Army Major Heinrich Klaus, star commanding officer on the battlefield. He's the reason why the captain doesn't want to push ahead."

Anthony looked at him, puzzled.

"When we first took Sicily, Klaus was leading the German defense on the ground. He was only a captain then, a Wehrmacht Hauptmann. We found him when we attacked and captured a German outpost, except we didn't know then he was with the Wehrmacht. He was wearing an American army uniform."

"What?"

"He pretended to be an American army captain and a prisoner of war captured by the Germans."

Anthony looked more closely at the man in the photo.

"He spoke perfect American English. We found out later he spoke perfect Italian too. We questioned him every way we could. His answers were impeccable. He had us all fooled."

Anthony thought about how Klaus might have come to possess an American army uniform, but he didn't want to ask what had happened. Most likely, Klaus and his men had captured a real American army captain, interrogated him, and killed him. That must have been how Klaus could deceive even Wesley. Klaus had enough information to pass himself off as one of them.

"We verified everything as best as we could, but all the troops had just landed in Sicily. Communications were terrible. Everything was disorganized. All the units were still trying to link up. He was with us for two days. He and the captain spent quite some time together. They hit it off like brothers. He was very helpful too when we were making our way in and needed to gather information from the locals. Unfortunately, he also gathered a lot of information from us." Wesley's eyes tensed. "Including some that were military secrets. He got most of that from Captain Harding himself."

Anthony widened his eyes. "What happened then?"

"Then he disappeared. When we finally regrouped with the rest of our division, we found out who he really was."

Anthony exchanged glances with Warren. Warren looked as surprised as he was. Anthony picked up the photo. "Did regiment know?"

Wesley smiled but didn't answer.

"There were reports of Company M finding a captain from the 45th Division who was reported missing," Warren said, his voice hesitant as he too was still taking in what Wesley had just told them. "He was lost again, presumed dead."

Wesley took the photo of Klaus. "The captain vowed he would never let Klaus off if he finds him again." He gave Anthony a grave, cautionary look before putting the photo back into the file. "Well, we just learned, Klaus is now a major. He's someone high on division command's radar. He's commanding and leading the German's Anzio ground defense under Kesselring."

"That means Klaus is on the way here," Warren said.

"Is that why the captain doesn't want us to push on?" Anthony asked.

Wesley glanced at the entrance. When he was sure no one was near, he said, "The captain won't give up any chance to get Klaus. If Klaus is coming here, the captain is ready to meet him here." Without waiting for Anthony and Warren's response, he gathered up the files. "You're never to discuss this with anyone else," he said and left the tent.

Still trying to get his mind around what Wesley had told them, Anthony remembered that Wesley had warned him that it was up to the two of them to look out for their men because the captain had his own agenda. Wesley had known all along that Harding would sacrifice those he commanded if it served his own purposes. Realization finally dawned on Anthony. They were lucky Wesley was their XO. Wesley was not merely an executive officer doing Harding's bids. He had been protecting them the entire time despite the captain.

With a heavy heart, Anthony walked outside with Warren. He looked out to the sea. The breezy air and smooth ocean waves made a peaceful beach scene that felt surreal considering what was happening here.

The calm before the storm, he thought.

The sound of a distant bomb explosion brought him back to reality. Two days ago, there were only scattered pops of gunfire and occasional *rat-a-tats* of Luftwaffe airplane engines overhead. Now, the artillery noises had grown more frequent. Not constant, but undoubtedly increasing. He could feel the German forces closing in.

"Come here," Warren said. "I want you to see something." Anthony followed him as they climbed on top of one of the empty tanks nearby. "There." Warren pointed out to the mountains miles behind the beach and took out his binoculars to survey the view. "This is not going to be good."

Apprehensive, Anthony waited to hear what Warren had to say. Warren always had exceptional insights when he assessed their immediate situation. Anthony also knew Warren often told him more than he would to other army officers, including opinions that Warren kept off the record. Warren never forgot how Anthony had helped and supported him when they were classmates back in Chicago. Their friendship came before the army took over their lives. Ranks and military rules hadn't changed that.

"The beachhead is wide open and the mountains are all around it." Warren lowered the binoculars. "It's Monte Cassino all over again." He pointed his finger across the mountain ranges. "The Krauts are gonna see everything we're doing down on the beach from every direction."

Anthony's heart sank further.

"No. I take it back," Warren said. "This is worse than Cassino. We have no barriers or protection down here. None at all. We're a front without a rear, unless you count the sea as our rear."

Anthony looked from the mountains down to the beach and to the ocean and beyond. He wondered if anyone in high command saw what they were seeing. From where they stood, the beach stretched fifteen miles between Anzio and another small town called Nettuno. In between the two towns, there was not even a tree or a building behind which anyone could hide. Coming from inland, the Germans would set up their defense at the top of the mountains. From there, they would have a wide-open view to observe the Allies' every move.

Even if their own troops got to the mountains first, there was no way they could defend the entire span of the mountain ranges. Their best chance was to take over Highway 6 and cripple the Germans' life support before they arrived.

"Can't you do something?" Anthony asked.

"I can only pass on the information and analysis. I've made my recommendations. It's up to command and the combat forces to decide what to do." Warren gave him a regretful smile.

Anthony tensed. "This is so frustrating." He looked out to the beach again. The arriving convoys and the staff units were still busy transporting loads of vehicles and containers from the Navy vessels to land. Large piles of supplies and equipment as high as houses had been dumped on the beach, awaiting collection. Trucks and vehicles were circling about everywhere, while servicemen tried to direct traffic and maintain a semblance of order. No one seemed to be aware of the dire situation they were in.

"Can I see?" he asked Warren, pointing at the binoculars. Warren handed them to him, and he took a closer look at the sites beyond the crew transporting their supplies.

Further down the beach, the first platoons of the medical battalion had arrived. They were setting up the tents of the field hospital. He could tell because each tent was marked with a giant red cross. Tessa was due to arrive in a few days. She would soon be joining the medical units there.

Tessa ... Panic seized him. He looked at the mountains again. The field hospital was entirely exposed. It was within the range of enemy fire.

He lowered the binoculars and looked out at the full stretch of the beach. The entire Allied base was exposed to direct enemy attack.

Tessa would be at the center of the battlefield.

Chapter 2

First, there were the long, high-pitched whistles of airplanes. Then, the booms of exploding bombs. The fiery sounds roared louder and louder with each step they climbed. When the passengers reached the deck of the medical ship, the noises had become so unimaginably deafening that, for a brief second, Tessa thought the raging noise might shatter and crack the shell of the earth.

The sounds were only the beginning, a prelude to the horror she was about to see. Outside on the deck, a haunting theater of hellfire greeted her eyes. Billows of black smoke filled the sky like sick, corroded clouds. German planes zoomed above her in every direction, chased by the lights of artillery fire shooting up from the Allies' ships and anti-aircraft units on the ground. To retaliate, the German planes dropped a storm of bombshells into the sea, creating geysers of exploding water that erupted all around them. Undeterred, the Allies returned fire. Lethal missiles from their naval forces sped through the air toward the enemies in the mountains behind the beach, the same beach where Tessa and the 33rd Field hospital unit were preparing to land.

"Tessa, I'm scared," Gracie said as they walked toward the nets of rope ladders hanging off the side of the ship. To get to their landing craft, they would need to climb down one of those like monkeys in a jungle. She took Gracie's hand and held it tight. Inside, her own heart was pounding.

Was this how Anthony had lived since he came to battle in Italy? He never told her things were this bad. Her heart ached to think that this was what he had been living through. He had arrived at Anzio days earlier. She wondered where he was now. Was he safe?

While she waited for her turn to disembark, she looked out at the landing crafts that had already gone ahead. They were just boats, really. They floated in groups except for the few that were straggling behind, separated from the rest by the formidable tides of the sea. All were trying to follow the pilot boats in the front guiding them ashore. Against the thundering gunfire in the sky and the furious waves in which they floated, they looked so small and fragile. So insignificant. Like clusters of discarded matchsticks tossing around in the sea.

For the first time in her life, she was facing something she could not surmount by the sheer force of will. Her body trembled and her legs shook as she climbed down the ladder.

She stepped onto the landing craft and nearly tripped. The landing craft swung sharply back and forth and the planks beneath her feet swayed. People all around her were shouting and shuffling but she couldn't make out what they were saying. She felt lost in the chaos. A corpsman grabbed her arm and pulled her in the direction of a spot where she could sit down. She took a step and, losing her footing, slammed into another man. "Sorry," she said, but she couldn't even hear herself. Almost crawling, she continued making her way there, grabbing on to anything she could to avoid being knocked about by the rocking of the boat. She finally got to the spot. Once there, it was all she could do to hold on and not fall over.

The landing craft motored toward the beach, but there was no hope of smooth sailing. The relentless waves thwacked them and splashed water all over the boat. The violent waves made Tessa's stomach churn and she wanted to throw up. People were still shouting and yelling all around her. The bombs and shells were still thundering from above. She felt like the whole world was spinning.

"Why aren't we landing?" someone yelled.

"We can't land until the Krauts stop shelling the harbor," another person hollered.

Tessa took a deep breath and looked at the beach ahead. The shores were within their reach, but the helmsman kept them circling around and around. The queasiness in her stomach had risen to her chest and her throat. She could no longer think. She only wanted everything to stop.

After what felt like endless hours, the sounds of gunfire subsided. The beach became quiet and only the splashes of ocean waves and the drumming of their boat's engine remained. The German planes were gone.

Tessa glanced at her watch as their landing craft began to steer ashore. She couldn't believe they had been circling around for only forty-five minutes.

They had no time to rest once they reached the shore. They needed to set up the hospital and their camp quarters, which were approximately six miles from the front line and barely off the beach between the small towns of Anzio and Nettuno. She tried to determine where they were in relation to everything else going on, but it was hard to orient herself to her surroundings. So many units from different army divisions were moving around, each preoccupied with their own set up and transport of equipment.

She followed the authorities' instructions and helped with the setup of their own hospital. They had to prepare the operating rooms, the beds, and the pharmacy at once. There was no time to lose. But even with Captain Fran Milton, their hospital's chief nurse, going around shouting orders in her most commanding voice, nothing could be done quickly. Equipment and supplies arrived in sporadic order. Their surgical equipment had been contaminated by sea water and needed to be sterilized. X-ray machines were damaged in transit and required repairs. A host of problems arose before they were even up and running.

Thankfully, the kitchen staff came and brought them refreshments. Wanting to find someone to join her for a short break, Tessa looked around for Ellie, the young nurse who had recruited her to become a cadet nurse back in Chicago and her closest friend here at the 33rd. Ellie was bringing a cup of coffee to Dr. Haley. Immediately, Fran Milton came and sent Ellie away. Dr. Haley's eyes, though, followed Ellie as she hurried away. Not pleased with the way her friend was being treated, Tessa gave Milton a cold glance and returned to the tasks at hand.

Setting up the hospital with the rest of the medical staff was a challenge, but setting up their own sleeping tent was outright impossible. A corpsman was supposed to come and help them, but no one had shown up. Tessa stared at the canvas and the poles. She had learned how to build a tent back when she was training in Chicago, but it was useless. The instructor had not imagined the rough conditions of the beachhead. Gracie was of no help. She was too much of a girly girl.

"My father used to take me and my brother on camping trips when we were little," Gracie said. "If I had known I would have to build my own tent someday, I would've asked them to teach me. I didn't think a girl would ever have to set up camp. When they taught us to build tents back in training, I didn't think we girls would really have to do it."

Having no other choice, they tied the pieces together and erected the tent as best as they could. When they finished, Tessa stood back and looked at what they had built. The poles were tilting to one side. No doubt, it would eventually topple over.

"It'll hold for now, I guess," she said.

"No it won't," a familiar voice said from behind her. "It's going to collapse on you while you sleep."

She turned around right away when she heard that voice. "Anthony!" How did he find her? Until this moment, she hadn't even been sure when they could meet up again after arriving at Anzio.

She ran up to him as he approached her with a shovel in his hand. Relieved to see him safe after the horrifying scene she had witnessed upon her arrival, she embraced him. His ragged uniform was covered with dirt. He wrapped his free arm around her and looked down with tired, weary eyes. She had never seen him look so drained and exhausted.

"You look beat," he said, stroking her back.

"I was going to say the same thing about you," she laughed. "How did you know where to find us?"

"It's easy to find everything on this beach." His voice was oddly cautious and she wondered why.

"Hi, Lieutenant Ardley," Gracie said. Anthony gave her a half smile. She gave them both a knowing look and said to Tessa, "I'll go check and see if anyone else needs help."

With Gracie gone, Anthony laid down the shovel and straightened the tent poles.

"What's the shovel for?" Tessa asked.

"I'm digging you a foxhole."

"A foxhole? Is that necessary?" It hadn't occurred to her that she would have to dig a foxhole for herself.

He frowned and tightened his lips, but didn't answer. She watched as he tightened the strings holding the tent together.

"Better safe than sorry," he said after he secured the tent in place. "I guess I'll dig one for Gracie too." He picked up the shovel and dug into the ground adjacent to their tent. The digging and shoveling were wearing him out further.

"You don't have to do this," Tessa said. "Why don't you leave that to us? I can dig one myself, or we can find someone to help us later."

"No!" The firm tone of his voice surprised her. She stood by until he finished. He dug one foxhole on each side of the tent. He then took her cot inside. She pushed aside the opening flap of the tent and watched him unroll her cot by the side of the tent next to one of the foxholes.

"If you're sleeping, you can roll under the tent into the hole." He lifted the bottom of the canvas next to her cot to show her. He looked so serious, she didn't know what to say.

He came back out of the tent and looked out at the mountains behind the beach. She wondered why he was acting so strange. Even though they were both tired, they should be happy to see each other. Instead, he had barely cracked a smile. He hadn't said much either. He didn't even ask her about her journey here. His mind seemed preoccupied with something else.

He put his hand on her shoulder and looked at her. She couldn't understand the expression in his eyes. He tightened his grip on her.

"I have to go," he said. "I'll try to come see you whenever I can."

She touched his arm. This was not how she thought it would be when they met up again, him digging her a foxhole and them having hardly a chance to talk. She wanted to ask him to stay longer, but her instincts stopped her.

"Get into the foxhole whenever any gunfire or bombing gets too near. Okay? Promise me you'll do that?"

"I will."

He let go of her. "It's okay to sleep in it."

She glanced at the foxhole. It was a temporary shield from gunfire, wasn't it? Why would she sleep in it? Had he been on the front line too long? Was his experience out there making him paranoid?

"Anthony, are you all right?" she asked.

He looked startled. Then his face relaxed. "It's a running joke between the guys. We call it a hotel. Jonesy has a sign stuck above his foxhole. It says 'Waldorf-Astoria'." He smiled. A natural, genuine smile.

"I'm thinking of putting a sign up in mine and calling it the Ardley Estate and send a photo of it to Father and Uncle Leon. They'll be proud to know I'm acquiring property for us in Italy."

She gave him an uneasy smile back. She still didn't know what to make of his bizarre behavior.

Then his smile was gone again. A shadow of fear fleeted past his eyes. He stroked her cheek and gave her a light kiss on the lips. "Be careful," he said.

"You too."

She watched him walk away. His lonely figure disappeared into the chaotic traffic of army units. Although they were no longer oceans apart, she still could not truly be with him and share all his burdens.

Chapter 3

Eight days had passed since Anthony and his unit had landed in Anzio, and nothing about their mission was going as planned.

Operation Shingle was planned to be a quick amphibious assault. Improbably, the Allies succeeded. The joint American-British Fifth Army forces had waltzed onto Anzio beach with virtually no resistance from the Germans. The outcome was beyond their wildest hopes. The siege of Anzio was quick and should have been over already.

But then, things began to falter. Their army had let the opportunity for a decisive battle slip by. Instead of pushing inland to force a German retreat, the Allied command had stalled. They chose to hunker down to secure the beachhead and stayed put. And now, with all their battalions convened and going nowhere, their troops sat on the beach like a giant flock of sitting ducks waiting to be culled. While they stalled, masses of German troops had moved in, surrounding them with Panzer tanks. Kraut guns were always pointing at them and firing from every possible direction. There was no more hope for a quick end to the battle.

"I had hoped we were hurling a wildcat into the shore," British Prime Minister Winston Churchill reportedly said, "but all we got is a stranded whale." His remark was widely repeated on the radio.

Alban Hills was no longer an easy option to cut off the roads that served as the German supply line. To cut off the railroad and Highway 7, the Allies must now seize the town of Cisterna, and the Third Division troops were being sent to complete that task. The plan was for the Ranger battalion to enter Cisterna in the middle of the night to spearhead the attack. Their infantry battalion would then follow as reinforcements, fanning out by company to surround the town when daylight came.

The Rangers had gone ahead hours ago. As he marched with his company toward Cisterna, Anthony couldn't help but wonder if he, Wesley, and Warren could have made a stronger case to convince Captain Harding that continuing their assault after their Anzio landing was their best course of action. If Captain Harding had relayed the urgency of forging ahead to command, perhaps they would not be in this situation now. He replayed their meeting with Harding when they first arrived in his mind, questioning whether he could have tried harder or done anything differently.

The sudden rattle of machine guns jolted him out of these thoughts. Without warning, the enemy opened fire from a web of interlocked machine gun nests about two hundred yards ahead. The guns unleashed a hail of bullets, slicing down half their men in the lead. A barrage of artillery followed. The Krauts lobbed shells in from behind the line of machine gun nests. With weapons exploding around them left and right, everyone in their unit who could still run scrambled for cover.

Anthony dropped to the ground, trying to think amidst the tempest of gunfire and screams. How could this be happening? Cisterna was still two miles away. A German counterattack at this juncture wasn't supposed to happen. This was not how their Cisterna mission was planned. What had happened with the Rangers up front?

He looked behind him. Where were the Sherman tanks that were supposed to be right behind their company? Why couldn't they ever show up when infantry needed them?

Nothing about this hellish operation was going as planned.

He surveyed the field around him. Although the bushes and weeds could provide temporary cover, there was no good place for them to hide on these flat grounds. They couldn't turn back either. If they tried to run, they would be out in the open and the enemy would annihilate them. They had only one choice. They had to try to take out the enemy.

Wesley was already ahead, waving his hand from the ground for everyone to follow him. They crawled forward behind Wesley, waiting for his signal.

The German guns were still spitting out bullets in the air above them. Anthony could hear them zipping by just inches above him. Crawling with his Tommy gun pointing forward, he took another quick look ahead. He saw bodies of their own men spread out across the field. Not just the bodies moving forward, but also dead bodies. Maimed bodies. Bodies of men shot and writhing in pain.

The Germans fired round after round. Under the blasting machine gun and artillery noise, he could hear the pounding of his own heart.

# # #

From where he was crawling on the ground, Jesse Garland could see the two wounded men lying next to each other about fifty yards in front of him. One of them was Clayton, the signal company officer. The other was a new replacement, a young boy whose name he didn't know. A few other soldiers near them had tried to get closer to rescue them, but they barely moved a few feet before a torrent of machine gun bullets forced them to dive back down onto the ground. No one could get to them.

Even if they could get to them, Jesse knew he was still the only one who could help them. There was no other medic nearby. Should he take the risk against the unrelenting enemy fire?

The replacement was howling in pain, wailing for his mother.

This was something that he kept seeing over and over again. When the GIs were hit and feared they were about to die, they didn't cry out for their fathers. They didn't cry out for God. They didn't cry out for Uncle Sam. They cried out for their mothers.

If he were ever hit and mortally wounded, he hoped he would remember not to cry out for his mother. But of course, he would not cry out for her. He couldn't remember a single instance when he had ever asked for her help or when she had come running to his aid. In any case, he didn't need her. His best protection was right here in his pocket.

He reached into his pocket and turned the lucky seven dice between his fingers. They were hooked to a chain that he used to wear around his neck. He no longer wore the chain. Instead, he had wrapped it around his belt to make sure he would not lose the dice in case the chain broke. He had had these dice since his eighteenth birthday when Quayle took him to Atlantic City where he had won his first high-stakes poker game. That game was not just another small-time bet against two-bit chumps. He had won it for real money. When the game ended, he wiped everyone empty at the craps table too. Afterward, he easily talked the pretty croupier into giving him the pair of dice before he left, telling her he would carry them as his lucky charm because of her magic touch. And with that little bit of flattery, he got lucky with her too, making a clean sweep of the night.

When the night ended and all was left behind him, he found the dice still in his pocket. He had all but forgotten about them after he left the casino with the girl, but when he saw them again the next day, he had a strange thought that they wanted to follow him home. He decided to keep them. It felt right having them on him. They were a souvenir to remind him of his streak of good luck the day he turned eighteen. A few days later, he passed by a street artist selling miniature sculptures near his brownstone apartment. On a whim, he paid the artist to put an extra dot in the centers of the sixth faces. He had carried the dice with him ever since. He liked to think that, if nothing else, he could always count on them to give him good luck. He turned them between his fingers one more time.

Spurts of gunfire continued to erupt, pinning them all down. A soldier crawled up next to him. "Garland, let's try—" Before the soldier could finish what he was saying, a stray bullet zipped toward him and struck him, killing him instantly.

Jesse watched him fall flat onto the ground and let out a quick breath. That was a close call. If the soldier hadn't crawled up to talk to him, the bullet would have hit him instead. He closed his hand around his dice and squeezed. The dice had come through for him once again.

Or maybe, the dice had nothing to do with anything. Sometimes, he thought the three Fates liked to play a game of cat and mouse with him, denying him what everyone else had but giving him what everyone else wanted. Such pranksters, those three malicious sisters of Moirai. Of all the people here, he was the most dispensable. If anyone must be KO'd, he should be the first to go. And yet, Death had spared him more times than he could count since he was deployed. The odds kept favoring him even though no one would miss him should he disappear from the face of the earth. Meanwhile, Death continued to pick off the others, one after another.

He glanced at the dead soldier. He wondered if the man had any loved ones waiting for him back home. As the army battled on, he watched everything that happened like an outsider observing how fate unfolded for the others. These men, they all carried pictures of their girlfriends or wives or kids or parents and whatever other mementos of people who were waiting for them to return. They tried to keep a symbolic closeness to the people who would remember them in case they didn't return. It was a form of solace, perhaps, to carry such items. Maybe it was the only way a soldier could believe he was significant when, every day, there were shells and gunfire to remind him that he was nothing but insignificant.

Unlike these men, he had no one waiting for him. He had no photos from home to carry, and he already knew he was insignificant. No matter how badly the war went, it couldn't take anything more from him. He had nothing to lose. He felt detached from it all.

He carried nothing except his dice, the tokens to remind himself that he still had luck on his side.

The replacement was still bawling. He and Clayton were lying there, exposed. Someone needed to rescue them soon or they would die.

Jesse loosened his hand and turned the dice one more time. Could his luck rub off on the others? Those two sure needed some of that luck right now.

The fiery gunfire above them continued.

He decided to make a go of it to get to them. If the Fates wanted to play, he was in. After all, what higher stakes game was there than the game of tempting Fate?

With a smirk, he glanced up at the sky.

Take me. I dare you.

He wondered if the Fates could hear him.

"Mama… I want my ma. Where's my mama?" the replacement blubbered on. "Help me! Help me! Somebody help me!" His cries turned to hysterics and his words slurred.

Staring at the boy, Jesse felt a spate of resentment and his smirk disappeared. The senselessness of the world and everything around him repulsed him. He looked up at the sky again.

Take me then. I dare you.

Unfazed by the bullets crisscrossing the air, he crawled toward the two wounded men. His movements drew the enemy's attention. Immediately, they targeted him. A bullet knocked his helmet and it fell off his head, landing two feet away from him. He rolled away from it just in time before another followed and hit the helmet where it had landed. The impact of the bullets sent the helmet bouncing up from the ground and further away. When the firing stopped, he stared at the helmet, stunned.

What? A double dare?

Leaving the helmet, he turned his attention back to the wounded men and resumed his movement their way, crawling toward them until he came close enough to see how severely injured they were. The replacement was lying on his back with his hand over his stomach. Blood gushed out between his fingers. Beside him, a few feet away, Clayton lay trembling in pain. A sheen of sweat spread across his face and he was having difficulty breathing. Jesse looked around, wondering where he could take them. He saw a dip in the field not too far from them. The spot, about eight feet wide, could give them temporary cover if he could get them both over there.

He crawled over to Clayton. "Hold on," he shouted out to the replacement. "I'll get you next." Without waiting for the boy to answer, he pulled opened Clayton's jacket and revealed his sucking chest wound. As he did so, he noticed two of Clayton's fingers were gone.

Jesse got up on his knees to retrieve bandages from his bag. A barrage of gunfire came at him again.

"Cover him!" someone shouted, calling for the others to save him. It might have been Fox, Company M's young sharpshooter, but he couldn't be sure.

He patched up Clayton's wound with vaselined gauze and sealed the bandages as tightly as he could, leaving one edge of the bandage free so the excess air in Clayton's chest cavity could escape. All the while, bullets were flying past him. The bullets did not let up when he dragged Clayton to the safe spot he had found. Miraculously, the storm of bullets had left them both unscathed. Luck had not abandoned him.

He took a deep breath, then left Clayton and crawled back over to the replacement. This time, he didn't even try to hide. Ignoring the continuous gunfire blazing around him, he got on his knees to help the boy, jabbing a shot of morphine into him and spattering sulfa on the flesh of his open wound. Somehow, despite making no attempt to conceal himself while he tended to the boy, all the enemy bullets missed him until a shell exploded near them. The blast pounded his eardrums and left his ears ringing. A piece of shrapnel pierced his left arm while he was retrieving bandages from his bag and another pierced his thigh. Searing pain shot through his body and he yelped.

He fell back and grabbed the part of his arm where he was hit. When the sharp pain subsided into a duller burning pain, he let go and glanced at the wound. Blood was staining his sleeve. He tried closing his left hand. His fingers and palm could still move. He looked down at his thigh and moved his leg. A sharp pain cut into him again as his own movement caused the metal stuck in his thigh to wedge further into his flesh. He took a few seconds to breathe and checked his own injuries. Just flesh wounds. Nothing broken. Nothing life threatening.

He got back up and finished bandaging the replacement's wound, then pulled him by his armpits to the spot where he had left Clayton. The shrapnel in his arm and leg dug into his wounds when he pulled. He gritted his teeth and pulled again. Once they got there, he dropped to the ground.

He won. The three Fates lost and Death had spared him again.

He grabbed the remainder of the bandages he had left in his bag and hastily wrapped them around his own wounds.

# # #

Crawling on the ground, Anthony watched as Wesley tried to lead everyone forward to attempt a counterattack. The German machine gun fire kept coming. The indiscriminate bullets continued to slash their troops, striking down every soldier who made the slightest move. They could not retreat and they could not get ahead. Sniper fire could now be heard too from behind the trees surrounding the field. The Germans were trying to surround them.

Was this it? Anthony tightened his grip around the barrel. Was this the end for them? Memories of his parents and Tessa flashed across his mind. His cross dangled from his neck as he crawled another inch. He shifted his arm to point his weapon at the machine gun nest closest to them.

Suddenly, Wesley sprang forward. Alone and staying low, he sprinted from bush to bush toward the machine gun nest Anthony was aiming at. In horror and amazement, Anthony watched as Wesley slipped across the field. Somehow, in the short time while he was pinned down, Wesley had configured a strategic line to the enemy that could give him just enough cover behind the foliage. When the Germans noticed him, he was already within twenty feet of their nest. They turned their fire at him but he unleashed a burst of fire first, taking down the men inside.

Roused by what they saw, the rest of their company rose up and pressed on, sending their own rain of fire at the German machine gun nests. Anthony got up off the ground. Behind them, the sputters of a Sherman tank finally arrived. The tank fired off a shell and demolished one of the German gun emplacements. A second hit took out another.

Encouraged, Anthony raced to Wesley's aid, firing his Tommy gun as if his shots were his shield. Wesley had entered the machine gun dugout he cleared. When Anthony reached him, the three German soldiers inside were already dead on the ground. Wesley had killed them all. He had taken control of the gun emplacement and was shooting at another machine gun with the enemy's own weapon. Taking advantage of the tactical position, he struck down the German soldiers behind one nest, then turned to aim at those in another. Unable to counter Wesley and the American soldiers coming toward them from the field supported by their arriving tanks, the remaining German soldiers in the other nest ran and dispersed in different directions.

When they were all gone and the rest of the enemy soldiers had retreated, Wesley let go of the machine gun and leaned back against the wall.

"You okay?" Anthony asked him. His arm was bleeding.

Wesley took several deep breaths and nodded. "Just a scratch. I'm okay."

Anthony watched him recover, in awe of how Wesley had led them out of such a treacherous situation and come out with "just a scratch."

Out on the field, the sounds of gunfire had subsided. Their own troops were moving up. Anthony relaxed slightly and was about to breathe a sigh of relief when a communications sergeant came running to them with a radio. "Lieutenant! Lieutenant! Retreat! The captain ordered immediate retreat!"

"Retreat? Why?" Anthony asked. "What did the captain say?"

"The Rangers failed. They were ambushed. The entire Rangers battalion's gone. Only six of them came back."

This couldn't be right, Anthony thought. "Six? Six of them came back?"

"Yes, sir."

How could this be? Anthony could not register what he was hearing. There were seven hundred and sixty-seven men in the Ranger battalion, all of them elite fighters. "What happened to them?" he asked, still skeptical of the news the communications sergeant had given them.

"Don't know, sir. The ones who returned said a lot of them were killed. The rest were captured. We all have to retreat now!"

Before Anthony could say more, the sounds of gunfire had resumed. He held up his binoculars and looked to the back of the field. The Germans had returned. They had come with reinforcements. A formidable force as large as sixty riflemen was coming their way. Three German Panzer tanks were approaching right behind them.

"Holy shit!" shouted the communications sergeant.

Wesley grabbed the German machine gun again. "Ardley, get everyone out of here. I'll cover you."

Unsure if he should stay and help, Anthony hesitated.

"Go!" Wesley hollered back at him. "Get everyone out of here. Now! I'll follow!" He turned the machine gun toward the direction of the Germans and fired.

Anthony picked up his pace and ran off. On the field, he shouted to get their troops to set up firing positions to provide defense, but the assault of enemy gunfire spreading across the field derailed all their attempts. Their company was faltering.

He turned around and caught a glimpse of Wesley firing a rapid succession of rounds at the oncoming German troops. Their own men were falling further and further back. If Wesley didn't get out soon, there would be no one to cover him.

Anthony continued to run. As he ran past a small crater, he spotted a team of his men setting up their mortar tube to shield the rest of the company. That might be enough to hold the Germans, but not for long. He turned to shout for the men to retreat just as one of the Panzers fired. The Panzer's shell struck the machine gun dugout and blasted it to shreds, obliterating Wesley along with the nest. Stunned, Anthony fell back a step and froze while the nest burned.

"Lieutenant! Run!" Fox shouted, running past him. Devastated but helpless to change what had happened, Anthony gripped his gun and looked away from the scene where Wesley was slaughtered. The team of men who were setting up the mortar had abandoned their weapon and were now running for their lives. Hastening his speed, Anthony joined the rest in escape. When he reached the edge of the field, he jumped into one of the vehicles that had pulled up to take the retreating troops away. The truck sped down the road. Sniper bullets followed, pinging and popping against the vehicle's sides. Just as the bullet sounds died down, a shell exploded behind them. Had they been a minute slower, they would all have been blown up.

In the truck, he looked at the men around him. They had all seen what had happened to Wesley. Fox's face looked as solemn as death as he stared at the direction where the machine gun dugout once was. Jonesy lowered his head. His lips tightened into a line and tears rolled down his cheeks. The rest of the men in the truck sat quietly in shock. For a long while, no one said a word. Only the sound of the truck's engine and stray shots from the Germans accompanied them as they trudged on.

In silence, Anthony tried to grasp the chain of events that had just occurred.

The entire Ranger battalion was gone.

Of the seven hundred and sixty-seven men, only six had returned.

Wesley Sharpe was dead.

A lump rose in his throat. He swallowed hard and looked down. Clayton was lying on the floor of the truck. Someone had loaded him onto the truck in the midst of their escape. His lips were white and his face pale.

"Clayton?" Anthony asked.

Clayton squeezed out a smile, but it came out more like a grimace. "Don't worry, Ardley," he wheezed. "I'm alive." His voice was so weak. Clearly, he was in pain. Anthony felt as if their entire operation was failing. Everything was broken.

"It's all right, Ardley. It's all right. I made my fair trade with God. My body's a mess, but I'm going home. Yes, sir. I'm going home."

Anthony looked away. He could think of nothing to say. Words were useless.

He thought of Wesley again. Wesley, the rock that held them all together. He was their center of gravity, and he was gone.

Anthony felt as if the wind had been knocked out of him. He felt empty to the core.

He felt the world shifting around him.

What would happen to them now that Wesley was dead?

Chapter 4

There was no warning at all. In a matter of minutes, the dreary, quiet night turned into a scene of frantic madness.

It was past midnight and Tessa was making her rounds checking up on the patients when wounded soldiers began to arrive by the hundreds, then thousands. Soon, the floors of the hospital tents were covered with litters holding injured men. Most of them were so severely hurt, it was impossible to determine whom to treat first.

They had only arrived three days ago. She did not expect to be thrown into an emergency of this scale so soon. Good thing Captain Milton was on duty and in charge. Despicable a person as Milton was, Tessa couldn't help but admire her ability to stay calm and mobilize the medical staff. Swiftly, Milton organized the nurses and medical corpsmen into groups and assigned them to tend to different patients according to the severity of their injuries. With just one look, she was able to determine which patients needed immediate surgeries and which ones could be given morphine shots and wait. Those whose surgical treatments could be postponed were dispatched to the evacuation hospitals. Those with minor injuries were patched up and sent off to make room for new patients who continued to arrive.

Tessa herself wasn't handling the situation so well. When the patients first arrived, she had rushed to assist. As they arrived by the hundreds and thousands within the hour, she started to lose her handle on the situation. She wasn't helping the wounded as fast as she wanted, and the backlog of patients was piling up.

Gracie reacted even worse. When they were in Naples, they had only treated patients in recovery. Now, seeing the fresh, horrific wounds of the soldiers and blood spilling everywhere, Gracie broke into tears. Milton had to pull her aside.

"I have no patience for drama, Lieutenant Hall. I won't have you going around my hospital upsetting patients with your sobs and waterworks. Stop this nonsense now, or I will take disciplinary action. Is that clear?"

Still distraught, Gracie wiped her eyes. Tessa watched them from a few beds away. There was nothing she could do to help Gracie. She could barely manage herself.

Despite her threats, Milton sent Gracie away and reassigned her to the group treating minor injuries instead. Tessa lowered her head and returned to work cleaning the mud off a patient's wounds.

"Graham." Milton came toward her.

"Yes, Captain." Tessa looked up.

"When you're done with this one, go to Ward One. They need help there." Milton said, her eyes as hard as ever.

"Yes, Captain," Tessa said. Following Milton's order, she went to Ward One. She knew that ward was where they took patients in the most critical condition, but she didn't know it would be a place that would haunt her memories forever.

Ward One was set up in its own separate tent. When she entered, Ellie was beside a soldier's bed, uncovering a soldier's chest wound. The bandages came off, revealing a hole in his chest. A piece of flesh as big as a small orange was missing. Tessa had never seen such a grotesque sight close-up. She couldn't take her eyes away from the grisly sight.

The chest wound was not his only injury. One of his legs was twisted at an unnatural angle. His face was scrunched up in pain. He looked like he was about to pass out. Quickly, she took his boots off. Ellie glanced at her to thank her. A surgical team had now arrived to help Ellie.

"There are simultaneous surgeries going on. I'll finish prepping him. Will you check on that one?" Ellie looked over to the soldier lying on another operating table near them.

Tessa walked over to him. The first thing she noticed was the diagonal blue-and-white striped insignia on his sleeve. It was the insignia of the Third Infantry Division. Anthony's Division. The Rock of Marne.

Alarmed, she grabbed the patient's arm. The hospital had been so inundated with new patients, she hadn't even had time to think about Anthony.

Was Anthony safe? Her lips started to quiver. She wanted to ask the soldier where their division had been and what had happened to them, but she couldn't find the right words. The soldier had multiple wounds on his chest and legs. She didn't want to upset him further by asking him questions.

"It's okay, nurse," the soldier said. "Don't feel bad for me. The shell that hit me, it killed my friend. It blasted him to pieces. We don't even have his body to bring back. I was lucky the shell didn't have my name on it."

She gazed at the soldier. He was worried about her!

No. She must not think about Anthony now. She had a job to do. She had to get all other thoughts out of her mind no matter what.

She unfolded the bandages wrapped around the soldier's legs to clean his wounds and prepare him for surgery. His legs were yet another ghastly sight. They were filled with metal debris. Some of the jagged shell fragments were embedded in his flesh. She could not believe so many pieces of metal could be inside a human leg. Nothing she had seen at the Chicago Veterans Hospital or the army hospital in Naples had prepared her for this.

She looked at the tent's entrance. Hundreds more patients here and elsewhere were still waiting their turn to be treated. How would they be able to take care of everyone?

She felt a reassuring touch on her shoulder and turned around. Dr. Haley, fully dressed in his medical scrubs, smiled at her. "You'll do fine," he said, as if reading her thoughts. "Come on. Let's get him started."

Another doctor and two nurses joined them and they brought the patient to the operating room. She looked at the wounds on the soldier's legs and his chest while she gave him an anesthesia shot. It disgusted her what the war had done to him.

"It'll be a few minutes before the anesthesia takes effect," Dr. Haley said. "Can you talk to him?" he asked Tessa. "Get his mind on something else so we can get started? We don't have time to wait."

"Talk to him?" Tessa asked. "About what?"

"Whatever diverts his attention."

She put down the needle and stared at the soldier. He looked so weak. He must be in so much pain, and yet he hadn't complained once. She tried to think of something to ask him.

"What's your name?" She picked up his hand.

"Kyle."

"Hello, Kyle. I'm Tessa."

The soldier tried to smile. Now what? She thought. What else could she talk to him about? An odd thought popped into her mind. "Do you like baseball?"

Kyle chuckled through his pain. "Yeah. Love it."

She smiled. She didn't know why she had thought of baseball, but she suddenly remembered the time when she had gone to a baseball game with Henry and Ruby.

"Do you like it?" Kyle asked her.

Actually, she knew nothing about it. What did Henry say about the game again? She tried to remember. She mentioned the only thing that she could recall. "There's the World Series."

"Yeah, the World Series." Kyle's face eased. She wondered if the anesthesia was starting to take effect. "Me and my buddies... we went to see the '42 Series live... Game One, just before we all enlisted... It was a treat to ourselves, you know... in case we don't come back, you know..."

"Yes."

"Who'd you root for?"

"Who did I root for?" In the '42 Series? She had no idea. She didn't even know which teams had played. "The Yankees?" She took a wild guess. Henry said the Yankees always won everything.

"That's too bad... I hate the Yankees. I rooted for the Cardinals all the way." His voice grew weaker. "We almost had them too... when we scored... those four runs in the ninth inning..." His voice trailed off and he passed out. She stroked his forehead, then said to Dr. Haley, "He's asleep."

"Good. Can you monitor his heart rate and blood pressure?"

"Yes." She watched the doctor and the team begin the surgery. It was the first of a string of surgeries they would perform as the hours passed. Their first shift continued on to the second shift. Those who had any strength left after that were then asked to stay for a third shift.

By the time she was relieved from the hospital, it was almost nighttime. More than a full day had passed since her first shift began and she had worked for twenty-seven hours straight. In that time, she took only one fifteen-minute break. Her muscles ached and her fingers felt numb. She could barely recall when she had last eaten, but she didn't feel hungry.

The scene at the hospital was much calmer now, although every bed was occupied and the floor was covered with litters. The soldiers who were awake were either smoking or talking very quietly amongst themselves. No one complained and all of them were putting on a brave face. It was amazing to see them taking everything so well. As she walked out of the tent, she noticed Captain Milton attending to a patient. Milton hadn't left since this all began either.

Leaving everything behind for the time being, Tessa hustled from the hospital to her tent with her head down. At this hour, there were very few people outside. The German air raid might come at any moment and no one wanted to be exposed. Several corpsmen who had arrived at Anzio before her had warned her. The enemy, they liked to attack at night.

No sooner had she finished that thought, the first sounds of attack began. The evening twilight had vanished. She had her small flashlight with her, but there was no need for it. The gunfire in the air had set the sky ablaze, illuminating the ground many times brighter than even the streetlights at night in London or Chicago.

It must have rained hard earlier in the day. She walked as fast as she could on the wet, muddy ground without slipping to a fall. Her breath quickened as she hastened her speed. The massive odor of diesel fuel in the air penetrated her lungs. She felt lightheaded. She covered her mouth and nose and hoped she wouldn't faint before she reached her tent.

She found her tent and hurried toward it. Once inside, she collapsed face down onto her cot and lay there until her heartbeat slowed back down to normal. Inside the tent, it was dark, but she could not turn on any lights. The army command had imposed a strict blackout policy on all units.

Gracie had already returned. Beneath the thunderous booms of explosions outside were the muffled whimpers of her cries only a few feet away. Tessa looked over and stared at the outline of her body lying on her cot, hiding and sniffling under her blanket.

The wheeling sounds of German Stuka engines hovered all over above her. Whistles of bombs dropping down from the sky whirled all around. The whistles grew louder as they fell nearer to the ground until the bombs landed with a thud. Tessa squeezed the corner of her blanket. She wanted everything to be over, but the noise would not let up. It only intensified as each minute went by.

And then, she understood. The night raid was not an anomaly. Here, at Anzio, this was how things would be. Anthony must have known it. This was why he dug the foxholes. This was why he looked so distracted and worried when he came to see her.

What should she do?

Maybe it was better to look the enemy in the eye. To see what was really happening.

She got up from her cot, opened the flap of her tent, and peeked out.

Outside, German planes were firing flares that were lighting up the sky and the entire stretch of the beach. The flares were profuse and constant. They did not allow for even a moment of natural darkness. She could see the entire beach, from the stretch of sand with the abandoned buildings lining behind it, to the dark waves flowing in while water erupted from exploding bombs dropped into the sea.

Although the beach was now as bright as daylight, the lights given from the flares were not like sunlight. They had an eerie, greenish quality to them. Under the greenish glow, the beach looked like a place that should exist only in a nightmare. The flashes of green light were followed by the drumming roars of anti-aircraft machine guns. When the machine guns fired their shells into the sky, they left behind traces of fire that looked like torn, falling threads and ribbons.

Horrified, yet mesmerized, Tessa stepped just outside of her tent to watch. The battle in the air was the most grotesque display of fireworks she had ever seen. This was what hell must look like.

Just when she thought that the noise around her couldn't be any louder, a Stuka dropped a series of shells onto the Allies' ammunition dump three miles north. Boom! A massive explosion followed. She covered her ears with both hands to block out the sound. The explosion burst into a colossal ball of fire. Its red and orange flames reached high up into the sky like the long claws of Satan's hand, followed by a giant mushroom cloud of smoke and dust.

Screaming car horns and wailing ambulance sirens now joined the cacophony of explosions and bombs. A breeze of night wind blew past her, carrying with it the thick, burning smell of smoke.

Boom! Another gigantic explosion. This time coming from the sea. She turned to the direction of the harbor. Three German Stukas were circling above a ship sailing away out into the ocean. One of the Stukas sent a succession of flares into the air, illuminating the sky above the ship. The bright light of the flares revealed the large marking of a red cross painted on the side of the ship. Tessa gasped.

A Stuka soared up into the night sky, then turned around, dove down, and dropped several bombs onto the ship. The bombs exploded and fire broke out at the front and the back of the deck.

The fire was soon extinguished, but another Stuka flew over the ship and released more bombs. The vessel caught fire again. A surge of smoke rose from its hull. Tessa raised her hand to her lips and watched. Then, all the lights went out and the ship went dark.

Terror gripped her heart. The Germans, they would attack a medical ship!

How many people were on board? Two hundred? Three hundred? More? She could only hope that they could escape and be rescued. She didn't want to watch anymore.

She went back inside the tent. On her cot, she sat down and hugged her legs close to her body, resting her chin on her knees. The cold, damp air around her offered no comfort. The booming sounds of exploding bombs continued.

The foxhole. Anthony had told her to sleep in the foxhole. She reached her hand behind her and slid it under the tent to touch the foxhole's edge. The soft, wet mud of the ground felt slimy under her fingers. She slid her hand further and felt a puddle of cold water.

Why was there a puddle of water? She lifted up the tent a few inches to take a look. The foxhole was flooded. Completely flooded. The heavy rain earlier had filled it like a bath tub.

She let the canvas fall back onto the ground. If she went to sleep, could she wake up to find that this was all just a nightmare? She lay down on her side, curled her body up and pulled the blanket over herself.

She closed her eyes and thought of home. What would her parents think if they knew what was happening in this place? They would be so upset. She came to find Anthony, but what if she was wounded? If medical ships could not escape, then how would she get back to them?

Her parents. She wanted to go back to her parents. They were waiting for her, waiting for the day they would reunite as a family. She couldn't be separated from them with no way of going home.

What if she were killed? What if she never saw them again?

No. Can't think like this, she told herself. If she hadn't come, Anthony would be here without anybody. They would all be in safe places, and he would be living this nightmare all by himself.

He was out there somewhere. Where was he? What was he doing now?

What if the shells falling from the sky hit him? The thought made her want to scream, but her throat was tight and no sound came out. Her body felt stiff and she was unable to move.

What if she never saw him again?

The thoughts haunted her until exhaustion took over and she faded into a deep sleep.

# # #

"Congratulations Lieutenant," said Colonel Callahan as he pinned the silver bar on Anthony's uniform.

"Thank you, sir." Anthony glanced sideways at the new insignia on his shoulder. Under different circumstances, this might have been an occasion for celebration. Instead, nothing felt right. The silver bar belonged to Wesley. It was a symbol of Wesley's fighting spirit and valor. On his own uniform, it was only a sad reminder that Wesley was dead. In his heart, he knew he didn't deserve it. He couldn't compare to Wesley. Not by a long shot. He hadn't done enough to earn the position that Wesley had held.

Next to him, Beck took his turn to recite his oath. The former first sergeant, now a second lieutenant, could barely hide his excitement. He beamed with pride when Colonel Callahan announced his promotion. The promotion of a noncom to a commissioned officer rank was a big deal. It marked a milestone in Beck's military career. Of course, Beck deserved it. He was an old warhorse. He had been with the company for more than two years. He had fought to hell and back and put his life on the line many times.

How would things go now that they must work together as first and second lieutenants? Anthony felt wary. When he joined the company last year, the hierarchy of command was clear. On the field, Wesley was in charge and he was the deputy, the backup. The same could not be said of him and Beck. While he outranked Beck, Beck had served his time and he had battle experience. There was rank, and there was respect.

Beck never hid the fact that he had little respect for ninety-day wonders like Anthony.

When the ceremony was over, Beck swaggered over to the sergeants and other non-coms to bask in his glory. His fellow officers heartily congratulated him and demanded to see his gold bar. Even the enlisted soldiers were happy for him. Beck's promotion was a true validation of his achievements.

Captain Harding walked over to him. "Congratulations, Ardley."

"Thank you, sir." Anthony shook his hand.

"We're all sad about Wesley," Harding said, although Anthony did not hear much grief in his voice. "Lieutenant Sharpe was a fine officer. You have some big shoes to fill."

Anthony didn't need the reminder. He had been worrying about that too. "I'll do my best."

"I can count on you the way I could count on Lieutenant Sharpe, can I?" Harding looked him in the eye. The question was straightforward, but Harding's look wasn't. The captain was not asking about his commitment to fight. He was questioning his loyalty. Loyal in what way? Anthony couldn't quite understand.

"I'll do my best," Anthony repeated.

"Captain, Lieutenant," Colonel Callahan came and interrupted them. "We'll meet again at 1800 hours. I'll brief you on your next mission. Captain, may I have a word with you?"

"Certainly, sir." Harding smiled at Anthony, then walked away with the colonel. Anthony watched them leave. Jonesy and Ollie came and congratulated him. Distracted, he thanked them. He didn't know why, but the captain's question left him feeling unsettled.

"Congratulations, Ardley!" Warren slapped him on the back.

Relieved to see him, Anthony smiled for the first time since the ceremony began. Finally, a sincere well-wisher. "Thanks."

"You look glum for someone who just got a big promotion."

Anthony watched the crowd of soldiers as they began to disperse. "I don't think I can replace Wesley. I don't think those guys trust me the way they trusted him. Or even the way they trust Beck."

"You'll do fine," Warren reassured him. "Wesley trusted you, and that says a lot. Come on, let's go grab a beer and celebrate."

They began walking toward their quarters. Before they had gone far, Anthony paused and put his hands in his pockets. "The captain might not be so easy to deal with."

"They never are. I should know. I'm one," Warren joked. "You'll manage."

Anthony wasn't so sure. He still felt uneasy about the way Captain Harding had spoken to him. What kind of loyalty did Harding expect? "Have you heard anything new about that German major, Klaus?"

"Oh yes. He's here. He's leading the German troops, and they are energized. We found out he orchestrated the capture of the Rangers a few days ago." Warren's voice tensed as he spoke of the Rangers. "That was a disaster. We're still trying to come to terms with it."

Anthony winced at the reminder of the Ranger battalion which was totally wiped out. His own company had suffered a high number of casualties that day too. The sight of Wesley being blown up in the dugout remained fresh in his mind.

The Captain has his own agenda. Wesley had warned him back in Salerno.

He thought back to the first few days after they had arrived in Anzio. If Harding didn't have his own agenda to confront Klaus, they might have been able to make a more persuasive case to the command to push their forces inland before Klaus and his men arrived. If they had not hunkered down to wait, Wesley might still be alive.

He stopped again and kicked a small piece of rock on the ground. The rock rolled a few feet forward and came to a stop. The captain didn't even seem too distraught at Wesley's death.

It's now up to you and me to get everyone through this. That was what Wesley wanted them to do, but Wesley was gone.

If something should happen to me, someone else will need to take charge and do what needs to be done, or a lot of them are going to die.

It was all up to him now.

The silver bars on his shoulders felt heavier than he had ever imagined.

PART TWO

Night Raid

Chapter 5

He knew it. Jesse knew Lady Luck was always on his side.

His last mission had left him with two surface wounds. It turned out, those wounds were a stroke of luck. They landed him right in the 33rd Field Hospital where he could watch Tessa Graham at work for hours on end.

A couple of non-lethal injuries in exchange for days of lying around watching Tessa. What an excellent bargain!

She had been working the night shifts. Every evening, he quietly watched her at work from his bed.

She's so beautiful.

He didn't want to take his eyes off her.

At the moment, another nurse was helping her prepare medications for the patients. He watched her force herself to smile, trying to be amenable, even though she seemed uninterested in whatever the other nurse was saying to her.

But she looked so sweet when she forced herself to smile. Her fake smile brought an adoring smile to his own face.

He grabbed his pack of cigarettes from his bag on the floor. Crap. He was out. He hoped Irene or Alice would come by and bring him more soon. He chucked the empty cigarette pack back into the bag.

He clasped his hands behind his head and sat back to watch Tessa again. A young corpsman had been assigned to be her assistant today. He watched her lead the aide as they made their rounds, dispensing drugs and changing dressings for the patients. The aide, a short kid with a round chubby face, was obviously new at his job. He kept messing up, and she seemed unable to give him the right instructions. She directed him this way and that way, but the aide only got more confused as he bumbled along. Plus, they could barely communicate. Between her British accent and his Southern drawl, Jesse wondered how they could possibly finish the night working together.

"Good heavens! What are you doing?" she asked the aide.

"I'm changin' his ban'dages, ma'am."

"No! You're doing this all wrong. You need to wrap it round like this." She took over the patient's arm, undid the mess the aide had made, and rewrapped the patient's wound herself.

"But that's what aah was doin'!" the aide said.

"No, it wasn't." She finished and showed the aide. "Like this. See? Easy peasy."

"Easy paysey. Hey, aah like the sound of that!"

Tessa gave the aide an irked look. "Can you give the chap in bed number twenty-five his medicine please?"

"Aye, Lootenant Graham. Easy paysey!" He tossed the bottle of medicine up in the air and caught it like it was a toy.

"Don't do that!" she told him.

Jesse chuckled. The more agitated she got, the stronger her accent became. Why did she have a British accent anyway? He wanted to ask her.

"Wait! Excuse me! Where do you think you are you going?" she called out after the corpsman who was walking away.

"Aah thought aah'd throw out the ole ban'dages first, ma'am."

"First of all, rubbish can go into this bin right here." She took the used bandages from his hands and pulled out a bin on the lower shelf of the supplies cart. "And don't worry about throwing those away for now. The gentleman in bed number twenty-five. Give him his medicine!"

Looking lost, the aide said, "Lootenant Graham, sometimes, the way you talk is very hard on my ears."

"The way I talk? Well frankly, I can hardly make out a word you are saying!" Irritated, she dumped the used cotton into the bin.

Jesse laughed and crossed his arms to hold himself together.

And then, the menacing ritual began, the first blasts of the German Flak 88 anti-aircraft guns that assailed the skies when everything outside had gone dark. The night raid had arrived.

Within minutes, 88-millimeter shells rumbled all around and above them. The booms of long-range missiles followed, spreading far and wide and filling all areas of space. A chorus of machine guns broke out, interspersed with shrill, high-pitched whistles of falling bombs that sounded like someone shrieking in pain. The shell of a German anti-aircraft gun struck an American plane, producing a metal-scraping screech that grated his ears and made his skin crawl.

The patients who could move scurried to hide, ducking under their beds and scrambling to the floor. The ones who could not move recoiled nervously in their beds. Unperturbed, Jesse remained still with his arms crossed over his chest. Solemn, he cast his eyes down.

The stench of diesel fuel suffused the air. Pops of debris pelting the tent joined the symphony of horror as shell fragments tore holes in the canvas behind the cots and the beds. Jesse frowned without turning to look at where the shrapnel had hit. It was a wonder that nothing had pierced through and killed anyone yet.

But the terror of the night had only just started.

Amidst the booms of artillery fire came the growing mechanical clacks of an engine that sounded at first like an express freight train passing them overhead. The sound surged until it ended with a harrowing blast somewhere farther away.

"Hell, that one came from the Anzio Annie!" a man crouching on the ground shouted to the people near him.

The Anzio Annie. Jesse recognized its earsplitting screech on the tracks just before the strike. The monstrous K5E railway gun had a barrel as long as seventy feet and a maximum firing range of forty miles. In comparison, America's own Long Tom could only fire as far as fourteen miles. Positioned in the Alban Hills over the tracks of the Ciampi-Frascati railway line just thirty miles away from the beachhead where they were now, the Anzio Annie could obliterate them.

Like a leviathan, the Anzio Annie lurked stealthily inside the train tunnels. At unexpected times, it would emerge from its hideout and open fire against the Allies' storage dumps. It would bombard any place where the Allied troops congregated. It would strike at the Allies' supply ships to keep them at bay and out of the harbor. If the Allies tried to retaliate with aerial and ground artillery attacks, it would disappear again into the tunnels and reemerge elsewhere later without warning. When its shells exploded, they sounded like the awakening roars of a dragon disgorging a colossal breath of fire.

He looked at the men hiding under the beds. Someday, if these men lived to survive this war, they could tell their children that real-life monsters really did exist in this world.

The same sequence of sounds from the Anzio Annie repeated again and again. Wherever the Anzio Annie was tonight, it had found good vantage points and wasn't about to stop.

"Man! We gotta get out of here," said the soldier in the bed next to Jesse. "This place's a Goddamn death trap."

"Hey, Garland," another fellow soldier said. "Why are you still here anyway? I'd be long gone if I were you. They don't call this hospital Hell's Half Acre for nottin'."

Jesse did not answer but glanced up at Tessa.

"I don't care what these doctors and nurses say," the soldier in the next bed continued. "I'm heading back to the front tomorrow where the foxholes are." He shifted uncomfortably in the narrow space between the bed frame and the ground. "You know how Marty got slashed by some flying shrapnel last time? It was a big gash too! He let the medic sew him up but he wouldn't come here or go to any of the evac hospitals. Just wouldn't. He said if they want him at the hospital, he better be already dead."

Jesse's eyes remained fixed on Tessa. Her corpsman aide was now in hysterics.

"What da ya mean we cain't leave? They're fa'aring at us! We gotta git ourselves to the foxholes when the shelling starts!"

"There are no foxholes here, Toby!" Tessa said. "And we can't leave. If we leave, who's going to take care of the patients?"

"But that ain't fair! We shouldn't have ta ba'y here with no shelter or protection!" Just as he said this, a series of bombs went off. The fury of the artillery fire continued and the earsplitting noises would not stop.

"Aah am done here. If y'all want to die, it's your business but aah sure ain't staying here," the aide said and stomped toward the exit.

"Come back here!" Tessa chased after him. "You'll get yourself killed going out there." Distraught, the boy stopped and hesitated. Tessa, though, showed no sympathy. "If you leave, I will report you to Captain Milton, and she will take serious disciplinary action."

"You cain't do that!" the boy argued. "Y'all cain't punish me for trying to save mah own life!"

"I can and I will." Tessa stood firm. Her face was stern and serious. "We are on duty. We don't leave our patients unattended no matter what happens." The boy strained to hold back his tears. "Try to stay calm, Toby. Please?" Tessa softened her voice. "Stay calm for the patients?"

Resigned to the situation, the aide picked up a cup of pills and another cup of water from the medicine cart and brought them to a patient cowering on his bed. Tessa gave them a watchful look and carried on with her work.

The raid continued throughout the night. Jesse sat motionless on the bed, waiting for the hours to pass. The thunderous explosions came again and again, meshing and overlapping and would not cease. The noise enveloped them. Trapped them. Oppressed them. He wanted the noise to stop but there was no escape. It drove him crazy. The sight of Tessa was the only thing that kept his sanity intact. He tried to block out the rest of the world and focus on her.

He imagined that there was another world where she could be his. Another world that was at peace and untainted by evil, violence, and death like where they were now. A world that was free of lies, hurt, and deceit, like the cesspool inhabited by whores and scoundrels from where he had come.

Could he wish for that? Could he dare to imagine being with her in a world that was honest and simple?

The idea felt so unattainable. She was out of reach. She was already in love with someone else.

The night wore on. But dawn did arrive to dispel the darkness of the night. A sliver of sunlight peered through the slit of the canvas tent's entrance. It grew brighter and brighter. The whistles of plane engines began to fade. The sounds of guns dissipated, and then, they were gone.

Across the tent, Tessa was now saying goodbye to a nurse who had arrived for the morning shift. On her way out, Tessa picked up a large box of medication. Seeing her leave, Jesse hustled out of the bed, put on his boots, grabbed the bottle of whiskey next to him and followed her. In his hurry, he forgot the wound on his leg hadn't yet healed. Pain shot up his thigh as he stood up. Gasping through clenched teeth, he inhaled, shifted his weight to his uninjured leg to ease the pain, and hobbled after her.

Chapter 6

Jesse followed Tessa to the underground cavern about thirty yards from the hospital ward where he was staying. The cavern contained a room for storing hospital supplies and another room for the medical staff to conduct administrative work. To protect against the daily air raids and constant danger of enemy shells, the army engineers had decided to dig underground and put everyone and everything important below. The entire beachhead had turned into a honeycomb of emergency shelters made up of trenches, pits, and dugouts. Underground wine cellars and catacombs that the locals had built into caverns before the war were converted into army headquarters and operational outposts.

He went down the stairway inside the cavern where Tessa had entered and came to one of the "rooms" where she was putting away bottles of medication.

"Hi," he said.

"What are you doing here?" she asked.

"I want some company." He came into the room. "I see your shift has ended."

"You want some company?" She put down the bottle in her hand. "All you've had is company since you got here. Everyone's treating you like a VIP guest. Good thing you'll be released soon. No one's getting any work done with you around."

"Don't talk like that. You sound like that old hag Milton. Besides, I can't help it if the ladies can't get enough of me. You just don't know what you're missing." He came close to her and said into her ear, "I'm a great lover, if you care to find out."

She stared blankly at him the same way she did the last time he tried to flirt with her. Unable to elicit any reaction from her, he backed away. "Okay. Never mind. This is the real reason why I'm here." He held up the bottle of whiskey and put it on the table. "I thought you might need this after putting up with that yokel aide of yours all night. Not to mention the very exciting air raid."

She looked suspiciously at the liquor on the table. He picked up two medicine cups on the cabinet shelf, put them on the small table in the center of the room, and poured each of them a shot.

"Unless, like all the other girls, you can't hold your liquor." With a challenging smile, he offered her a cup.

"Who says I can't hold my liquor?" She took the cup from him and drank the entire shot.

Quietly thrilled that he had found a way to provoke a reaction from her, he waited until she finished her drink, then downed the other cup himself while she continued putting the medicine away.

"How are your wounds?" she asked him after she locked the medicine away. Her voice sounded personal, more than just professional concern for a patient. Or at least he thought so. She looked sad that he was hurt. He wasn't expecting that. Her tenderness made him feel self-conscious. At the same time, a strange, unfamiliar feeling of warmth filled his body. It was a sweet, happy feeling he had never felt before. He looked down at the ground. "Better. Thanks for asking."

Just then, Gracie entered with a tray of medication bottles. "Hi Tessa, I…" She stopped mid-sentence and her face froze when she saw

Jesse. At the sudden interruption, Tessa and Jesse both turned to look at her. Quickly, Gracie looked away from him. Her cheeks flushed although it was not obvious under the dim light in the room.

"I'm about to finish up my shift," she said to Tessa in a nerve-stricken voice. "I came to put these away." She looked at the tray of medicine she had brought in. "Would you please unlock the medicine cabinet for me?"

Tessa took the key out of her pocket and unlocked the cabinet. Gracie came over, turned her back to Jesse, and began putting the drugs away.

Turning his attention back to Tessa, Jesse picked up the whiskey bottle and asked, "Want another one?"

This time, Tessa relaxed and walked back to the table. "Yes. I think I could use another one. My friend Jack back in Chicago, his family's Irish. He was a bartender and he really knew his whiskeys. He used to treat me to some of the best whiskeys in his stock."

"I bet you my stuff's better than anything your friend's got. This one's top shelf." He poured her another cup. "I got it direct from a nobleman's private collection."

A loud crash disrupted their conversation. "Sorry!" Gracie said. She had dropped a bottle of pills on the ground, and it rolled toward Jesse. She rushed to pick it up but was not fast enough. The bottle stopped rolling at Jesse's feet. He picked it up and handed it to her. As he did, their eyes met. Her face burned red again. Embarrassed, she took the bottle from him. "Thank you."

He looked away. He recognized this girl. She had been coming by his bed every day, filling his water pitcher and leaving him candies and chocolates but not daring to talk to him. She stole glances at him when she thought he wasn't aware. He knew she had a crush on him and it was starting to annoy him. He wished she would finish up and leave already. He wanted to be alone with Tessa and she was in the way.

Gracie rushed back to the medicine cabinet and fumbled to put the rest of the drugs away. Noticing her odd behavior, Tessa asked, "Gracie, are you all right?"

"Yes!" She slammed the cabinet doors shut. Looking straight at Tessa while avoiding Jesse's direction, she said, "I'll see you back at the tent."

"See you." Tessa picked up her drink. Gracie rushed to the room entrance. Jesse turned his head away from her as she passed him on her way out.

After she left, he asked, "She shares your tent?"

"Yes," Tessa said, sipping her second cup of whiskey.

His mind started churning. "You got any other tentmates?"

"No."

He broke into a smile. "I've got a proposition for you."

"What's that?"

"It must be hard for you to be apart from Ardley all the time, isn't it?"

Tessa paused at the mention of Anthony's name. She lowered her cup. "Why do you ask?"

"I come here regularly to pick up supplies and deliver the sick and wounded." He sidled up to her. "If you want, I can help you pass messages on to him."

A spark of hope came to her eyes, but she hesitated.

"I can bring his messages to you too. I can be your messenger."

She stared at him. He could tell she wanted this, but she leaned back and narrowed her eyes. "What's in it for you?"

His smile widened. "Help me get together with Gracie."

"No." She refused to entertain the idea at all.

"Why not?" He leaned closer to her. "Don't tell me you're jealous?"

"I'm not jealous." She pushed him away. "I am not getting involved with your love life."

"Not even if I can help you stay closer in touch with your boyfriend?"

"No. Absolutely not. I don't want any part of your nonsense."

He sighed and pulled away from her. "All right then. Guess I'll just have to go after her myself." He crossed his arms. "How about this instead?" He leaned close to her again.

"What?"

"You carry the key to the medicine cabinet."

"Yes. So?"

"I have a constant supply of fine liquor that comes my way every time a ship arrives from Naples," he said, his expression now serious. "I need a place to store my stock. How about you help me keep my supply of liquor safe and locked away in the medicine cabinet?"

Tessa considered his offer. Still wary, she rested her lips on the rim of her cup.

"It's not that big a deal," he said. "I have no good place to store it. If you do this for me, I'll be your personal runner and mailman."

He watched her struggle to decide. Knowing he was getting closer to convincing her, he softened his expression to an earnest smile. Slowly, she dropped her guard. "How do you get your liquor supply anyway? What do you do with it? Drink it yourself, or pass it around to the other soldiers?"

"Well," he laughed. "Aren't you a curious cat? So many questions."

"If I help you, I want to know what I'm getting myself into."

Not bothered by her suspicions, he took his time and poured himself another shot. "I get it from a very special supplier. I'd rather not say who he is. I gave him my word I won't disclose his identity. As for what I do with it…" He took a sip of his drink. "Money has no value here when supplies are scarce. You know that. We're always short on supplies. These fine spirits are my currency. I trade them for what I need to get for our boys. Is that so bad?"

She lowered her guard again. "No. I guess not." Intrigued, she smiled at him. "You've been pulling strings to look out for your unit."

He shrugged.

"I thought so," she said. "Anthony told me you could always somehow get extra blankets and socks for everyone in your company. Not to mention the booze and cigarettes." She gave him a mischievous look. "Even pin-ups of naked girls, I heard."

He felt a tad embarrassed when she mentioned that. "I drink it myself too, you know." He changed the subject. "Sometimes, I'd even offer to share it with the woman I love." He switched to a playful tone again and poured another shot into her cup.

Taking his attitude as another meaningless attempt to flirt, she ignored his last remark. "You know, I'm not the only one with the key to the cabinet."

"Who else has a key?"

"Ellie."

"It's no problem then. I'm sure you can work something out with her." He watched her reaction. Her hesitation was waning. "Think of Ardley. Think of how happy it'll make him every time he gets a message from you."

She bit her lip. He knew he was making an offer she could not refuse.

As he expected, she agreed. "Okay. Deal."

"All right then!" He raised his cup. "Bottoms up to celebrate?"

Still looking unsure, she nonetheless smiled and raised her glass. But instead of drinking, she asked, "Why do you want me to help you get together with Gracie? She's not even your type."

"How do you know she's not my type?"

"You can't be interested in Gracie, not when you have Irene and Alice and all those other nurses fawning all over you."

"What do you mean? Are you saying Gracie's not as good as the rest of them? That's a pretty low view you have of your tentmate."

"You know that's not what I mean. What I mean is, Gracie's a nice, simple girl, that's all. I can't see what your interest is in her."

"You really want to know why?" He lowered his voice, his eyes serious.

She stared at him. Clearly, she did not know.

"No particular reason." He switched back to his flirtatious tone. "I'm a cad. It's what I do. I told you that before. It's in my nature to go after every woman and ruin her."

Instead of taking offense, she observed him. There was no judgment in her eyes, only concern. "Jesse, that's not true."

"Of course it is. What do I have to do or say to convince you? I'm a fraud. I lie, I con people. That's what I'm good at." He felt a sudden rush of anger. Anger at himself. "What else am I good at? Let's see. Oh, yeah. Gambling. I'm good at that too. And skirt chasing. Definitely one of my specialties. So there! That's the kind of person I am." He didn't know why he said all that. He thought he must have put her off, but she only watched him without saying anything. The way she was looking at him made him feel even more exposed.

Trying to deflect her doubt, he finished the rest of his whiskey. "I'm a cad. Don't let those stupid little favors I do for the boys fool you. I've never done a good deed in my life. You better believe that."

"You're doing something good now. You save lives."

His hand trembled. He tightened his hold of the cup to steady himself. "That's nothing," he dismissed. "Uncle Sam's making me do it."

"You were drafted, that's true, but you're here because you want to help."

"What makes you think that?" he sneered, trying to hide his face from her, feeling too vulnerable to look at her.

"I came across your personnel file when I was doing paperwork after you were admitted. You were stationed in Casablanca before you came to Italy. The war was over in Africa. They gave you a cushy desk job handling repatriation of patients going home. If you're such a cad, why didn't you just stay there? Clean sheets. Comfortable bed. Hot meals and fine wines. You could romance ladies there day and night. You requested a transfer to join the Third Division to come to the front line. Why?"

He played with his cup for a while, then, instead of answering her, he turned away. "I'm tired. I'm going back to bed. See you later." Without waiting for her response, he picked up his bottle of whiskey and left.

Outside, he passed a pile of dead bodies on his way back to his ward and stopped. Casualties were mounting so fast each day, the graves units couldn't even keep up. Staring at the mound of deceased soldiers, he thought of what Tessa had asked him.

You requested a transfer here to the front line. Why?

He didn't initially choose to be on the front line. Like everyone else, he didn't even know where he was going when the army shipped him out of America.

Fedala. He didn't ask to be dropped into that nightmare.

It was his first mission, and everything was still vivid in his memory. The amphibious landing in the middle of the night on the African coast. The poor navigation of the landing crafts. The destruction of boats that capsized or smashed onto the rocky shores. The consequent loss of supplies and the chaotic scattering of medics and soldiers. People, weapons, and equipment were all separated. Communication was hopeless. In the midst of all that, they had to try to set up aid stations and hospitals on the beach while under enemy attack. It was a nightmare he hoped he would never have to relive again.

But there were things worse than nightmares. In the hours and days that followed, he saw hundreds of people arriving at the make-shift aid station the medics had built. The station was made out of nothing but sand dunes, but those seeking to survive came anyway. People who were able-bodied only hours before came to them. They came mangled, burned, maimed, and covered in blood. What he saw made him sick.

None of the medical staff or officers took any rest. Alongside them, he worked nonstop through the day and night, rescuing casualties and doing what he could to keep the wounded alive until he couldn't stand up anymore. At one point, he stopped to take a good look around him, trying to understand what was happening. The world, it seemed, had spun out of control. Madness. It was all madness around him.

Back in New York, he had always thought his own world was mad. His world was an aberration, a sphere of insanity where scoundrels and whores and every garden variety of parasites leeched onto whatever they could to survive because they couldn't help themselves. Perhaps they didn't know any other way to live. They were the rotting, decomposing patch that marred a world that was generally all right. It was unfortunate, but he could live with that. The rest the world was normal. He could live with himself as long as he could sometimes look from the outside and see glimpses of the inside of the normal world.

All that he understood of the world changed in Fedala. Suddenly, the perversions of his own world could hardly compare. The rest of the world had spiraled into a bottomless pit. It had become a vile, sinister place filled with depravity beyond anything he could ever imagine. Everything happening around him was surreal. The laws of physics had turned upside down. He was normal and the world was mad.

He recalled being at the evacuation hospital a month later. Fedala by then was under American control. He was leaving the hospital when a boy called out to him for help. The boy looked no more than eighteen, but his face looked whipped and haggard. "Please. Help me," the boy cried. His voice was so meek. "Can you give me some morphine please? Can you stop the pain, please? My legs are burning."

The boy had no legs.

After that, by a stroke of luck, the army reassigned him out of the medical detachment. The war in North Africa had ended in March of 1943. The army asked him to return to Casablanca, where evacuation and general hospitals had been set up to receive casualties from the European front. They needed someone to fill an administrative role managing the transfer of wounded veterans who required longer term care or repatriation home.

With the Germans gone and no more threat of war, life in Casablanca was bliss. After his reassignment, his life was a whirlwind tour of exotic places—Marrakesh, Fez, and of course, Casablanca itself. In the dark hours of the night in Morocco's largest city, the music was smooth, the wines were sweet, and the girls were plenty.

But every night, there was that voice, pestering him in his sleep.

"Please. Help me. Can you give me some morphine please? Can you stop the pain?"

Two weeks later, he put in a request for a transfer to the front line.

Soon afterward, he was on his way to join the forces for the invasion of Sicily. And now, here he was. He turned away from the pile of bodies and continued back to the hospital, unaware of Tessa standing not too far behind, watching him.

# # #

Back inside the hospital tent, Gracie was getting off her shift and saying goodbye to her patients. Jesse stood by the tent entrance, checking her out. She was petite, a few inches shorter than Tessa. A cute girl with light blonde hair and a heart-shaped face who might as well have the word "naive" written across her forehead.

He knew her type well. He could practically read her like an open book. She was the kind of girl whose head was filled with dreams and fantasies of romance that existed only in her girlish infantile mind. Girls like her could be clingy and whiny and they never knew when to quit. They were nothing but trouble. Generally, he stayed away from this type except for naive heiresses and daughters or sisters of men who could make for far more lucrative financial transactions.

He put his bottle of whiskey back under his bed and walked over to her. When she saw him approaching, she looked away and pretended not to notice him.

"Hi," he said, putting on his most dashing, all-American-boy smile. "Gracie, right? We haven't officially met. I'm Jesse. Tessa said you're her tentmate?"

With her chest heaving and her face flushed, she nodded.

"Nice to meet you." He took a step closer.

"Nice to meet you too." She gave him a shy smile, her voice almost a whisper.

"Are you done with work? I'm sick of lying around in bed. Would you mind if I walk you back to your tent? I could sure use a walk and some exercise."

She stared at him with her mouth open, then nodded again.

"Let's go." He moved aside to let her pass the narrow gap between the litters of patients. A wide, ecstatic smile lit up her face. He followed her. When they exited the tent, he deliberately brushed his arm against her shoulder as they began to walk.

PART THREE
Carano

Chapter 7

Anxiety had spread throughout their company since the day Wesley died. Anthony could sense the apprehension among the noncoms when they gathered for the briefing for their next mission. Without Wesley's reassuring presence, everyone floundered. The only exception was Beck. Beck went about business as usual like he had seen it all.

Anthony put on a brave face, never letting on that he, too, was full of doubts. He wanted to do the best he could to fill the role that Wesley had left behind, not because he thought he could replace Wesley, but because the soldiers needed someone they could put their faith in to keep up their morale. Yet no matter how hard he tried, he couldn't inspire confidence the way Wesley had done. Everyone had grown to like him well enough, but they weren't convinced he was ready. They didn't trust him as they had trusted Wesley.

They didn't trust the captain either. As a leader, Captain Harding was not always approachable. He liked to keep to himself and the reasons for his orders were not always obvious. If Wesley hadn't told him about Heinrich Klaus, Anthony wouldn't have known that capturing Klaus was part of Harding's plans.

Wesley had known how to navigate between the captain's motives and protecting their men. More than that, he had everyone's trust. Now, with Captain Harding, Beck, and Anthony serving as their company's commanding officers, the dynamics had changed. Anthony was now the first lieutenant, but the captain valued Beck more for his battle experience. Which one of them would the captain put in charge? Anthony didn't think Harding would rely on him if the outcome of the captain's plans was at stake.

Even if Harding chose him over Beck, would he be able to carry out the captain's demands without unnecessarily risking the lives of their own men? The captain was not above sacrificing anyone to achieve his own aims. That was something Anthony had learned from his first battle back when they were fighting their way from Acerno to Naples. He was reminded of this again when the captain made the fateful decision not to urge the command to forge ahead after they arrived at Anzio. If the captain wanted him to do something that exposed their men to unnecessary risks, could he find a way to protect them like Wesley had? He wasn't sure.

"Our ultimate objective is to cut Highway 7 above Cisterna," Colonel Callahan explained to Captain Harding in the tent that served as their company's temporary command post while Anthony, Beck and their company's noncoms listened. "Company B will clear the regiment's right flank." He ran his finger along the blue-colored line on the map. "Paratroopers will drop down here along the Mussolini Canal to divert the German troops while units from the 1st Armored Division move into the area. They'll try to blow these two bridges to stop any counterattack. That'll give us a chance to push ahead from the left and stake our front position right here." He stopped his finger at a site marked Carano. "Your job, along with the rest of your battalion, is to take this town. Your company will advance toward here." He pointed at a route on the map near a small village called Borgo Flora. "We want to take Carano and hold our position here to set up our base of operations."

"Do we have information on the German's movements here, sir?" Anthony pointed to the inland area past the blue line beyond Carano.

"We have some." The colonel showed them a series of aerial photographs. "These were taken yesterday. They're mobilizing and their troops are in Cisterna." He flipped through the photos on the table. "It doesn't look like they are fully organized yet. It looks to me like the area around Carano is still undefended."

Anthony picked up the photos and studied them more closely. Earlier before the briefing, Warren had warned him that the Germans were amassing their troops much faster than what their intel reports suggested, although the information Warren had heard hadn't been confirmed.

"Our goal is to seize the area before the German battalions arrive. 45th will try to hold the south. The Third will go after the north. You saw the surveillance photos. The German troops are still mobilizing. Not all of them have arrived yet. In the meantime, if you come across them, do your best to push on ahead. Don't give them an inch. Keep me informed. Keep communications open."

"What about our artillery support, sir?" Captain Harding asked.

"You'll be covered, Captain." He handed the captain a file.

"We'll get the job done, Captain," Beck said, looking ready for a good fight. "Those German pigs are no match for us. The damn Krauts won't even know what hit them when we're through with them."

Anthony lowered his head to avoid looking at Beck. He didn't like the way Beck talked big around superior officers like the colonel. Perhaps given the fact that Beck had risen to his position from being a noncom, he felt the need to impress, but that kind of talk only created higher expectations that they might not be able to deliver.

"We'll smite them before they see us coming. I'll see to that." Beck stood with his chest puffed out, his legs apart, and his hands on his waist.

His posture reminded Anthony of a penguin. Jonesy looked away, his lips twisted as he tried to suppress a smirk.

Unlike Jonesy, Anthony found no humor in any of this. The capture of an entire Rangers battalion had been a severe blow to their division. After that, their own company had fought for days without a break to hold the front line. Their troops were tired. Wesley's death, of course, further crushed their morale. Their men needed someone who would look out for them, not fill the room with empty talk.

"That'll be all, gentleman." The colonel gave them one last look. "Good luck, and Godspeed."

After Colonel Callahan and the noncoms left, Captain Harding held Anthony and Beck back. "We're not done yet."

Anthony glanced at Beck. Beck gave him no more than a flippant raise of his eyebrows.

"There's one more thing." Harding tapped his pen on a spot on the map. "After our regiment secures Carano, and I'm counting on it that they will, I want you to try to take this village right here."

Anthony looked at where he was pointing on the map. "Borgo Flora?" It was a tiny village south of Carano that didn't fit into the plan they had just talked about. He couldn't see any tactical reason for taking this place. "Borgo Flora's further away from Cisterna. What advantage would we have to divert our men there? Shouldn't we concentrate our forces in Carano? We'll have a better chance to defend against the Germans that way if more of them arrive."

"Perhaps," Harding said, his tone not at all concerned. "I got word Klaus is in Borgo Flora." A fervid gleam flickered in his eyes.

Anthony's mind jumped. He had seen this look on the captain's face before. It was the same look he had when they first arrived in Anzio, when he, Wesley, and Warren were trying to convince him to advise their regiment command to continue their assault rather than to halt.

The captain had refused their recommendation then too. He was thinking of Klaus even back then.

"You're right, Lieutenant." Harding glanced at him, his lips turned up into a maleficent half-smile, "Borgo Flora serves no tactical advantage, but we've received information, a suspicious German convoy showed up there last night. There could be only one reason for this. I believe Klaus is setting up a covert command base there. That village is inconspicuous. He can remain concealed and be close enough to observe our movements." His voice tensed, he leaned forward with his hands on the table. "This is just like him. Everyone would expect him to be in Cisterna where their stronghold would be, but he's too cunning for that. He's running the German defense from Borgo Flora." He fixed his eyes on the spot where the tiny village appeared on the map. "We won't let him outsmart us this time."

Confused, Anthony observed the captain. Harding's intensity made him feel uneasy. Everything he said sounded like wild conjecture. "Captain, you're saying that we don't know for sure Klaus is there. Shouldn't we gather more information on what the Germans are doing there first? They know this region better than we do. Maybe we shouldn't rush in until we know more."

"Oh, he's there. That snake. He is stealthy. I'd bet my money he's there, watching our moves."

Anthony wasn't convinced. He had come to realize that, when it came to Klaus, the captain often could not act in a rational manner. Worse, the direction to split up their company made little sense. He threw a glance at Beck, but Beck was of no help. The battle-tested lieutenant would not support him in the slightest.

"It's too risky, Captain." He tried again to persuade Harding to take a more sensible course. "After what happened to the Rangers, we shouldn't go into any area blind. We can't assume any area is undefended. Why don't we send a recon patrol team there first and find out what we're dealing with?"

"Send a recon patrol team?" Harding balked. "Time is our advantage, Lieutenant. Recon will just waste precious time. What we need is speedy action to get Klaus before he knows we're on to him. Believe me, Ardley, Klaus is a wanted man. Regiment would be pleased if we can capture him. We can't afford to delay."

"What if they are mobilized in that area and they outnumber us?"

"I doubt that. I doubt they're even in Carano. Besides, the whole reason why Klaus is holding out in this armpit is so he could be under our radar, so what would be the point for him to build up his troops there? Our own reports said the Germans are still organizing their defense. Their forces are still weak."

"We can't underestimate them, sir. We shouldn't spread ourselves too thin."

Harding lost his patience. "There is nothing to worry about! Borgo Flora is a tiny farming village. If you see a chance to go in, you're to regroup, reassess your positions, and do what you can to take Borgo Flora. That's my order. This discussion is over." He tapped his pen on the table, then pointed it at Beck. "Lieutenant Beck, how would you like to lead our company's first platoon into Carano? It'll be a good chance for you to show everybody you deserve your gold bar."

"Be glad to, sir," Beck answered without missing a beat. He didn't even look at Anthony.

"Good," Harding said and glared at Anthony. "Good to know I can count on you in case others get cold feet."

Anthony let his last remark slide.

"Any more questions?" Harding asked.

"No, sir," Anthony said. There was no use objecting any further. The captain had made up his mind. He would have to deal with the situation when the time came.

On his way back, Anthony walked past their company's temporary base camp where their troops were resting by their pup tents. With empty ration boxes littered around them, a chorus of men sang, or rather, shouted out the words to "Dogface Soldiers," a song that the Third Division had adopted as their own anthem during their invasion of Anzio. The title of the song told of how the troops, living in pup tents and wearing dog tags, felt like they were dogs in training. The lyrics, however, showed off their pride.

Tomorrow, he would be taking these men on another dangerous mission. Between Harding hell-bent on capturing Klaus and Beck being all too eager to please the higher ranking officers, could he alone keep these men from unnecessary harm? If Harding was indeed sending them into a death trap, what should he do?

What would Wesley do?

The burden weighed on him as he continued on his way.

Chapter 8

The winter sun glided slowly down on the horizon over the sea. Outside her tent, Tessa splashed her face with the water in her helmet to get ready for her evening shift. Earlier in the afternoon, she had tried to sleep, but these days, she could never sleep well. She hadn't seen Anthony for a long while. Every hour of the day, she wondered if he was safe. She had heard so many rumors about the horrifying conditions on the front line, it was hard to know what was true and what was not. Sometimes, she couldn't help thinking the worst when she saw the staggering number of injured men entering the hospital. Here in Anzio, her mind was never at ease. The fact that Anthony's unit had not returned to reserve didn't bode well either. Why hadn't the army relieved his unit yet? He must be so worn out by now. Her heart ached thinking about him.

Nearby, the army engineers continued their work of digging an underground bomb shelter for the nurses quartered in this patch of the beachhead. The brass higher up the chain had decided it was necessary to protect the off-duty nurses and medical personnel from the nightly bomb raids. That was good. They needed it. She looked at the foxhole that Anthony had dug for her. The rain had rendered it useless.

How was Anthony? What was he doing now? She longed to see him again. She was glad she had made a deal with Jesse after all. If she hadn't, she would worry about Anthony even more.

Her shift didn't start for another hour, but as she was unable to rest, she decided she might as well go to work early. The hospital could always use more help. Keeping busy also helped to keep her mind off her worries. She could stop by the canteen and have a quick dinner before she started.

She dried her face with a small towel and tied her hair up into a ponytail. Before she took off, Gracie returned from her day shift. For the fourth day in a row, Gracie had returned with Jesse in tow. She strolled with him hand-in-hand, smiling ear-to-ear.

"Tessa!" Jesse called out to her.

"Hi, Tessa!" Gracie shouted. Her walk turned to a skip, like a young girl hopping on a playground.

Tessa returned their greetings with a reserved smile.

"You're off to work already?" Gracie asked.

"Yes. I couldn't sleep. I might as well go help out. I'll grab dinner at the canteen on the way."

"I'll go back with you." Jesse let go of Gracie's hand. "We can have dinner together."

"You can't stay a bit longer?" Gracie looked at him with longing eyes. "Tonight is your last night at the hospital. You'll have to go back to your unit tomorrow."

"I wish I could," he said, "but it's getting dark. I have to get back before the night raid starts. Besides, I want you to get some rest. You've been working hard all day." He stroked her cheek like she was a child.

"Okay," Gracie pouted. "We'll have lunch together before you leave tomorrow? You promised."

"Of course!" He raised her hand and kissed the back of her fingers. "I'll see you tomorrow."

"See you tomorrow," she called out after him, looking ever more sweet and smitten.

While Jesse and Gracie were saying goodbye, Tessa had left without waiting for him. Realizing that Tessa had walked on ahead, Jesse dropped Gracie's hand with a quick smile and left her to run after Tessa.

"Tessa! Tessa! Wait up!"

Tessa kept on walking, neither slowing down for him nor quickening her pace. He hastened his steps. When he caught up to her, she looked him over once up and down and said, "Running now, huh? Guess you've fully recovered."

"Yeah. It's too bad." He ran his hand up and down the side of his leg where he was wounded. "I kind of enjoyed staying at the hospital doing nothing."

"I'd say!"

They continued walking in silence. Tessa didn't have a habit of making small talk. If she were anyone else, he would have tried to make conversation. He always took one-on-one opportunities like this to charm people when he wanted something from them. With Tessa though, he didn't try. His charming ways with women had no effect on her. She wasn't easily enticed or impressed by anything he could offer the way most other people were, so he no longer bothered. What he didn't expect was how much he liked her that way. Around her, he could finally drop his facade. He didn't have to play a role or put on an act to be who someone else wished him to be. When he was with her, he felt a sense of peace he had never known before. He liked that feeling. He could simply walk with her and be with her. He felt relaxed and at ease. He could be himself.

He didn't get any sense from the silence between them that she wanted to keep him away either. On the contrary, the quietness between them made him feel close to her, as if they understood each other and words were superfluous. As they walked along, a flood of warmth filled his heart. It flowed from his heart to his veins and extended to every part of him. His lips softened into a tender smile that was barely noticeable.

Next to him, Tessa's straight face suddenly turned playful and she let out a chuckle.

"What's so funny?" he asked.

"That she buys your phony act," she said, still snickering.

"Phony?" He feigned indignation. "I take offense to that. I'll have you know that I know exactly how to please and impress a woman. No woman who has ever fallen for me ever doubted me."

"Okay. If you say so."

"What do you mean if I say so? Didn't you see how happy she was back there?"

"Sure I did, but it's not as if it's hard to fool someone as nice and trusting as Gracie."

They walked on again without talking, but now he started to doubt himself.

"Do I really look phony to you?"

She paused. "It's not that you look phony. You're pretty convincing, I suppose. It's more that men who like to seduce women, they like women's attention and they flaunt it. They like showing off they have a lot of different women around them." She stopped and looked at him. "You, though, you always look like you're going through the motions of it. You'll have a lot of girls around you and you'll do and say all the things a womanizer would, but you never look like you enjoy it. I don't know how to explain it. When you're around the girls, you look like you'd rather be somewhere else. So I think you're faking it. It's all a phony act."

He started to dispute her, but said nothing and resumed walking. She followed him. "I don't know why you bother if you don't enjoy it. I especially don't understand why you've decided to make Gracie your next project. You've been walking her back from work for four days now. Only her. Some of the other girls are not very happy about that. Some are getting jealous. It's one thing if you really like Gracie, but if you have no intention of being serious with her, then I don't know why you're causing all this discontent among everyone. Why are you doing this?"

He halted his steps. "Why am I doing this? Why…you don't know?"

She stared at him, curious.

"If I'm with Gracie, then I can keep coming to your tent, and that means I can see you more often."

"Oh, for heaven's sake, Jesse! Stop joking." She walked on. "I am talking seriously with you. Maybe you should stop making everyone jealous. They'll resent her and it'll be all your fault."

"I am serious. I—"

"No!" Tessa cried out in alarm, interrupting him before he could say anything more.

He turned to the direction where she was looking. About ten yards away, a military jeep moving at high speed crashed into a stray dog that had run in front of it. The jeep braked to a stop. Tessa ran toward the dog and Jesse ran after her.

"You idiot!" he yelled at the driver, who had gotten out of the vehicle. "Do you know how to drive?"

"I didn't see it! It came out of nowhere!"

"Shut your trap! Moron."

Tessa examined the dog. Jesse got down on the ground to help and felt its body to check if any part of it was broken. Blood was oozing from the nasty scrape marks on its skin. "I don't have my med kit with me." He grimaced as the dog labored to breathe, annoyed at how helpless he was without his bag of supplies.

"The pulse is slow," Tessa said. "We have to take it to the hospital."

He went back to the jeep. "I need something flat. Something we can use to carry the dog," he said to the driver who was standing by, looking lost. “And bandages. Do you have something we can substitute for bandages?”

“Nothing, I don’t think.” The driver glanced at the supplies he was transporting. Annoyed and losing patience, Jesse ignored him, climbed into the back of the jeep, and rummaged through the loads in the truck.

The driver climbed in after him. “Look, I really didn’t see it. Besides, it’s just a dog—”

He grabbed the driver’s collar. “You say that again and I swear I’ll beat the sh—”

“Jesse! Hurry!” Tessa yelled out to him. He let go of the driver’s shirt and flipped through the loads in the jeep again. The only thing he could find was the lid of a large metal container carrying new army uniforms. He took the lid off and snatched a pair of pants along with some belts and went back to where the dog lay. The poor animal looked lifeless on the ground. He wrapped the pair of army pants around its torso and tightened the belts around it as best as he could. “I don’t even know if this will work. Maybe it’ll slow down the internal bleeding. Let’s take him in.”

She agreed without saying a word. Together, they lifted the dog onto the container lid and carried it to the back of the jeep.

“Take us to the field hospital,” he told the driver as they climbed into the back of the vehicle.

“All right, but I didn’t mean to hurt it—”

“Go!”

The driver got back in and started the car. Every time the car hit a bump, Jesse cringed. If they didn’t get there soon, the dog would never make it.

They arrived at the hospital. At once, Jesse and Tessa took the injured animal and set it on the ground outside the emergency aid area. He grabbed the first bag of saline drip he saw. Frantically, he searched for the dog’s jugular vein and inserted the catheter while Tessa monitored its breathing and tried to find its pulse. He tried to clean and treat some of its wounds, but before he could even get through its front leg, Tessa touched his arm and stopped him. "It won't help." She lifted the dog's upper lip and showed him the pallor of its gums, which had turned pale and dull. "It's got massive internal bleeding. It's going into shock. There's nothing we can do."

Still holding the dog's leg, his hands froze.

Quietly, she told him, "We should put it to rest." She filled a syringe with an overdose of anesthesia and handed it to him. He took the syringe, stared at the dog, and dropped the dog's broken leg from his hand.

"You do it." He gave the syringe back to her.

She took the syringe back. Jesse pulled a pack of cigarettes from his pocket, lit one up, and inhaled while she injected the drug into the saline line he had placed in the dog's jugular vein. He watched her stroke the dog's forehead as its breath waned. When it stopped breathing, they looked at each other. He took another deep drag of his cigarette and walked away.

Chapter 9

In the morning, Anthony took their company forward toward Highway 7. Carrying only their essential weapons and equipment, they hiked up the road behind the tanks that led the way. The artillery units followed not far behind.

The early February sun emitted only languid rays of light through the grey clouds looming above. The cold, dank air and the dreary sight of trees bare of leaves depressed their moods. Trekking along, Anthony watched the wariness on everyone's faces. He could feel the nervous tension of the replacements who had recently joined them. He wished he knew what to say or do to boost the troops' spirits.

Beck, who should be his right-hand man, kept his distance. The new second lieutenant still thought of him as an upstart.

Jonesy, who had been promoted to first sergeant in Beck's place, walked past him. Their eyes met, and he gave Anthony a thumbs up. Anthony smiled. Jonesy might be a loudmouthed jokester, but everyone liked him and Anthony was glad that the sergeant was behind him. He could use all the support he could get.

While they walked, Fox stayed close by his side like a squire. The young sharpshooter used to do this with Wesley too, staying close to the one in charge, always ready to be the first to answer the call.

The incline steepened and the road became harder and harder to tread. Darnell walked to one side and stopped.

"Are you all right, Corporal?" Anthony asked.

"I'm fine." Darnell bent forward, holding himself up with his hands resting on his knees. "Just catching my breath." His face flushed from the physical exertion. Not an athletic man to begin with, he could not keep up with boys more than a decade younger than him on such a demanding climb. Anthony wanted to tell him to take it easy, but couldn't. They had to keep going.

Darnell understood that too. "I'll be fine," he said and started walking again.

"I'll take that," Fox offered, pointing at Darnell's rucksack.

"Thanks." Darnell didn't refuse. Still puffing from the walk, he could use the help.

Approaching the road beyond the area already secured by the Allies, their company advanced in rotations of platoons. Their surroundings were strangely quiet. Anthony detected no sign of the enemy. Could the captain be right after all? Could it be that there were no Germans here? The truth was, he would gladly be wrong if Harding was right that the Germans had not yet arrived. He would gladly admit that his worries were unwarranted if it meant that nobody would get killed.

They continued forward for a long while and came upon no resistance. But the farther they went, the more nervous Anthony felt. He couldn't shake the feeling that something was wrong. The Germans had been gearing up and mobilizing for days. They couldn't have left this entire area unguarded. There should be at least some signs of German activity here. Why was everything so quiet?

What if this was a trap? What if they were walking into a trap like the one the Germans had set up to capture the Rangers?

As they closed in on the area they were trying to reach, he surveyed the terrain, all the while keeping his eyes and ears alert to any hint of enemy presence. He marked in his mind the areas where they could run for cover in case they came upon a surprise attack.

"We could waltz right into Carano and be home in time for dinner," Beck said. "Carano's just a few miles ahead, and there's no one here."

He spoke too soon. Without warning, gunshots broke out and smashed the silence. Up ahead, the enemy had opened fire. Enemy shells began to drop and black smoke rose from the ground, obstructing their sight. The roars of cannons followed as their own tanks fired back. The puttering pops of machine guns raged all around.

Everyone dove for cover. Anthony lunged into a ditch on the side of the road. While bullets flew above him, he moved down the ditch to try to find a position from which he could shoot. A bullet struck a soldier in front of him, piercing his jaw and knocking him down. Another soldier tried to get to the fallen man and was hit himself. A mere glimpse at their bodies and Anthony knew that they were both dead.

In a matter of minutes, everything had descended into hell.

The battle continued into the afternoon without end. In the chaos, Anthony managed to organize the troops around him. Luckily, with their tanks shielding them and the artillery units moving up to provide support, their forces were able to stave off the attack against them.

The Germans, too, refused to back down. Sounds of gunfire would break out as the two sides exchanged shots. The shooting then tapered off, only to break out again as the hours wore on until, eventually, the sun began to descend. The troops on both sides tired and the fighting halted except for the occasional sparring of sniper shots.

"Lieutenant! Lieutenant!" a runner came up to him in the ditch.

"What?" he asked.

"Lieutenant Beck said to tell you he is taking his platoon to Borgo Flora."

"He what?"

"He has taken his platoon to Borgo Flora to look for Klaus. He said we're holding fine here and now's a good chance to try to capture Klaus before our fighting resumes here tomorrow." The runner then made an incredulous face and said, "He said they'll be back before dark."

Anthony could not believe his ears.

"He said this was the captain's order," the runner added.

Anthony tightened his grip around his gun. Beck. That fool. The idiot didn't even clear it with him before he went off. He would not have dared to pull such a stunt with Wesley.

Doing his best to restrain himself, Anthony said to the runner, "Find First Sergeant Jones. Bring him here."

"Yessir." The private went off, clearly glad to take his leave after delivering the bad news.

"Beck, damn fool," Anthony muttered under his breath. Beck was not the brightest man among them, but this was stupid even for him. If the Germans had already set up such an efficient defense here, they would likely have done the same in nearby villages including Borgo Flora. Besides, it was utterly irresponsible for him to take off when they were still in combat here. He was an experienced veteran. How could he not know that? Why would he do something like this?

If only Wesley were still here. Without Wesley, their company had become dysfunctional. They couldn't even coordinate among themselves.

But you're leading the company, a voice said within him. The voice, harsh and unforgiving, laid the blame squarely in front of him.

He looked toward the direction of Borgo Flora. No matter what, he was at fault. He had let this happen. He couldn't control his own troops.

Frustrated, he played out all the possible options in his mind and tried to think of what to do. He wasn't sure. He felt like he was winging it and making up his plan as he went.

"What is it, Lieutenant?" Jonesy came up to him.

"Beck's gone to Borgo Flora."

"Why? Did you send him there?"

"No, I didn't send him. He decided to go on his own. He took his platoon with him."

"You're joking!" Jonesy looked at him in disbelief. "Why would he do that?"

"The captain ordered us to take Borgo Flora, although it wasn't the plan for him to take off this way. He's gone to look for Klaus."

"That's fucked up. What do you want to do?"

Anthony looked around at the troops still holding in their positions. Fox snuck his head up above the ditch, aimed, and fired a shot. He was still carrying Darnell's rucksack. Anthony looked at the direction of Borgo Flora again.

Darnell. Darnell was in Beck's platoon.

Beck could get his men killed.

Anthony's heart sank. He had to do something. He couldn't let their men risk their lives on a fool's errand under his watch. "Jonesy."

"Yes?"

"Tell Sergeant Oliver to bring the rear guard up. I'll take a platoon to Borgo Flora to back them up. Or better yet, get them out before tomorrow morning when the Germans start shooting at us again."

"Are you sure?" Jonesy asked, concerned. "You'll get yourself killed too."

Jonesy was right. This could be a lost cause.

It's now up to you and me to get everyone through this.

Wesley…

Anthony clutched his gun. "We can't leave them out there. If the Germans are there, they could get wiped out."

"Do you want me to go instead?"

Anthony considered his offer. Jonesy had a point. Perhaps he should stay. As first lieutenant leading the mission, his place was here, but sending someone else to get Beck might not work. No one else had ranking authority over Beck to order him to stand down and return. "No," he told Jonesy. "I'll go. You're in charge until I come back. Go get Ollie and get his men up here."

Quickly, Jonesy ran off. The sun was setting. The gunfire had calmed. The line between them and the enemy was drawn. Anthony got up, rounded up his own platoon and a tank to prepare for another fight. As soon as he saw that Ollie and the reserve unit had moved up, he took his platoon and the tank and began to make their way to Borgo Flora. He thought of Darnell and all the soldiers who followed Beck. They could be marching to their deaths. He needed to get them out before it was too late. From the east, the moon was rising. He only hoped he could get to them in time.

From the noises of artillery coming from the direction of Borgo Flora, Anthony knew the situation in the village was as he feared. The Germans had taken that village too. Captain Harding was right about that, but he was wrong that the Germans weren't mobilized. The noises of the battle sounded too fierce.

Could Klaus really be there as the captain had thought? There was no way to know.

He took his binoculars out and looked at the view ahead. The village of Borgo Flora was very small. From the number of houses he could see, there couldn't be more than a hundred people living there. He didn't see any German tanks. The fighting seemed confined to rifles and submachine guns. Grenades were exploding everywhere.

"Are we ready?" Fox asked.

Anthony lowered the binoculars and nodded.

Following the tank, they made their way in. The ground was strewn with bodies of dead American soldiers, slaughtered.

They came upon a narrow street where Beck and his men were pinned down by enemy fire coming from the windows above. The tank could not get through.

"We have to split up," Anthony said to Fox. "I'll get Beck. You stay with the tank and take the village from the other side."

Fox ran off with his squad at his order. Moving lightly, Anthony led his troops in. They came closer to Beck and the others trapped by gunfire, trying as carefully as they could not to draw attention to themselves. It was no use. A machine gunner from a second story window spotted them and sent a blast of bullets down, taking out two men behind Anthony as they dashed from one spot to another to escape. As he ran, Anthony saw out of the corner of his eyes the bodies of the men who were hit writhing on the ground. He felt a piece of his own soul perishing with them.

Another blast came at them. He ran behind a pile of rubble and crouched down to catch his breath.

Beck! If they got out of this alive, he would kill the cretin himself for this!

But the company is under your command, not his. The inner voice taunted him. *It's your job to protect them.*

Angry, he raised his Tommy gun and shot at the window where the machine gunner was shooting and killing his men.

The enemy gunner behind the window sent several blasts his way, then turned to target a group of men hiding next to a pile of wreckage across the street. The gunman's shots were relentless. He was determined to obliterate them. Another soldier fell.

Watching the man die, Anthony couldn't take it anymore. Abandoning his own safety, he darted along the buildings toward the machine gunner. When he got close enough, he hurled a grenade through the window. The gunfire stopped and everything inside stood still. Then, the window and the wall exploded. Debris from the explosion rained down all over him as he ran away. He could taste the dust and dry specks of rubble in his mouth. He spat them out and strode ahead, calling for the soldiers in hiding to follow him.

Scrambling from building to building, they continued on, searching out the enemy, searching out their own. The Germans hidden inside kept up and retaliated, killing more of his men and thwarting them from getting through the street to escape. Desperate to defend his troops, Anthony returned fire. Saving his soldiers was the only thought in his mind.

When they came close to the end of the street, the hum and sputters of the Sherman tank coming from the other side sent him a rush of relief. The tank fired a shell and struck the building where the Germans were barricaded. The building's wall crumbled. German soldiers staggered out and ran.

Among the Germans on the run was a soldier in a commander's uniform. Instinctively, Anthony ran after him. The man turned his head slightly. Anthony, taken by surprise, stopped. The man's face looked familiar. His icy eyes unnerved him. And then, it struck him. Klaus.

Klaus ignored him and dashed behind another building. Anthony chased after him, but when he reached the other building, Klaus was nowhere in sight.

Outgunned by the Americans, the remaining German troops soon surrendered. Borgo Flora was under their control. Klaus, though, had disappeared.

Anthony wasn't the only one who had encountered him.

"I saw him," Beck said. "I could've gotten him."

"You could've gotten everybody killed," Anthony shot back at him. Beck's platoon had lost half its men. Anthony's own platoon suffered casualties too. Behind them, Darnell and Fox were lining up the German soldiers they had captured.

"At least we took this place," Beck retorted. "Now we won't have to report back to the captain empty-handed." He glanced at the German prisoners of war. "Believe me, Lieutenant, the captain will be happy to hear this."

The captain? Anthony thought. He didn't care about pleasing the captain. He looked at their weary, remaining troops. He had failed them. He couldn't control Beck and lives were lost because of it. He had failed to protect them.

Chapter 10

Despite their casualties and failure at capturing Klaus, Harding was not disappointed with their mission's outcome. Two days after their company took Borgo Flora, their battalion advanced into Carano. When the city was secured, the captain invited Anthony and Beck to the small abandoned shack which was their temporary command post for a private toast to congratulate them.

"Well done, gentlemen." The captain poured himself a hearty shot of whiskey and guzzled it, then smacked his lips, savoring the taste. "I cannot be more pleased to hear we gave Klaus a good scare and took the village from him."

Unlike the captain, Anthony couldn't revel in their victory. Yes, the captain had been right about Klaus hiding in Borgo Flora. And yes, they had sent Klaus running. But Harding was wrong about one thing. Klaus wasn't scared. In that split second when Klaus turned around before he ran off, all Anthony saw was the cold, calculating eyes of a man who could stay calm even in the face of death.

As for taking Borgo Flora, it was a worthless victory. The place offered no vantage point for their continuing mission to take Cisterna. All it did was deliver a win for the captain in his personal duel against

Klaus. The number of men they had lost to take this little rural village was not worth it.

"Lieutenant Beck, here's to you." Harding poured Beck a shot. "Thank you for leading the way."

Anthony winced. Beck, though, didn't show the least bit of regret. "Thank you, sir." He accepted the drink and finished it in one gulp. The story of his storming into the village to go after the infamous German major had now spread like a heroic tale and he wasn't shy to take the credit.

Things could not remain this way, Anthony thought. He must find a way to keep Beck in check. This was not simply a matter of rank and respect. If Beck disregarded him again, the consequences would be on him too.

"Now, gentlemen, be sure to get your beauty sleep," Harding said. "Get a good night's rest tonight. Tomorrow, we'll move on."

"Move on?" Anthony wasn't aware that their battalion command wanted to press forward yet.

Harding took out a map and laid it on the table, then gestured for them to come over. "I want us to scout out this area." He pointed at a wooded area in the mountains north of Cisterna.

"Why?" Anthony asked.

"Because this is where Klaus is now." The fervid gleam had returned to Harding's eyes. "We questioned the German soldiers we captured in Borgo Flora. One of them told us this is where Klaus is. He's gathering his men there. We should try to capture him before his troops are fully mobilized there."

"Sir, we've been ordered to hold our position in Carano, and we should. We should concentrate our forces here in case more Germans arrive. Diverting our troops into the woods would spread us out too thin. Did regimental HQ authorize this?"

The captain threw him a dismissive glance. "It's just a precautionary measure. We can handle it. Regiment's got enough forces here at Carano, and we took Borgo Flora from Klaus too, didn't we?" Sensing Anthony's doubt, he gave Anthony a wickedly friendly smile. "I have full confidence in us, Lieutenant. Don't you?"

Anthony stared at the area on the map where Harding wanted to send them. The forest terrain had too many places for the enemy to hide, and climbing up the mountain could put everyone in danger if the Germans were in fact there. "Captain," he said, mindful not to sound argumentative, "we don't have enough information. We're relying entirely on the words of a German prisoner. For all we know, the Germans might have staked out this whole area. It's too risky. We lost a lot of men in Carano and Borgo Flora. Our troops are tired. Division says they're sending replacements, but they aren't arriving fast enough. We could be outnumbered."

"Or we could be losing our chance for a quick victory if we don't act," Harding said. "Have you forgotten, Lieutenant, that you were the one who urged us to push ahead and not wait when we first got here to Anzio?"

Stumped, Anthony felt lost for words.

"I'm taking your advice from then under consideration now, so what could be wrong?"

"Captain," Anthony said, flustered. "There was no German defense here when we first arrived. They could be here now."

"There is no basis to believe that." Harding raised his voice. "Our intel reports said they're still mobilizing. There weren't enough of them to hold us off in Carano. Even with Klaus in command, they couldn't defend a nothing village like Borgo Flora." His excitement grew as he talked. "If we can find Klaus, we may even be able to capture him and take down his troops. If we do that, our battalion would be able to move up and expand our occupied zone behind Cisterna. If we succeed, we'll be able drive into Cisterna when the rest of the regiment gets here. We'll deliver Klaus his final blow." Then, realizing he had lost his composure, he checked himself and calmed down. "The Germans are not ready. What I'm asking amounts to nothing more than essentially a recon mission, Lieutenant. There is nothing to worry about."

Anthony tried again to object, but the captain cut him off. "Lieutenant Beck, what do you think?"

"Bring it on, sir. The boys and I can handle it."

Satisfied, Harding relaxed. "That's the spirit."

Anthony didn't know what to do. Everything was slipping away from him. Just now, he had been thinking about reigning Beck in, but the captain was making it impossible.

"I don't want to let Klaus get away again," Harding said. "Find him in the forest. He's got to be there. He couldn't have gotten far."

"Yes, sir," Beck said, looking smug.

Anthony glanced at the captain. How could he be so sure Klaus was in the forest? He wondered if the captain had lost his mind.

"Oh, Lieutenant Beck, why don't you lead this mission? Take First Sergeant Jones and Sergeant Oliver with you. Looks to me Lieutenant Ardley's got a case of cold feet. Or maybe he needs some rest. The men are tired, he said. He can stay behind with the reserve unit."

"Will do, Captain." Beck gave Anthony a haughty grin.

Anthony tightened his fists. He had become useless.

Before Anthony left, Harding pulled him aside. "Ardley."

"Yes, Captain."

"Let's not talk like we're afraid of the Gerries again. It's demoralizing for the troops."

Unable to contradict him, Anthony said, "Yes, sir." In his mind, he didn't agree. He could not overlook the risks to their own men. He had promised Wesley he would look out for them. He couldn't disregard their troops' lives because of Harding.

But what he thought and what he intended didn't matter. It was his actions that counted. At that, he was failing. At Carano, he didn't keep Beck under control. Now, all he had done was get himself sidelined. He wouldn't even be on the field tomorrow. If something could be done to save them from suffering more casualties, he wouldn't be there to make it happen.

He thought of the first time he had gone to battle when the captain assigned him to lead a deadly assault. He thought of how Wesley had changed their plans at the last minute during their mission to protect him. Why couldn't he learn to work the system like Wesley?

Defeated, he returned to his tent.

Nearby, Jonesy and Ollie were playing cards by their tents. "Want to join us, Lieutenant?" Jonesy joked. He knew Anthony couldn't.

Instead of saying no as usual, Anthony came over to them. "Ready for your next mission tomorrow?"

"Will you be coming with us?" Jonesy asked.

As he could not say yes, Anthony only looked at him with regret.

"Beck?" Ollie asked. Anthony did not deny it.

"Hell, no then." Jonesy sucked his cigarette and took a swig from his bottle of cheap wine. "Not if you're not coming with us."

Anthony thought he was joking, but Ollie looked at him and bobbed his head up and down in agreement. "We really don't want to go without you."

"Things weren't like this when Lieutenant Sharpe was around." Jonesy blew out a cloud of smoke. "We didn't used to run headlong into the lion's den like this with no good plan. Lieutenant Sharpe always had a plan. I don't want to talk shit about Beck, but if he's running the show, fuck me, my days are numbered."

"Yeah," Ollie concurred. "Another snafu like Borgo Flora, we'll be all done for."

Anthony couldn't believe what they had just said. Jonesy and Ollie were both experienced fighters. To hear them say they wanted to follow him in battle, it meant they believed in him. He wished he could tell them how much he appreciated their words. Their faith in him was a greater validation to him than the silver on his shoulders.

At the same time, he felt he had let them down. Not only had he failed to convince the captain to change course, he got himself put on reserve. Because of that, Jonesy and Ollie were saddled with this mess, with Beck calling all the shots. If anything happened to either one of them, he would never forgive himself.

Chapter 11

As Anthony feared, the mission into the forest was a disaster.

The chaotic return of the squads that made it out alive was the first sign of how bad things had gone. Those who were lucky to escape brought back with them a slew of bad news. Their company had come under attack within an hour after they began making their way into the woods. The Germans had staked out the area and their presence threw everyone into a frenzy. Beck tried to lead them to retreat, but the enemy's gunfire formed a wall of bullets between his platoon and those that followed him, separating him and his men from the rest of the company. Jonesy and Ollie got away in time, but Beck and his men were cut off, isolated and trapped.

As Jonesy reported in detail what had happened, Harding's face tensed. His expression changed from shock, to panic, then fury. He glared at the photo of Klaus on the table. "He lured us there," he said. "Klaus knew we would come after him in the forest because we captured his men, so he set up his army there. That was his plan. This is how he wants to destroy us."

Anthony exchanged a glance with Jonesy. Ollie looked up, then sideways, completely befuddled. What the captain was saying didn't make any sense. Klaus couldn't have known they would come after him in the forest. Besides, they had no proof Klaus was in the forest at all. Only the captain believed that he was.

"He's devious." Harding's voice turned bitter. Anthony noticed the tic on the left side of his face. "He wants to trap us in the forest and demolish us."

Anthony wondered if Harding might have gone mad. The Germans had been mobilizing for days. They knew the mountains and forest regions well, much better than the Americans. Fortifying themselves in the mountains and taking advantage of the terrain was their winning tactic back in Cassino, and it made good battle sense here. Their hiding out in the mountains was entirely logical and predictable. The forest gave them an even greater cover to solidify their defense. It was only a matter of when the Germans would employ their tactic of geographical advantage. No matter how devious Klaus might be, the enemy's set up was not the result of one man's plan. "Captain," Anthony said, hoping to refocus their attention back to their trapped comrades. "Our men, we need to figure out what to do."

Clearly frustrated, Harding slammed his hand on the table. "How are Beck and his men holding up?"

"I checked with them over the radio," Ollie said. "They're holding on for now. It's gotten dark and the attacks stopped, but they won't last if they don't make their way outta there soon."

"What about our tanks? Can we get our tanks in to get them out?"

"No, sir," Jonesy said. "The tanks couldn't get up and through the trees. The armored trucks and mortar vehicles couldn't either. When we first went in, we had to leave them behind at the bottom of the hills."

Harding's face darkened.

As much as Anthony wished there were other options, he knew there was only one way to save them. "We have to go get them. We have to go back and get them out."

Everyone fell silent.

He also knew the only way he could ensure their success would be for him to lead the rescue himself. "We'll regroup," he said. "I'll take us all back in tomorrow morning."

Without any other solution, Harding gave his tacit consent.

# # #

Their company took off before the crack of dawn. It was a rescue mission from which all Anthony hoped was that they would make it out alive.

Just as Jonesy had described, the forest spread across a hill which the tanks could not climb. They walked along the ridge leading into the forest, treading as lightly as they could. There were no sounds except the crackle of branches and leaves under their feet. The early morning fog began to dissipate, but the tension among the troops hung thick in the air, weighing them down.

They had taken the entire company with them except for a rear guard of three squads, but their forces were hardly invincible. Half of the soldiers he was leading were replacements who had only joined their company in recent weeks. They were inexperienced and terrified. The other half were already worn down by the fighting in Carano and the battles before that. Their exhaustion was obvious.

Faint noises of a gunfight grew as they went further into the woods. Instinctively, some of the soldiers halted and clutched their rifles.

"Fox," Anthony said to the young soldier next to him. "Go in and scout the area. See if you can find Beck and his men. If you can find him, ask him if he knows whether the Germans have a weak spot we can break into?"

"Yes, Lieutenant." Fox went ahead without hesitation. Anthony watched him go. He prayed he was not sending Fox to his death.

While Fox was gone, he surveyed the area. Their way ahead would continue to be an uphill climb. This was a bad sign. The Germans could lob grenades down to stop them.

Feeling anxious, Anthony glanced at his watch. Fox returned less than half an hour later. Anthony felt a wave of relief to see him alive. The reliable young soldier brought back with him a private who was among the trapped. Cross-eyed and frazzled, the private's face exhibited a mixture of desperation, fatigue, and fright. He was nothing more than a terrified boy, but he managed to tell them where the trapped troops were hiding and the conditions up ahead.

Armed with the new intel, they moved up until they came to a flattened area near where Beck and his men were hiding. Anthony took out his binoculars and assessed the scene. The first thing he saw were the bodies of American soldiers dead on the ground. The sight wrenched his heart.

"Our troops are right there." The private pointed to a spot ahead. "They're in the foxholes."

Anthony looked at the area near the spot, trying to determine the safe perimeter around Beck and his platoon. The sun was now out of the shadow of the night. With the rising daylight, the area was turning into a war zone once again with clacks of guns and rumbles of exploding shells. The Germans were zeroing in on the trapped men. Worse, the German fire was blocking him and the rest from reaching their comrades. They would have to run head on into the storm of German bullets to save them.

"It's going to be tough to find everybody with all these trees," Jonesy said. He too, was scanning the scene with binoculars.

Anthony turned his sight higher above the ground. With all the trees blocking their view, it would be hard to tell the Germans from their own men. Besides the German guns, they would have to watch out for their own friendly fire. This would be the worst hide-and-seek game he would ever play.

He turned to Jonesy and Ollie. "This is the only way in." He pointed to a path by the ridge. They answered with subdued silence, knowing all too well that when they tried to cross, many of them would be shot.

"We'll have to be quick," Anthony said. The longer they took, the more chance they'd be dead.

Leaving a platoon behind to keep their escape route open, they moved in. Inching forward into positions and camouflaging themselves as best as they could behind the trees, they waited for Anthony's signal. Anthony felt himself tensing up. His heart hammered. If this mission failed, it would be all on him.

He waved "go." When he did, everything became a blur.

Their troops rushed in, zigzagging between trees while firing at every spot where they saw their enemy. As soon as they opened fire, the Germans fired back. Anthony raced forward. In the rush, men—his men—fell all around him. Harrowing cries and shouts for help seared through the cold mechanical hisses of guns. He ran behind a tree and threw a grenade at a German soldier manning a machine gun, then sprinted to another tree near where Fox and the cross-eyed private were returning fire. He grabbed the private. "Take me to Beck!"

In fear, the private nodded and lurched forward. Fox followed, covering them and fending off hits coming their way until they came to the foxhole where Beck was hiding. Anthony slid inside.

"We got to get the rest of your men," Anthony said to Beck. With a dour face of someone who knew he had committed a fubar, Beck nodded. They jumped out of the foxhole. Crisscrossing from tree to tree, they checked every foxhole and pushed everyone toward the escape route. The German snipers continued their fire, forcing them to stop again and again to avoid being hit.

Darting behind a tree, Anthony held his Tommy gun close, looking for the best way out. The cross-eyed private was behind a tree not far from him. A sniper about thirty feet away sent a shot. The bullet hit the tree behind which the private hid. In a panic, the boy started to run. The sniper fired another shot. His bullet hit the private in the chest and the boy fell to the ground. Anthony aimed at the sniper and struck him down, then ran to try to help the private, but the kid was already dead. His blood seeped out of his chest, staining his jacket. Anthony looked away. His stomach tightened.

They must get everyone out of there. He did not want to see any more of them dead. He rounded up his troops as best he could. For once, Beck followed him, gathering the remaining men to retreat.

When the area was cleared, they turned to escape. A shot rang out from a tree behind them and Beck fell to the ground.

"Beck!" Anthony ran back.

"Ah! Those fuckers." Beck pounded his fist on the ground. "They shot my ass."

Holding his weapon with one arm, Anthony pulled Beck up and dragged him forward to help him get away. More bullets were now coming at them. A grenade exploded near them, sending dirt and debris their way. Thankfully, no shrapnel reached them.

"Lieutenant, Lieutenant, let me help you!" someone called out to him. In the haze of smoke, Anthony saw Jim Darnell running toward them. Before he reached them, a stray bullet hit him in the front of his neck. Blood spurted out of his wound and he clutched his throat with both of his hands. For a split second, he looked confused, as if he couldn't believe what just happened. Then his eyes widened. He looked at Anthony, as if begging for help. Gurgling sounds escaped from his throat as he fell to the ground.

Stunned, Anthony stood. Everything happened so fast, he couldn't process his thoughts. Jim was alive only seconds ago. He had come to try to help them.

Another grenade exploded. The blast sent splinters of wood flying past him, cutting his pants and slicing his skin.

Fox appeared. He pulled Beck up by the other side. "Lieutenant!" he shouted. "Run!"

Acting now entirely on instinct, Anthony continued on. With Fox's help, they hurried toward the escape path back to the ridge.

They finally reached the troops guarding the path and waiting for the last of the escapees. Following everyone in retreat, they hurtled down the hill. Grenades flew down at them as they raced away. Men continued to drop around them.

When the noise of the German fire tapered off and his mind became clearer, the only image Anthony could see was Jim Darnell, with a bewildered look on his face and blood flooding out of his throat.

On his way to report to Harding, Anthony felt a tightness seizing his entire core. His throat was so constricted, he could hardly swallow. Their company had been depleted to nothing more than a few squads of able men. Of the one hundred and fifty men in their company, only twenty-three had made it out unharmed. The rest were dead, injured, or missing.

"Ardley! You made it back! That's great. That's really great." Harding said, oblivious and relieved to see him return. No one had told him yet that their mission had turned into a massacre. "I got your radio report. You got them out. Great job. Great job. Could you gather everyone in the field? I want to personally commend everyone."

Anthony stared at the captain. Suddenly, he felt tired. Tired inside. Tired throughout. Without saying another word, he turned and walked away.

"Where are you're going? Ardley. You can't leave yet. I'm not done talking to you."

Ignoring him, Anthony walked on. He might be reprimanded later for walking out this way, but he was too tired and numb to care.

# # #

In the chapel of the little village church in Carano, Anthony sat alone on the pew before the altar. The cherubic sculptures of two baby angels on the wall smiled mercifully at him even though he didn't feel he deserved forgiveness.

An elderly caretaker lit the candles and illuminated the place. When he finished, he took one curious look at Anthony, then walked away and disappeared behind a side door.

Anthony slouched forward and laid his forehead in his hands. The image of Jim Darnell's violent death played again and again in his mind.

Darnell was just a man who sold ice-cream. Anthony remembered the photo that Darnell had once shown him. He had four small children. Those children had now lost their father.

What did Darnell do to deserve this?

Since coming to Italy, Anthony had seen his share of deaths. He thought he had learned to deal with it. He thought he had accepted that death was a necessary part of war. In the big scheme of things, they were each nothing but a number to be added or subtracted when needed. But the massacre in the forest depressed him far more than he ever thought anything could. It was not just the death of Darnell, but the staggering number of people who had died. More than two-thirds of their company was now wiped out. The death toll had mounted from Carano to Borgo Flora and then to the forest. The accumulation of casualties felt worse this time. He felt responsible. If he had been as astute as Wesley in dealing with the captain, maybe he could've stopped all the misguided missions from the start.

The echoes of footsteps up the aisle broke the silence in the sanctuary. He ignored it, but the person who entered sat down next to him.

"I saw you coming in here," Warren said. "Sounds like you all got clobbered."

"It was a blood bath."

"You did your best."

"Did I? I'm not so sure." Anthony dropped his hands onto his lap and held them together. "The whole time we were fighting, I tried to think what Wesley would've done if he was here. I tried to do the same thing. He knew how to command the troops. People like Beck wouldn't defy him. He knew how to manage the captain. I don't. I can't. I'm doing the best I can to fill in for him. I'm not sure if I can do it anymore. I can't do what Wesley did."

"So don't."

"Don't what?"

"Don't do what Wesley did. Don't fill in for Wesley."

Anthony looked at him, puzzled.

"Maybe that's your problem," Warren said. "You're trying too hard to be Wesley, but you're not Wesley. Wesley's dead. Maybe it's time to close his playbook. What worked for him, obviously it's not working for you. What would work for you? You're the first lieutenant now. What would you do?"

What would he do? Anthony hadn't thought of asking himself that question.

"It's time to set your own playbook." Warren gave him a sympathetic smile and left.

Alone once again, Anthony stared at the altar.

What would I do?

Take control, a voice inside him said.

He realized then that he would not let the captain risk the troops' lives anymore. If Harding's vendetta against Klaus was clouding his judgment, he would have to make sure their troops wouldn't be sacrificed for it. There was only one person still looking out for everyone. That person was him.

From now on, he would make sure he was in full command of the operations when they went out on a mission. He would not lose control of Beck or anyone else again. He would no longer stand by helplessly when Harding gave his wild orders, only to watch tragedies unfold before him. Not if he could help it. He would have to find a way to take control of the situation.

That meant he must take on every major battle himself. If he were to take control, then he must get out on the field. He could not be with the reserves when his company's platoons went out like last time when Beck took the troops into the forest. If he were to stop Harding from risking everyone's lives, he would have to be out on the field where he could command the operations and take control.

It might not be apparent to the others, but Harding was not always in his right mind, especially when it came to Klaus. If Harding lost his senses again, he might have to take the most drastic action and defy him.

It's now up to you and me to get everyone through this.

Yes. This was what he had to do. Get everyone through this. The army was sending all the people in his company into dangerous battles, asking them to fight a war. These people were innocent men. Men like Darnell who might be an ice-cream parlor owner with small children. They were told to follow every order, even orders to sacrifice themselves.

They had no one other than their commanding officers to look to, to make sure that someone was in turn looking out for them. Right now, he was all they had to look to, to hope that they could get back home.

He couldn't let them down again.

Beck. He had to reign in Beck. He had to keep him on a tight leash. He would have to make Beck listen and follow his orders.

He stared at the cross on the altar in front of the stained glass window and reached his fingers to touch his cross. It had become a habit now whenever he needed reassurance. He looked down at it, a bit startled to see it. With everything that had been going on, he almost forgot that the cross was with him all along.

Tessa.

The beachhead was less than ten miles away from the Allies' front line. If their army failed to hold, the Germans would invade the beachhead and push their entire force out into the sea.

The Allies could not fail. His company could not fail. They could not let the Germans defeat them. He would do whatever he had to do to keep the beachhead safe, to keep Tessa safe.

He took their photo out of his pocket. It was the one they took together over a year ago at the Museum of Science and Industry in front of the Christmas tree. The theme of the tree was Christmas Around the World. It was a beacon for peace.

The photo took him back to a time when he could still live without a care in the world, back to a more innocent time before they both saw the true depth of human evil and depravity. It was the last time when they could love without the burden of all the world's miseries thrust upon them.

He was only an ordinary person. He never sought to be more. That day, in front of the Christmas tree, all he had hoped for was for the girl standing beside him to fall in love with him. How maddening it was back then, when he wanted so much to have her and yet could not for the life of him figure out how to let her know his feelings for her.

But she did fall in love with him. More than that, she braved oceans and mountains to come to him, placing herself in the center of war to be by his side. She risked everything, even her own life, to be with him.

He looked at the cross and prayed that he and Tessa would make it through this war. Not for his own sake or their own survival above everybody else's, but because, for the days to come, he wanted to have many, many more days to make her happy. He wanted to return her love and give her all the love that he could give.

No. He could not risk his own life unnecessarily for Harding anymore either.

He looked at the beauty of Tessa's smile in the photo. Seeing her image comforted him. For a brief moment, it drew his thoughts away from death and misery.

He still remembered how hard she cried the night before he left home.

Tessa. He held on to the photo. There were still things to live for in this world.

Somewhere, not too far away, she was waiting for him. She was waiting for a future with him when there would be peace. Before the cross at the altar, he made a vow that he would not let her down.

PART FOUR
Stolen Kisses

Chapter 12

Tessa wrapped up the last of her remaining duties of the day and checked her watch. In another few minutes, she would be off her shift. She couldn't wait to be done. Anthony was waiting for her at her tent. It had been more than three weeks since she last saw him.

She had never before prayed as hard as she had in the last three weeks. Only when she found out his company was back on reserve did she feel like she could rest easy again. When she got his message from Jesse that he would be coming to see her today, she began counting the days, then the hours.

The war was not going well here at Anzio. As the days passed, the German attacks on the Allies intensified. The sounds of gunfire never let up, they only escalated. The entire region seemed to be infested with German troops closing in on them. After nearly a month, the Allies still couldn't make any headway inland. They were barely holding on to the front line surrounding the beach. If the Germans broke through their line of defense, the Allies would have no place to retreat except into the sea.

The atmosphere was not the only bad sign. By the sheer number of people admitted to the hospital every day, Tessa knew everything had taken a turn for the worse. Most harrowing were the dreadful injuries they suffered. When the casualties rolled in, it was all she could do to block Anthony out of her mind. She didn't want to think that, at any time, one of the casualties could be him. She didn't want to be reminded of that terrifying thought.

Thankfully, he was back again. All she wanted was to run to him, to see him alive and well and in one piece, but her hope of spending a few good hours with him was dashed when Captain Milton showed up and asked her to stay longer.

"Alice and several of the medical corpsmen are coming down with the flu," Milton said. "We're shorthanded. Can you stay and see to it that the patients in Ward Three have gotten their morphine shots? I know you've worked all night, but there's no one else."

Saying no to Milton was not an option. Her request was in fact an order. "Yes, ma'am," Tessa answered without showing her disappointment and reminded herself that her duties were her priority.

Her work didn't stop with the morphine shots. After that, there were supplies to be restocked, equipment to sanitize, and items to collect for the laundry. Unlike her work back at the Chicago Veterans Hospital, or her mother's hospital back in England, so much of her work here involved manual labor, so much hauling of things from one place to another.

The hours went by. Her work seemed endless. She checked the time in between tasks, her heart sinking further and further as the minutes slipped away. When Milton finally let her leave, she had lost all hope of seeing Anthony today. If he was waiting for her, he would probably be gone by now. She wondered why he hadn't come to the hospital to look for her. Perhaps he had, but she was moving around in so many places, he couldn't find her?

She left the hospital and hurried back to her tent. To her delight when she approached, Anthony was still there. He was sitting on the ground, asleep with his back against a tent pole.

Excited, she ran to him and kneeled down beside him. She was almost afraid to look away from him. If she could, she would etch his image into her memory. Before Anzio, she hadn't realized how precious it was to be able to see him. In this place, in this living hell, everything could be lost in a split moment. Any life could perish to dust and be taken away without an ounce of mercy. She wanted to remember everything about him, his every look and every feature. Just in case.

*Just in case...*She frowned and stopped herself from finishing that awful thought.

She took a closer look at him. He must be so tired to fall asleep like this. Asleep, he was scowling. His face was tensed. The hardship of war had left its mark on him.

She thought of the Anthony she knew before they came to war, the one whose smile was like a ray of sunshine. The one who radiated goodness and personified everything that was upright and decent. The one who made her feel that Chicago was where she belonged. The one who showed her for the first time what it felt like to be in love.

She watched him, sound asleep but tormented by a troubled mind. What was he dreaming about? What horror had he seen that was haunting him in his sleep?

It made her wonder. Would the old Anthony remain unscathed if the war continued to take its toll on him?

She reached out her hand and gently touched his face.

He opened his eyes. When he realized that her hand was on him, he rubbed his face against her palm.

"I'm sorry," she said. "I couldn't get out. Captain Milton asked me to stay and help."

"It's all right. What time is it?" He looked at his watch. His face dropped. "I have to go soon. We've got training this afternoon."

They stared at each other, disappointed. There was so much she wanted to say to him, and time had run out.

"Come here." He pulled her into his arms.

She sat down against him, trying to hold on to every moment that she could feel his warmth and hear the beating of his heart. His heartbeats were melodies to her ears. They were clear signs that he was alive.

He kissed her forehead. She closed her eyes, relishing the feel of the touch of his lips.

"I guess the foxhole didn't work out so well." He glanced at the hole he had dug for her. The bottom was filled with muddy water that never drained away.

"Nothing ever works right in this place," she said. "It rains so much. What do you do when your dugout gets wet?"

"I stay in it," he said, resigned. "We're used to it." He tightened his arm around her. "Sometimes we try to slant the bottom of the foxhole so the water drains from one end to the other end. Mostly, I just pray that I don't get trench foot."

Trench foot, the awful condition that afflicted so many soldiers after their feet had been immersed in cold, dirty water for a long time. After a while, blisters would form. Skin and tissue would start to fall off. If left untreated, gangrene could grow and the sufferer could lose his toes or heel. Even his entire foot.

She reached out and touched his leg. She wished she could soothe him and dispel all the discomfort he had to endure. It hurt more to think of him hurt than if she were hurt herself, but there was nothing she could do.

"I'm safe. You don't have to worry." She pointed to a concealed entrance into the ground about twenty feet behind her tent. "Some brass made the engineers build us an underground shelter over there. They decided the nurses should be protected. Want to see it?"

"Sure." He got up and pulled her up.

Holding hands, they walked over. The entrance to the shelter was in a large hole about five feet down into the ground. It was a small opening secured by wooden logs. Its two sides were held in place by stacks of sandbags.

Anthony jumped into the hole and Tessa slid down after him. He peeked inside. It was pitch dark. A small lightbulb hung at the inside of the entrance and he switched it on. The shelter was about the size of two large elevators. A group of ten people could huddle in here if they needed to hide quickly.

"Everything is underground," she said. "All the nurses joke that we're living like groundhogs. They even built the central command headquarters underground in Nettuno."

"Do you hide in here often?"

"Sometimes. Gracie and I, and some other nurses too. We've spent some long, dark hours in here. Gracie always runs in here as soon as the night raids start. I don't. I'm usually too tired. I sleep through the bombs," she said. "Not a lot of people come by here during daytime. The German planes don't tend to fly when our anti-aircraft units can see them."

Taking her by surprise, he turned around with a smile and pushed her against the wall. "Not a lot of people come by during the day, you say?" Without waiting for her to answer, he kissed her. He did this so suddenly, she lost her footing. Her body weakened at the sweet taste of his lips. She embraced him, burying her face against his chest. How good it felt to be in his arms once more. She couldn't hold her tears back any longer.

"I've been so afraid. So afraid," she said. "I was so afraid something bad would happen to you."

He stroked her hair and kissed her again. She wished she could hold on to him and keep him from going back to those dangerous places. "What's it like out there? How bad is it?"

"Probably nothing worse than what you've already seen. I don't think about it. You just go on. But sometimes, when everything goes to hell and everyone around is dead, I would sit in the foxhole for hours and wonder if I could've done anything different to keep everyone alive. Sometimes, I think this war's never going to end. When I run out of things to think about, you're the only good thing left that I can think about to keep me going." He took her hand. "I know I should want you to be back home and be safe, but I'm so glad you're here. Every time they send us out, I know that if I can make it through, I'll be able to come see you again. Is that selfish of me? All I want is to come back to see you."

She closed her hand around his. "When I'm working, I get so busy, I don't even think about myself or where I am. The wounded soldiers arrive, and I see all the awful things that happened to them. But as awful as I feel for them, I'm always relieved it's not you. And then I feel so guilty for thinking that. Is it selfish of me to think that?"

He kissed her lips and pulled her close against him. She let the burden of her worries drop and gave in to the comfort of the strength of his arms.

"Let's make a promise to each other, okay?" he said. "Let's promise each other we will get through this."

She held him tighter. "I promise."

"No matter what happens here, we'll see ourselves though this. When the war's over, we'll put all this behind us. We'll live a happy life together. The way we want it to be, okay? We won't let anything that happens here take that away from us."

"No."

He loosened his arms around her. "I have to go."

"I know."

"When's your next day off? I'm on reserve this week. I heard the USO built a rec center in Nettuno. Shall we go take a look? Or shall we watch a movie in one of the underground cinemas?"

She lowered her chin and smiled. "Are you asking me out on a date, soldier?"

"I'm asking you out on a date."

"It has to be a really romantic date if I'm going to accept."

"The most romantic. Dinner by flashlight on the beach with the best C-rations served by the United States Army."

Imagining the two of them sitting on the beachhead in their helmets and shabby uniforms eating C-rations, she laughed. He embraced her one more time. She felt his breath quicken as he kissed her neck, her cheek, and her lips. His warm breath full of longing more than he had ever shown her. He moved his hand down her arm, her back, her waist, caressing her. He had never touched her like this. It was as if he was driven by an uncontrollable force. A force filled with life and vitality. A force that was primal and determined, hungry to be unleashed.

Her own desire swelling within her, she kissed him back, wanting more than anything to feel the force of life emanating within him. Here, in Anzio, they were all at the mercy of Death. In this place, Death mocked their mortality, threatening at all hours to yank away their lives and crush them by the scores. She wanted to feel something that rivaled the shadow of Death. She wanted to feel him. She wanted to feel him wanting her. She wanted the irrefutable sensation that they were both alive.

Slowly, he released her. She could see how reluctant he was to have to tear himself away from her. Her own heart ached too when he said goodbye.

She watched him walk away. "Come back," she whispered. Maybe the wind could carry her words to him. "Come back to me."

Chapter 13

Standing with his arms crossed, Jesse watched as Tessa went through all the items she had received from the packages her parents and friends had sent her. When he offered to bring her messages to Anthony, what he wanted was to have an excuse to be around her. It seemed like a brilliant idea at the time. It gave him a legitimate reason to visit her every time he came to the field hospital. So what if her notes and letters were going to Ardley? Who cared about letters when he was the one who got to talk to her regularly in person?

That was the plan when he made that deal with her. The way he saw it, each time he got to see her was an opportunity. He never passed on a good opportunity. His own end of the bargain, delivering messages, was a simple task that would cost him nothing.

Or so he thought, until the hurt came. He didn't know it would hurt. It hurt every time he saw her smitten expression when she gave him letters to pass on to Ardley. It hurt to see the delicate way she held Ardley's letters in her hands. It hurt to know that Ardley alone had the privilege to write to her words that he himself wanted to say to her.

Anthony. Anthony. It hurt to hear her say his name. It hurt to listen to her talk about him.

Why couldn't he have met her before Ardley ever showed up in her life? Why couldn't he have met her under different circumstances without Ardley being in the picture?

Why did she have to love Ardley so much?

He had never had trouble attracting a woman. Even women who were married or engaged found him hard to resist. So why was it so impossible to get Tessa to pay attention to him? Why didn't she see anything about him that might tempt her to feel something—anything—for him?

He could try to make a move. He could pull one of his usual tricks for coaxing women to fall for him. Women had fallen for that before. Some gave up everything for him even to the point of their own ruin. They did it for his sake in the name of love. Seduction. He could try to take her away from Ardley.

But he couldn't. Not her. He disdained the idea of manipulating her. The things he did to seduce other women were low. Tessa Graham was not just any woman. He wouldn't treat her the same way, even if in her case his feelings were real. He would not taint or mar her with tricks and deceptions.

He didn't want to either. How could he do something that might hurt her? She was so happy with Ardley. He didn't want to take that happiness away from her. Even if he could win her over, she would be caught in a moral bind. He didn't want to see her torn and distraught, having to choose between two men.

So he watched her happy in love while his own pain grew. At first, it only annoyed him. Then, it frustrated him. The hurt mounded, layer upon layer each time he saw her, stinging his heart and leaving him with a wound which scabs kept peeling away before it could ever heal.

How could he have known that it would hurt like this? No woman ever made him feel hurt before. None. This wasn't part of the bargain when he made the deal with her.

So now, here he was, in the field hospital once again to see her. Anticipation gripped him every time he came. Riding toward the hospital, his heart would race miles ahead thinking of seeing her again. But as soon as he saw her, pain would cut into his joy, torching him even as all the sweetness in the world poured forth and immersed his entire being.

If he could, he would stop himself from falling in any deeper. He couldn't. He didn't want to stop seeing her. Maybe the pain would eventually do him in. Maybe in the end it would crush his soul and break his heart. If that was the case, then so be it. He would bear any pain as long as he could see her and be near her.

Oblivious to his feelings, she carried on as usual. Only this time, she was not just giving him medical supplies and letters. She wanted him to bring a box of gifts to Ardley.

Here in Anzio, homesickness and boredom reigned. Everyone craved letters and words from home. Mail was a big deal. Receiving packages was an even bigger deal, especially since the Germans had sunk several Allied ships. Mail from home and cargos they carried had sunk with them.

"Look what my parents sent me, Jesse." Tessa took out a dozen pairs of socks. "I told my mother about the soldiers having trench foot and those awful American government-issued socks. I told her I was worried Anthony might get trench foot. She sent me these thicker ones." She picked up a pair and showed him. He forced himself to smile.

"She sent extra pairs for him to pass around. Do you want one? The boys are going to be so happy when you bring these back." She didn't notice the wooden look on his face.

"She sent biscuits too." She took out a tin box. "I hope they're not stale by now. Oh, look! Little soaps. Yardley!" She picked one up and smelled it. "Can you give the rose-scented one to Anthony and tell him to share the rest with the boys?"

Give Anthony the rose-scented ones? Why would she want Anthony to smell like roses? Jesse himself wouldn't want to smell like flowers. "Yeah, sure," he said, feeling less than enthused.

She hardly heard him. She was looking at the rose-scented soap in her hand, obviously thinking of something known only between her and Ardley.

So infuriating. Jesse frowned and looked away.

"Sweets!" she looked into another smaller box. "My friends Ruby and Henry sent these. They must have gotten them from the black market. Must have cost them a fortune!" She laid out several bags of different kinds of candies on the table. "Do you like sweets?"

Jesse looked at her, confused.

"Candy, I mean," she said, taking another bag of treats out of the box. "Butter cup candies! They are Anthony's favorite! He will be so surprised." She put everything into one box. "Do you like candies? You can take as much as you want, except for the butter cup ones. The butter cups are for Anthony, but you can have first pick of any of the rest if you like. My gift to you for helping me bring these to Anthony?"

Gift for being her mule? "No thanks," Jesse said. He hated candy.

Noticing the strain in his voice, she asked, "Are you all right? You sound upset."

"I'm fine. I'm not upset."

She hesitated a moment, then looked at the bundle of letters on the table. "Oh, these too." She took the letters and gave them to him. "For Anthony."

He snatched the letters from her and stuffed them into his medical supplies bag.

"What's gotten into you today?" she asked.

"Nothing." He closed his bag. "Bye." He picked up the box and left without waiting for her to say goodbye. He didn't want her to see the hurt he felt.

Riding in the military jeep on his way back, he stared out at the dreary, desolate fields. The abandoned, bombed-out farm houses were now a familiar sight, no longer worth a second look. His mind was somewhere else, some place better. Someplace like Central Park back in New York on a lazy Sunday afternoon, where he could bike down the path with Tessa by his side. Or someplace like the top of the Empire State Building, where he could show her the breathtaking view of his world. At night, they could stroll through Greenwich Village. While people whisked past them and cars zoomed down the streets, he would slow down, pull her close, and whisper in her ear how much he loved her.

He took her letters out of his bag and looked at them. From the way she wrote Ardley's name on the envelopes, he could see she had a pretty handwriting. Or did she only take special care when she wrote his name?

How he wished it was his own name she had written on those letters.

Fragrance of roses fused with the wind as the vehicle moved along. Where did it come from? Curious, he held the letters to his nose. He had smelled this scent before. Rose perfume. Tessa wore this the night she came with them to see the Army band back in Naples. He caught whiffs of it when he danced the tango with her. He never smelled it on her again after that.

Did she wear this only for Ardley?

Soaps. *Yardley! Can you give the rose-scented one to Anthony?*

He laughed to himself. Of course. So Ardley would be reminded of her, even feel her on his skin.

Jesse looked at the letters once more. Closing his eyes, he held the letters to his nose again. This time, he inhaled the fragrance until the scent ran through every cell of his body.

He opened his eyes. The jeep drove over a bump on the road, shaking her box of gifts and the butter cup candies in orange wrappings on the top bounced. *They are Anthony's favorite!*

Annoyed, he looked away, then looked at them again. He looked away and looked at them one more time, feeling crankier each time he saw the loathsome butter cups of gunk. Fed up, he reached into the box and grabbed a piece, unwrapped it, and popped it into his mouth. The goo of peanut butter stuck to the roof of his mouth and the salty sugary taste left him thirsty.

He hated candy. Especially butter cup candies.

He took another piece and put it into his mouth, letting it melt on his tongue and tasting every last bit of its sweetness.

The vehicle stopped. At their camp, all the soldiers were lolling around in their dugouts, chatting and smoking, bored with nothing to do to pass the time while waiting for the next order to attack.

He got out of the car, slung the strap of his bag of medical supplies over his shoulder, and reached into the car to grab the box of gifts. The candies were still there, mocking him. He took a deep breath and picked up the box.

He found Anthony reading in his foxhole by himself.

"Ardley." He dropped the box into the foxhole. "For you. From Tessa."

Anthony jerked back from the box dumped in front of him.

"These too." Jesse pulled out the batch of letters and tossed them into the foxhole.

"Thanks!" Anthony picked up the letters and looked to see what was in the box. "Butter cup candies! Where'd she get these?"

Jesse didn't answer but walked away.

"Hey, Garland, you want some?" Anthony called out to him.

"No. I hate candy." He took off without looking back. He didn't want to show the sadness he could no longer hide on his face.

PART FIVE
Sabotaged

Chapter 14

Gathering the soldiers for their next mission to press toward Highway 7, Anthony saw mostly the faces of strangers. They were the fresh faces of replacements about to witness the horrors of fighting in Anzio for the first time. In the aftermath of Carano and the misguided mission into the forest, the troops in his company had a near total change of guard.

Not too long ago when he became the first lieutenant, he had tried to make an effort to learn the replacements' names. Get to know some of them even. He didn't do that anymore. There were too many newcomers. If these boys would not make it to the end, it was easier if he didn't know them. Many would join them for only a few days before they became casualties themselves, never to return.

Most of the men he had met when he first joined the company were no longer with them.

There was one person he did not miss, Beck. Injured, Beck was out of commission recovering at the hospital. He would deal with Beck later. For now, it was a relief not to have to worry about his second lieutenant going rogue. Without Beck and without the distraction of having to search for Klaus, they should have better luck this time.

At 0200 hours, their company took off and began the long night march to the line of departure with their battalion. They were instructed to make their way up the route that passed a field of evenly spaced hedgerows, and cut the highway before daylight. The battalion command had told them the hedgerows would make good cover to shield them if the enemy waged a counterattack.

Everything went as planned except that the hedgerows were not hedgerows. What appeared to be hedgerows in aerial surveillance photos were in fact rows and rows of long drainage ditches. The ditches ran as long as a football field and their walls reached at least twenty-feet high. The battalion tanks, unable to cross the drainage ditches in the dark, had to stay behind while the infantry troops pressed forward. Taking his company, Anthony spent the miserable hours that followed marching through shrubs and overgrown briars in the dark.

All that, though, was just the prelude. Before they reached the highway, a blizzard of enemy gunfire came blazing down. Anthony dove into the nearest drainage ditch. The troops scattered for cover, seizing any strategic spot they could find to return fire. Oddly, their own barrage did not counteract the enemy fire in the least. With his back against the ditch wall, Anthony listened to the eruption of sounds and tried to make out the directions from which the enemy fire came. Where were the Germans shooting from? He was desperate to know. He thought they were marching through a flat plain. Their maps didn't show any markings of hills or mountains, so where could the Germans be? Were their maps wrong? What was going on? In the dark of the night, he could not tell. He could not see.

An enemy flare blasted above him. The nightmarish green light illuminated his surroundings for a few seconds, long enough for him to see Jonesy pinned down about ten feet away from him. Jonesy saw him too and scurried over. "Where are they shooting from?"

Anthony still didn't know. "Sounds like they're up top. How can that be?"

The shooting continued. Trapped, Anthony slid down into the bottom of the ditch. The night wore on. Another battle at Anzio, another disaster. Could he ever wake up from this nightmare?

# # #

Eventually, sunlight emerged and the dire condition they were in unveiled itself.

Climbing to the top of the ditch, Anthony could see a series of small knolls directly in front of him. The German troops were entrenched on top of those low rolling hills. The Germans must have just built these recently, or the knolls were too small to be visible in the Allies' aerial surveillance photos. Watching and listening to the gunfire, he observed that the enemy had formed in a defensive line starting with their forward position to his right. From there, the German line curved north and ran horizontally in front of him along the knolls until it curved around to his left to form an L-shaped fort. During the night, their own battalion had marched unwittingly straight up against this German line and cornered themselves in the pocket surrounded by the knolls.

The oncoming daylight made their situation even more precarious. From where they were, the Germans had a clear view of the American troops hiding in the drainage ditches. He took out his binoculars and looked at the knolls. He could see links of German machine gun nests. While was he still observing the landscape, a German machine gun on top of one of the knolls fired at the end of a drainage ditch. The burst of gunfire rolled down the length of the ditch, obliterating everyone hiding below. Before he could blink his eyes, another German machine gun fired at the opposite end of the same ditch. The enfilade of deadly fire rolled up the ditch and killed off anyone running for escape. In an instant, a trough full of soldiers were blasted to death.

"Holy shit!" Jonesy said. He had climbed up from the bottom of the ditch too.

"We have to get out of these ditches. Go!" Anthony shouted. He pushed himself up above ground, calling for everyone he could see to climb out and run. By now, their troops were dispersed throughout the field. A shower of bullets chased after them. In front of him, a communications sergeant carrying a radio was running for his life. Anthony sped up, grabbed the sergeant and pulled him behind a bush.

"Is your radio working?" Anthony asked.

"Ye—yes." Breathing hard, the sergeant could barely speak through his clattering teeth.

Jonesy jumped behind the bush. "Lieutenant."

Anthony looked up at the knolls. "There." He pointed south. The artillery fire in that spot appeared lighter and less frequent. "I think their forward position is there. The heavy block of MG nests is at their rear."

Jonesy looked to the south. "That's our best way out."

"Yes." Anthony turned to the communications sergeant. "Can you get through to our command?"

Wide-eyed, the sergeant nodded.

"Tell them to send the heavy weapons units south. Tell them we're retreating that way. They need to take those nests down."

The sergeant did as Anthony ordered. As soon as he finished, they bolted away again.

Sprinting and scuttling from one spot to the next, they made their way south, all the while yelling for other soldiers in hiding to follow them. As they got farther away from the enemy's firing range, Anthony's hopes rose. Their command had followed through. Their heavy weapons had arrived at the southern edge where the knolls began. He lunged behind a bush. Holding his breath, he watched as their artillery unit inflicted strike after strike against the MG nests, creating an escape route for their troops.

Unable to withstand the Americans' attack, the German forward units began to retreat. Not losing any time, Anthony ran for safety as a group of soldiers followed him.

# # #

For those who were lucky enough to escape the ditches, the mood was a mix of confusion and relief. Their battalion had broken up and their units were in disarray with men having died or gone missing. Among those who had gathered, only one other officer had survived.

"Second Lieutenant Lee Dennison, Company H." The officer identified himself.

"Where's your CO?" Anthony asked.

"Missing," Dennison said, "presumed dead. Some of my men reported seeing him shot down. Our XO was killed too." His face looked grave.

Must be awful for him, Anthony thought. He remembered how sad he had felt the day when Wesley died. Thankfully, Jonesy and Ollie had both made it out. Fox too.

While they tried to regroup, Anthony took out his binoculars to observe the enemy. The German units at their forward position were pulling back. Their machine guns were no match for the Americans' artillery and mortars. The forces that formed the German L-shaped defense line, which threatened to annihilate the entire American battalion only a while ago, was breaking. They had lost their strategic advantage now that the Americans were no longer entrapped by the terrain. Moreover, he could see now that the German battalion was in fact quite thin. The Americans, even with reduced troops, could overwhelm them with superior artillery support. If their battalion attacked the Germans from their rear and flanked them from behind the knolls, they could cut off the enemy's retreat route.

Having determined their advantage, Anthony gathered Jonesy, Ollie, and Dennison. "We can launch a counterattack." He pointed at the direction where the enemy troops were retreating along the German line. "If we can find the gaps between their defense units, we can punch through from their rear."

"And wipe them out!" Jonesy said.

"And wipe them out," Anthony said.

"Yeah!" Ollie cheered.

"Should we radio command and tell them?" Jonesy asked.

"Yes," Anthony said. "We can do it."

Jonesy pumped his fist. Despite the hours of agony he had just endured, he walked away reenergized, ready for another battle.

Anthony watched the soldiers around him. They all looked to him now, especially the men in his own company. They trusted him. They stood and waited, soldiers and noncom both, ready to do as he asked. He felt a rush of renewed strength.

Before Jonesy could send his message to the command, a jeep carrying Captain Harding arrived with their reserve unit and the rest of the men from their battalion who had escaped from the attack at the knolls. Warren followed in another vehicle.

Mistaking their arrival as reinforcement support, Anthony quickly told the captain about their plan to launch a counterattack before it was too late. To his surprise, the captain disagreed.

Spreading a map on the hood of his vehicle, Harding showed him and Warren an area on the map three miles from where they were. "We'll set up our position in these caves. Command will be sending a reinforcement battalion. When they arrive, we'll be able to continue on and take Highway 7."

"Captain, we can take out the German forces that are here now," Anthony said. "We've got a chance. We can take the geographical advantage. If we don't, they'll return with more troops."

"If they return, we'll be ready for them."

"But Captain, if they return, they could outnumber us. We have a chance to weaken their defense now. We should let command know we can take them down."

"We will tell command no such thing, Lieutenant." Harding folded the map. "The German forces here are not important. We will build up our position in the caves. We'll launch our attack from there. If they dare to return," he said with a confident smile, "bring it on." The now familiar fervid gleam flashed across his eyes. "Gather our troops, Lieutenant. We're heading to the caves."

When Harding left, Anthony looked at Warren. "Klaus?"

"Yes," Warren said. "We've received reports, Klaus is directing the German defense at Highway 7. Harding's salivating at the chance to fight him." He took out a batch of photos. "Our mission is to establish our position around these caves. Before the war, the locals dug these underground tunnels to excavate for building materials. They'll make a good strategic base for us to set up our field command operations. Once we're organized, we'll launch our attack."

"But if command knows we can launch a counterattack now, they might change their plans."

"You may be right," Warren said, "but Harding's in charge. He doesn't care about defeating the German troops here. He wants to get Klaus. Command's directions are exactly what he wants. He wants our battalion to build up here. And then, he'll bring the fight to Klaus."

Anthony glanced at the photos. For reasons he could not explain, they made him think of tombs. "I don't have a good feeling about this."

"Harding's mind's made up. He's not going to give up a chance to defeat Klaus."

Chapter 15

For Fran Milton, today was another routine day. Within the sphere of the hospital, she had done all she could to keep everything routine. She could not control the enemy attacks or the number of wounded soldiers arriving, but she did what she could to maintain order and avoid surprises. For the hospital to run at maximum efficiency, certain things must remain in order regardless of outside interruptions. Those things included her daily breakfast and evening tea time with Aaron Haley. Their meetings were part of the routine.

Arriving at his tent office for tea this evening, she heard a familiar female voice from within. The voice belonged to Ellie Swanson. What was Swanson doing here? Fran stopped outside the entrance and listened.

"That's too bad you'll be leaving Naples the same day I arrive," Ellie said. "If our rest leaves could've overlapped for longer, I would have loved to help you find a birthday present for your sister. Anyway, would you like to join my friends and me for lunch? My ship arrives in the morning and yours doesn't depart until three in the afternoon. There's a Napoli pizza place everyone's been raving about. We all can't wait to try it."

"I don't want to intrude on you and your friends. I don't want to be the old man coming along and boring you all to tears."

"Doctor!" Ellie laughed, her voice blithe and effervescent like a breath of fresh air. "You're definitely not a bore. And… you're not old… " Her voice trailed off, nearly inaudible.

Listening outside, Fran's face darkened. When she heard Ellie mumble "you're not old," she reflexively clenched her hand into a fist until her fingernails dug into her skin.

"All right, you convinced me," Aaron said. "It'll probably be the last good meal I'll have for a long time."

His acceptance was more than Fran could take. She pushed the flap of the tent open and walked inside. "Good evening, Doctor," she said, keeping her usual stern demeanor. "Lieutenant Swanson, what are you doing here? Aren't you supposed to be on duty?"

"I am, ma'am. I came to give Dr. Haley his patients' charts and reports." Ellie touched the stack of files on Aaron's desk.

"You're finished here then. Stop wasting time and get back to work."

"Yes, ma'am." Ellie gave Aaron a silent look of apology and hurried out.

After she left, Fran went over to the small kettle and poured Aaron and herself each a cup of tea. "I tell you," she said with her back toward him, "It's tiring keeping these young nurses in line. If I take my eyes off them for one minute, they'll find ways to slack off. Young people these days, they don't have the same concept of responsibility that we do."

"I don't see that," Aaron said. "Our nurses work very hard."

"That's because you're a man. These young women only let men see their good sides. I'm not a man. I see everything." She turned and gave him a look of caution. "The younger ones are the worst. I've seen this happen at every place I've ever worked. They ingratiate themselves with doctors so they can get promoted faster without working for it." She walked toward him. "Some have ambitions beyond being promoted. A doctor is a very attractive choice for a husband. You need to be careful."

Aaron laughed, incredulous. "Captain, I find that hard to believe. Our staff is more than professional. Their work ethic is beyond reproach. Anyway, a doctor husband?" He held his pen to his chin with an amused smile. "I appreciate you think I might be a catch, but in case you haven't noticed, we're in a military base camp. They have their pick of strapping young men among officers of every stripe. An old fogy like me won't even make it to the end of the line."

She sat down. "What about Ellie Swanson?"

"What about her?"

"She has a tent full of patients to attend to. What's she doing coming here in the middle of work, chatting you up, if not to slack off and gain favors from you? Bringing you patients' charts and reports? That's a good excuse. Don't be fooled."

"Captain, you're being unfair. I asked her to bring me the charts and reports. She was writing them up when I left."

The way he came so quickly to Ellie's defense annoyed her. "You'll be going to Naples next week?"

"Yes. I have three days off. I'm looking forward to it. It'll be nice to get away from Anzio for a while."

"I agree. I haven't taken a pass in eight months. I think I'll finally make use of one." She took a sip of her tea.

"You should. You work too hard. No one deserves a break more than you. You probably have enough days accrued for a furlough."

"A furlough? I don't have time for that. I've got too much work to do here. But I will take a few days' pass. What do you say we go to Naples together?"

"Go to Naples together?" Aaron asked, confused.

Squeezing her hand around her cup, she cleared her throat. "What I mean is, I want to arrange a meeting with the supplies division at the army medical headquarters in Naples. The irregularity in shipment of our supplies is a huge problem." She lowered her cup and stared directly at him. "You should come with me. Our joint presence will show the officials in charge that this is serious."

Aaron didn't answer. Seeing his hesitation, she continued, "It would also be good for us to check in with everyone back there. We should get updated on the army medical's latest plans and keep ourselves in the know. We're too far away and out of touch here. We need to stay on top of everything."

"Captain." He clasped his hands on the desk. "Getting supplies is important, of course, and it's great that you care this much about our operations. Really, your dedication is admirable. I, for one, can't commend you enough."

"You'll come with me then?"

"I..." he let out an awkward laugh." I really want a break. I need it. I just want a few days' rest, a few good meals, and enjoy my time off. I'd much rather not spend a day at the Med Corps HQ talking business."

"I see," she said. Her expression remained unchanged. "As you wish. You could use some rest." She handed him a copy of a list. "Let's get to work then. We'll go over the patients to be transported to the Naples General Hospital."

Aaron turned his attention to the list, checking each name off, occasionally asking her a question or two about them. Fran held on to her notebook and tried to focus on the patients, but she was too distracted. The patients' names and their medical data were all meaningless letters and numbers. Subconsciously, she drew a small square on the right margin of the page. She traced the lines of the square over and over again, pressing the pen harder and harder into the paper. When the tracing cut through the page, she blurted out, "I hear an American ballet troupe is touring in Naples."

"Oh yeah?"

"I think I might go and see them perform when I'm there."

"I didn't know you like ballet. You should go. You never take time off for yourself. You work too hard." As always, his words were kind and encouraging, but he sounded no different than if he were talking to anybody else. It was not the response she wanted to hear.

"Peter Delaney." He went on to the next patient on the list. "Let's keep him here. I'd like to keep him under observation for a few more days."

Normally, she would question a decision to keep a patient when the hospital was filled to capacity. She liked to clear the beds and leave them free in case of new arrivals. But today, right now, she found the entire exercise of reviewing patients for transfer downright irritating.

"Sure." She made a quick note next to Delaney's name.

Aaron continued on. With his focus on the patient list, he did not realize how grim she looked.

"Saul Raymond… he's the one with the second-degree burns, right? He's ready to go. Be sure to include in his chart though that…"

Not letting him finish, she interrupted, "Dr. Haley… Aaron… Do you want…" Her voice tensed. "Would you like to…" Her words hung in an uneasy silence. Feeling ever more awkward, she darted her eyes to the floor and drew a long breath. "Would you like to examine Saul Raymond again before we send him off? I saw him earlier on my way here and he didn't look well." That wasn't what she wanted to say. She hadn't seen Saul Raymond when she was coming here, but it was impossible to say what she wanted. She couldn't do it.

"Of course. If you think so. I trust your opinion."

He continued down the list, but she was no longer listening. It irked her that he did not realize what she meant to ask him, and it annoyed her that she was unable to extend him an invitation when Ellie Swanson could do it so naturally. Most of all, it frustrated her that after all the time they had known each other, he hadn't shown any interest or taken any initiative. She didn't understand why he couldn't see that, at their age, with their shared medical background and experience, they were better off with each other than with anybody else.

It must be Ellie Swanson. He didn't know what was best for him because of Ellie Swanson.

Aaron Haley and Ellie Swanson. This could not be. She must intervene, not for herself but for his sake. A young girl like Ellie Swanson might be temporarily infatuated with an accomplished doctor, especially one as esteemed and successful as Aaron Haley. But young girls were ignorant. They cared too much about the superficial and frivolous. What would a young girl like Ellie Swanson know about the hard work and long hours that it took for Aaron to become the great doctor that he was. Ellie Swanson would only distract him from accomplishing more. Besides, young girls were fickle, especially the pretty ones. They didn't know what they really wanted. Here in the military, they had all the men's attention. They wouldn't value the feelings of a man as sincere as Aaron. A pretty young blonde like Ellie Swanson would be tired of him when the next exciting thing came along.

No, she decided. She couldn't let Aaron make such a huge mistake. She must stop the disease before it spread. One day, he would thank her for it.

# # #

Having finished their rounds, Tessa and Ellie sat down on a tree log by the canteen for a short coffee break. The coffee tasted horrible, but the hot mug warmed their hands on this chilly February day. Tessa wished she could have some tea, but the canteen did not always serve tea.

"Irene said you're having lunch with Dr. Haley in Naples. Is it true?" Tessa asked.

"Oh, she's exaggerating again," Ellie said with a dismissive smile. "It's not me having lunch with Dr. Haley. It's me and my friends from the 95th Evac who will be on leave in Naples. Dr. Haley will be joining us for lunch at Angelo's. Everyone says Angelo's serves the best Napoli pizza."

"So Dr. Haley will be coming for the food then."

"Of course. Everyone can use a break from the army rations. Besides, we thought Dr. Haley might enjoy having company while he's in Naples."

"'We'?" Tessa couldn't help teasing her friend. "Yes. I am sure the staff at 95th are quite concerned that Dr. Haley has someone to dine with and not be alone."

"Tessa!" Ellie pushed Tessa's arm in protest, but her eyes shone at the mention of Dr. Haley.

"Oh, no. Don't look." Tessa bowed her head. "Captain Milton's coming this way. Let's pretend we don't see her." She pretended to drink her coffee and hoped Milton would go somewhere else. To her dismay, Fran Milton walked straight up to them.

"Lieutenant Swanson," Captain Milton greeted Ellie, her voice unusually friendly. Tessa glanced at the captain, suspicious.

"Yes ma'am," Ellie answered.

"You're scheduled to go on rest leave to Naples next week."

"That's right, ma'am."

"It so happens that I need to take a leave myself next week to visit the army medical headquarters in Naples. You are aware that lack of supplies has been a consistent problem, to say the least. The situation is such that a personal visit by me is now necessary. I'm going to report the situation in person. Hopefully, someone will listen and things will improve."

"Of course, ma'am. Is there any way I can help? I'll be glad to come along if you need my help when I'm in Naples."

"That's not necessary." Fran brushed off the idea by a wave of her hand. "What I do need is your help to oversee our field hospital while I'm gone."

Ellie and Tessa stared at her. Tessa could not believe what the captain had just said. Captain Milton was always so critical of Ellie, the last thing one would expect was for her to assign Ellie to be in command while she was gone.

"That's right," Fran said. "I'm putting you in charge, Lieutenant Swanson. Perhaps I've always been a bit too tough on you. That's only because I recognize your potential. I want to see you excel. If you don't mind postponing your leave until the following week, this will be a good chance for you to prove yourself."

Tessa looked over at Ellie. Ellie looked bewildered and conflicted. Tessa wanted to shake her head to signal to Ellie to decline. Before she could, Ellie said, "Certainly, ma'am. I'm honored that you asked. I'll do my best."

"I'm very pleased to hear that." Satisfied, Fran straightened her glasses. "I'll notify personnel and let them know about your change of plans."

"Thank you," Ellie said. The spark in her eyes had disappeared.

"Don't disappoint me," Fran said before she took off.

As soon as the captain was out of hearing range, Tessa grabbed Ellie's arm. "Why didn't you say no? She's doing this on purpose. She's trying to sabotage you and Dr. Haley again. She doesn't want you and Dr. Haley to see each other in Naples."

"There's no way I can say no. It might as well have been an order. Anyway, she isn't sabotaging me. There's nothing to sabotage. Dr. Haley and I are not seeing each other in Naples. He's joining my friends and me for lunch. Anyhow, Captain Milton doesn't know anything about our lunch plans."

"Of course she knows. I don't know how she knows but I'm telling you she knows."

"Tessa, don't be silly. The captain's too busy to care about who's eating lunch with whom while they're on leave. Anyway, I should be grateful. She's giving me a wonderful opportunity. I'm surprised she actually thinks well of me." Ellie now looked at peace and continued to enjoy her coffee.

Tessa decided not to pursue the matter, although her suspicions about the captain's motives remained. She must have heard about Ellie's plans somehow. "But now you won't be able to have lunch with Dr. Haley in Naples."

Disappointment passed Ellie's eyes. Still, Ellie corrected her. "I won't be able to have lunch with everyone, not just Dr. Haley. I'll miss out on going to Angelo's with all of them. Yes, that is a shame."

Tessa felt bad for her friend. With Aaron Haley convinced that he was too old and Ellie being so stubbornly shy to admit her feelings, these two would never have a chance.

PART SIX

Catacombs and Caves

Chapter 16

As the battalion trudged along to the caves, Anthony felt his mind melding with the clanks and the hums of the convoy vehicles. The roller coaster of emotions he had experienced in the last eighteen hours had left him drained. From the moment they came upon the enemy at the knolls, he had gone from being overwrought with fright of being killed, to relief at his survival, to an adrenaline rush to wage a counterattack, only to be disappointed by Harding's order to halt and retreat. Now that it was all over, an odd sense of detachment had come over him. He stared numbly ahead as his jeep took him to yet another destination that would likely bring neither victory nor end.

Arriving at the caves, he got out of the vehicle and followed a ravine filled with shrubs and bushes to their main entrance. The captain and Warren had already arrived, and the support units were moving supplies and equipment inside. Together with Warren, he entered the maze of underground passages that were dug into a ridge of shale and sandstone. The staff sergeants had set up their command station near one of the passageway entrances, while the medical attachment took an area in a corridor to use as their medical aid station. The crisscrossing passages led to twenty other entrances. They came out of one of the exits that opened to the gullies and knolls outside.

"What do you think?" Warren asked.

"It's hard to say." Anthony looked out at the view of the surrounding area. "It's a natural fortress. It would be hard for the Germans to break through here."

"You don't sound convinced."

Anthony touched the wall of the ravine. A large battalion of troops could not move through the narrow access way for a quick escape. "It would be hard if we need to get out."

Back inside the caves, the captain was shouting at a group of civilians near one of the larger passages. About seventy of them huddled close to each other before him, bewildered. From the way they were dressed, they appeared to be local villagers. While he shouted, an older couple clung tighter to each other. A small child began to cry and her mother picked her up to try to calm her.

"Does anybody speak Italian?" Harding shouted at the soldiers standing with him. "Get me someone who speaks Italian. I need to know what these people are doing here."

Anthony walked over to the crowd. The group, mostly women, along with children and some older men, stepped back as he approached. There was not a single young man among them. Nonetheless, the older men moved in front of the women when he got closer. They stared at him, terrified. In as friendly a tone as possible, he asked, "Does anybody speak English?"

The men looked confused. A young woman raised her voice and stepped out from the group. "I'm Claudina." She looked about nineteen or twenty. Her hair was tied in a single long braid behind her back. "We're farmers." Her English had a heavy local accent. Her voice trembled as she spoke.

"Hello, Claudina. I'm Anthony. These are my fellow officers. We're American soldiers."

"I know."

He looked at the group behind her. "Why are you all here?"

"We came down here when you Americans got here, and then you all and the Germans started bombing each other."

"I see." Her accusatory tone surprised him. "The bombing must be frightening for all of you."

"Frightening?" She took a step closer. "You think we're only frightened? Your ships are shooting bombs at the Germans through our village and the Germans shot back the same way. Our village has been bombed out. We have no homes to go back to anymore."

"I'm sorry to hear that." He had no answer for her. Running into a group of angry locals in the caves was the last thing he expected.

The little girl who was crying before started to wail again. Anxious to diffuse the situation, Anthony said, "We can protect you."

"Protect us? You think you can protect us? You're bringing danger to us. The Germans will try to attack this place now because you're here."

He hadn't thought of that. He looked at Harding and Warren. Neither seemed to know what to do either.

"We want to be left alone, but you are not leaving, are you?"

Anthony looked at her in silent admission. He felt sorry for them, but there was nothing he could do.

Knowing she had no choice, she conceded. "Let us stay in this corridor then. We'll keep to ourselves. You stay out of our way and we'll stay out of yours." She turned around to go back to her people.

"I'm sorry," he apologized again. Claudina turned her head, but did not look back at him. She returned to her people and they surrounded her, talking to her all at once while she explained to them what had happened.

The tensions between the two groups now eased, Anthony rejoined his troops. Warren gave him an encouraging smile.

"Why didn't she speak up when I asked if any of them speak English?" Harding asked. "All right, fine. They can stay. Just make sure they don't get in our way." He scowled at the local villagers and left.

Thoroughly exhausted, Anthony took his duffle and found a spot in a corridor slightly farther away from the others. He had been awake for almost twenty-four hours. All he wanted was rest. Everything else would have to wait. As soon as he lay down, he passed out into a night of sorely needed sleep.

# # #

In the morning, Anthony was finishing his breakfast of yet another cold and tasteless K-ration when Fox came running to him. "Lieutenant! Lieutenant! The Germans are coming!"

Immediately, Anthony dropped the tin of food and followed Fox outside. On his way, he passed the group of villagers again and saw Claudina among them. For a brief moment, they looked at each other. The resentment in her eyes last night was still there, except now there was also a shade of inevitability and hopelessness. He wanted to apologize again, but there was no time. In any case, their current situation was beyond his control. He let it go and continued on his way.

The explosions of bombs could be heard even before they got to the entrance of the caves. Jonesy and Ollie were already outside.

"What's happening?" Anthony asked.

"Our patrol squad came back," Jonesy said. "The Krauts from those damn knolls are back. They've brought a mass of troops and Panzer tanks. They're coming our way."

"So fast?" He was hoping they could have a little more time. Their reinforcement battalion was not scheduled to arrive until that evening.

"Our forward units are still holding," Ollie said.

Yes, but for how long? "Where's the captain?"

"Inside? Don't know." Jonesy said. "The patrol squad leader already reported to him."

Anthony looked around. "Set up watch around all the entrances," he ordered and hurried to the command station. There, he found Harding hovering over a private on the phone with the battalion command. Clearly distressed, the captain kept shouting instructions to the frazzled soldier. Warren, looking grim, was examining a map on the table. He walked over to Warren.

"We've got bad news," Warren said. "The Germans are not just coming after our battalion here. They're launching a full-on simultaneous counterattack in a dozen places." He stared at a series of locations circled in red on the map. "If they break through any of these areas, they can send their troops straight into the beachhead."

"Can they defeat us?" Anthony was afraid to ask.

"The situation's critical."

Before Anthony could ask more questions, Harding shouted into the phone receiver. "We cannot wait. We need reinforcements, now!" He shoved the receiver back to the private. "Get Colonel Callahan on the phone. Can you do that? Do you know how to do that? Do I have to show you?"

"I'm trying, sir," the private answered. Frantically, he pressed the keys on the switchboard another time.

In a low voice to Warren, Anthony asked, "Our reinforcements are coming, aren't they?"

"They're coming, but the rain yesterday slowed them down, and they have to pass through those same lousy ditches you went through. There's no way to divert other units here either. They're all held up by the German offensive."

Anthony looked at the walls of the cave. Their precarious state slowly sank in. "We're isolated here then." His own voice seemed to echo in the chamber of the corridor. He noticed a hand-drawn map of the interior of the caves on the table among the notes and reports. Someone had made it in haste yesterday. He pulled it out for a clearer view. The twenty entrances jumped out at him. "We don't have enough men to defend every entrance of the caves." He thought of the ravines surrounding the caves. "If the Germans arrive before our reinforcements get here, we won't be able to retreat in time. They can surround us and cut us off. We'll be trapped."

"You think we should get out?" Warren asked, lowering his voice.

"If we get out now, we can try to link up with the reinforcement battalion. We'll have a better chance holding our position that way. If we fail to link up, we'll still have a better chance at escape."

"Do you want to tell him?" Warren glanced at Harding.

They had to. "Captain," Anthony called out to Harding. "We shouldn't stay here. We don't have enough men to defend these caves. If the Germans reach us before the reinforcement battalion arrives, we'll be trapped."

Harding frowned and came to the table.

"We should get out and try to link up with the reinforcement battalion," Anthony urged.

"You want us to go backward?" Harding asked. "If we leave to try to join the reinforcement units, we'll be ceding our position here."

"It's too dangerous for us to stay."

Rounding his shoulders with his arms crossed and his finger on his chin, Harding considered his advice. "No." His frown deepened. "Our battalion's been depleted by half. It's risky for us to move out. These caves aren't easy to get to even for the Gerries. We're safer here."

Anthony disagreed. For the time being, yes, the caves could protect them from artillery fire. But without freedom of movement, what would happen if the Germans encircled them? How long could they last?

"Reinforcements are on their way." Harding straightened up. "The Germans haven't arrived yet. We still have time. We'll take our chances here."

There was no way for him to dispute Harding, but this was a mistake. Every sense in him told him that remaining here would be a mistake. Every instinct told him they had to get out.

But the captain had already made his choice. "Let's not forget, Klaus is commanding the German troops in this area," Harding said. "I will not back down and give up our position to him so easily. Our order is to hold, we'll hold. Go tell the troops to set up wires, traps, and mines all around this area, Lieutenant. We'll set up guards at every entrance. Make sure the area is patrolled. We'll do whatever we have to do to hold this damn place until reinforcements arrive. And when they do, we'll give Klaus a good licking."

Anthony had no choice but to comply. "Yes, sir." He exchanged a glance with Warren, then left. As he walked down the corridor, an unbearable feeling of claustrophobia overcame him. The thought of a tomb returned to his mind as he passed the twists and turns of the passages that could soon lead to their doom.

Chapter 17

Standing at one of the cave entrances, Anthony could hear the orchestra of gunfire besieging all of Anzio. It seemed as if every weapon from the beachhead where the Allies were based to the rear of the German line behind Cisterna was firing off. In between, the Allies' naval cannons would join in the racket, adding their roars of constant, furious booms. He could smell the burn and smoke of exploded weapons polluting the air. The Allies' troops were on the move, and so were the Germans'.

The Germans might have gotten the edge. Klaus' troops were closing in on them. The explosions of artillery from the direction of Highway 7 were approaching closer and closer. Reports from their own battalion's units holding their defense against Klaus worsened as the day passed. Their own defense was breaking.

All day long, Anthony went from squad to squad talking to their soldiers, hoping in vain to keep up their morale. He did so even when the unbearable tension among their own troops within the caves oppressed him, suffocated him.

As the day turned to dusk, a German plane flew across the sky. He looked up. Surely, the enemy must know they were here. The Luftwaffe aerial surveillance pilots could easily see the congregation of American tanks and convoys near the caves. No doubt, they would reach them very soon.

Staying in the caves was a mistake. He was sure of it.

It only took the Germans one night. The moment Anthony feared had arrived. By noon the next day, the Germans had reached the fields outside of the ravines. The Panzer tanks were the first to show. Their own battalion's anti-tank units tried to fend them off and keep them at bay. But soon, the German mortar units appeared, followed by waves of German troops. Their own tanks, which were their strongest defensive force, were outmatched. Their weakened infantry units had no choice but to pick up their weapons to hold their guard.

Casualties began to mount. In a frenzy, the medics brought in the injured soldiers, laying them on the ground in the treatment area. The area continued to expand through the hours and the make-shift aid station turned into a madhouse.

When night fell and the gunfire ceased, Anthony walked through the grounds where the medics had gathered the wounded. He counted at least sixty people debilitated in various degrees. This was only their first day of fighting. The full force of German troops had not yet arrived. They wouldn't be able to sustain their rate of loss. Something had to be changed, quick.

In a corner, Jesse took off his helmet, sat down on a large rock, and lit a cigarette. Anthony walked over and sat down on the rock next to him. "How are you all holding up?"

Jesse blew out a heavy puff of smoke. "We got eighteen critically wounded. We need to get them to a hospital."

There was no way to do that. To take the wounded back to the beachhead, they would need to carry them through the ravines. They would need transportation afterward too. With the Germans closing in, this was impossible. They would be caught for sure if they tried.

"They never planned for us to take wounded soldiers in here." Jesse took another deep drag of smoke. "These caves are supposed to be a temporary command headquarters."

Jesse was right. The command had anticipated that their reinforcements would have arrived by now and any fighting would take place at least a mile from here. If things had gone the way they planned, the wounded would be brought to the rear, treated, and then transported to the hospitals back at the beach. Instead, they were inside the caves, barricaded.

"How long will your supplies last?"

"Four days? Five days? Hard to say. Depends on how bad things get."

Anthony looked at the injured soldiers. Since the fighting started, Captain Harding had not come here once to check on the wounded. The captain's disregard for those who were suffering under his command annoyed him. They were trapped here. The captain should be looking out for their men. "I'll talk to you later. Thanks for the update." He got up and went to the command station.

The moment Anthony saw the captain and Warren, he knew things had taken a turn for the worse. "What's wrong?"

"The reinforcement battalion's been attacked," Warren said. "The Germans are holding them up five miles from here."

"What happens if they can't break through?"

"They'll break through." Harding interrupted him. "They're not far now. We just have to hold on for another day."

"But, Captain, if they don't, we won't be able to hold on much longer if the Germans bring in more troops." He thought of the eighteen men they needed to get to the hospital. "Some of our men are badly hurt. Eighteen are critically wounded. We need to get them out to get help."

"What would you have me do, Lieutenant? How do you want me to transport them out of here? I can't send them out with a medic and an ambulance with no rear units to protect them."

That was the problem. They had no front and no rear. They were simply barricaded in. Anthony knew Harding would not agree, but against his better judgment, he said, "Maybe we should all get out, sir."

"That's ridiculous. Our job is to hold our position here."

"The Germans are already here. If more of them arrive, they can surround us and trap us here." The more he talked, the more Anthony was sure he was right. "We should get out now while we can."

"He may have a point," Warren said. "If we leave now, there are still enough of us to fend off the German troops for all of us to get out."

Harding thought to himself, then dismissed their idea. "We can't dismantle our entire offense strategy yet. There's a good chance reinforcements will break through tomorrow. When they come and we join forces, we'll be able to fight off the Germans." He smiled. "And more."

"You mean Klaus," Anthony said. Until now, he hadn't dared to suggest Klaus might be the true reason why the captain wanted to remain here.

The fervid gleam Anthony had now come to recognize beamed in Harding's eyes.

"We don't even know for sure Klaus is here, or if he'll be coming."

"Oh, he's here. I saw the Krauts' surveillance planes. They've got to have seen the regiment insignia on all the mortar vehicles parked outside. If their intelligence is worth a dime, he has to know I'm here." His lips curled into a disturbing smile, baring his teeth. "He won't give up a chance to come after me."

Anthony listened in disbelief. He had not seen any evidence that Klaus might have a personal vendetta against Harding. The captain's obsession with Klaus was clouding his judgment.

"Don't worry, Ardley," Harding said. "We'll be able to turn everything around tomorrow. I'm in continuous contact with regiment. If the reinforcement battalion is still held up after tomorrow, I will convince command to send more troops." He took a step back, signaling the end of their discussion. "I'm going to get some sleep now, gentlemen. You should too. We have to be a hundred percent awake and alert tomorrow." Satisfied with himself, he left to get his rest.

Coming out of the command station, Anthony passed a group of soldiers resting by a pile of rocks near an entrance to the caves. Worn-out and exhausted from the day's fighting, they ate the crackers and beans from their dinner rations. The scrimpy morsels of food hardly made up for their sweat and toil.

Needing fresh air, Anthony walked outside. Intermittent shots of sniper fire from afar pierced the silence of the night, reminding him that the enemy was nearby and closing in.

It's up to you and me now to get everyone through this. Wesley's voice echoed in his mind.

But Wesley was no longer here. He stared back at the group of soldiers. Somewhere, another shot fired.

It's up to me now to get everyone through this.

# # #

The morning did not bring good news. Noises of artillery erupted again from the areas outside where the enemy had concentrated their forces. The Germans had brought in more troops overnight in preparation for an attack on the American battalion hiding out in the caves. More casualties returned. Standing by the cave entrance, Anthony could smell gunpowder drifting toward him like the shadow of Death.

"Lieutenant Ardley." Lee Dennison caught Anthony outside the caves when Anthony returned from observing their field conditions. The second lieutenant of H Company had been doing all he could to rally his men to follow their plans. His company had suffered greater casualties and the loss of two commanding officers. It was to his credit that he was able to keep his men fighting. "I don't want to overstep the line but," he looked in the direction where some of his platoons were sent out, "my men are barely holding on. Will reinforcements arrive soon?"

Anthony wished he had better news to tell him, but he didn't. "They're on their way. That's all I can tell you." He started to walk away.

"Lieutenant," Dennison called out.

Anthony stopped. "Yes?"

"If I may speak frankly, I don't think we should stay here if reinforcements aren't coming."

Anthony turned around and glanced at the walls of the narrow ravine leading to the cave entrance. If he could, he would tell Dennison he thought the same thing. "Thank you, Lieutenant."

At the command station, Anthony tried again to convince the captain to make plans for escape. "We should leave tonight. If we don't, we might be outgunned by tomorrow."

Scowling, Harding turned to the private operating their telephone. "Where is the reinforcement unit?"

"They're still pinned down, sir," the private said, nervous. "Command is sending a British infantry squadron from north of Cisterna to see if they can get to us quicker through another route. They should be here soon."

"A squadron?" Anthony said. "That won't be enough."

"No," Harding said, "but it'll be enough to help us hold until the reinforcement battalion arrives. Lieutenant, do what you can to hold our positions. We only need to hold on for a while longer."

Frustrated, Anthony went to check on the troops rotating in and out. Ollie was taking out a platoon to replace the one that had just returned for relief. He glanced at Anthony. The solemn look on his face told Anthony their situation had worsened.

The medics had been working around the clock. An injured soldier sitting with his back against the wall bowed his head lower and lower. Anthony walked over to him to help him lie down. Before he reached him, the soldier's body tipped over sideways to the ground, causing a muted thud that only Anthony could hear. The man was dead. His cigarette was still burning. Anthony crouched down, took the smoke out of his mouth and put it out.

Fox and Jonesy came up to him with a British army captain. "Lieutenant, this is Captain Chandler of the Gordon Highlanders Battalion."

"Your squadron has arrived!" Anthony said.

"Yes, but I'm not sure we'll be of much help. We're out of artillery. We used up our ammunition on our way here. The Germans are not letting up."

Anthony looked at the British soldiers entering the caves. A sinking feeling washed over him.

"At least we got more bodies," Fox said.

"If you have enough guns, we'll help you fight," said Captain Chandler.

No. They did not have enough. Their own artillery was running low, but they would all have to make do with what they had. The British soldiers could replace their wounded for the time being. "Thank you, Captain." He turned to Fox. "Take Captain Chandler to Captain Harding. Let's regroup when the British are ready."

After Fox took the British captain away, Jonesy said, "I don't know how much longer we can keep fighting. Every time we take the Krauts out, more of them arrive."

"I know."

Before they finished talking, a group of the villagers came running to the aid station. A woman seized the arm of the first soldier she saw and uttered a jumble of Italian words. Behind her, an old man carried a crying boy with bloodied arms and charred legs. Claudina was right behind them.

Anthony rushed over. "What happened?"

"He's my cousin." Claudina came close to the boy, distressed. "A grenade fell into a crack in the cave's wall near us. He was playing around there when the grenade exploded."

Horrified, Anthony stared at the boy.

Nearby, Jesse saw what was going on and rushed up to them. "Give him to me," he said to the old man. He took the boy from them, laid him down on the ground, and started to treat him.

On the verge of tears, Claudina said, "You all brought this on. This wouldn't have happened if you didn't come in here."

"I'm sorry." Anthony apologized. He didn't know what else to say.

Her anger turned to despair. "No. No. I'm sorry. I know this isn't your fault." She covered her eyes and shook her head. Wiping away her tears, she went to the boy. Anthony came closer to them. He stood behind them, helpless.

"We don't want this," she said. "We're farmers. We don't care about governments, or war, or anything like that. We want to be left alone. We want things to be back to the way they were."

Anthony stared at the wounds on the boy's little body. As he watched the boy whimper in pain, his mind cleared. He knew what he had to do. "We'll be gone tonight," he said to her. "I promise."

Chapter 18

The Germans' assault showed no sign of letting up and reinforcements still hadn't arrived. It didn't matter though. Anthony knew what he had to do. He could not stand by and watch while Harding indulged in this wild pursuit. Their supplies were running out. Their ammunition would not last. Worse, their men were dying.

The day had come to an end. The fighting wound down, but his plan was only about to begin. He would get everyone out of this living tomb. Whatever the consequences, he would have to bear it later.

"Garland." He found Jesse kneeling on the ground giving a wounded solider a morphine shot. Jesse looked up. The entire front of his uniform was smeared in blood. "Can I speak to you alone?"

"Sure." Jesse followed him to a spot out of earshot of the others.

"We need to get out of here, especially the wounded." Anthony glanced at the injured soldiers on the ground.

"You don't say!" Jesse said. "You don't have to tell me." His face then turned serious. "We're short on plasma. We're running low on bandages, morphine, everything. We need more supplies. Will reinforcements be arriving soon?"

"No. I wouldn't count on it."

Jesse looked at him in disbelief.

"I need your help." Anthony lowered his voice. "I want to take everyone out of here. If we don't leave, we could be trapped in these caves when the Germans get here. We're running out of time. We have to leave tonight. I'm going to try to convince the captain, but if I can't, I'll need you to declare him medically unfit for duty so we can all get out."

"Are you talking about a mutiny?" A playful spark came into Jesse's eyes.

"I'm talking about saving everyone's lives. You don't want to die, do you?"

"Not if I can help it."

"Harding's not in his right mind. He's not doing what he should to look out for us. He's got a personal agenda."

Jesse stared at him, amused. "You don't have to justify yourself to me."

"So will you do it? Declare him medically unfit if he won't agree?"

Weighing his options, Jesse asked, "You got a plan to get us out of here?"

"Yes."

"I'm with you then," Jesse said as though he were placing a bet. The way Jesse approached everything like a game never ceased to amaze Anthony. Nonetheless, he was relieved to know he could count on Jesse. With the most important part of his plan resolved, he left to search for Jonesy and Dennison. If he could persuade them to go along, they might just have a chance.

# # #

Alone with Harding in the command station, Anthony tried to persuade the captain to take the right course one last time.

"We have to leave tonight," he told Harding. "Give the order and I'll get everyone started."

Staring at the maps on the table with his arms behind his back, Harding would not answer.

"We're running out of time," Anthony said.

"Reinforcements will come."

"They're not coming. They won't make it in time, if they make it at all. We're on our own. If we stay here, we'll all die."

Harding would not budge. "They'll get here. We just have to hold on a while longer. This is our best chance to get Klaus. I'm not letting him get away again. You will not interfere with my plan, Lieutenant."

Anthony would not acquiesce so easily this time. He had made up his mind, and he meant to follow through. He took a deep breath. "We're leaving tonight whether you agree or not. I'm taking all the men. Sergeant Jones and I will set up an escape route and provide cover. Lieutenant Dennison and his company will take the wounded. They'll try to get back to the hospital. Once they're in the clear, the rest of us will make our way to the reinforcement units. We'll try to link up with them."

"You will disobey my direct order?" Harding glared at him. "You wouldn't dare!"

"Try me."

"You're out of line. I'll order the troops to stop."

"Then I'll have a medic declare you mentally unfit to lead." Anthony looked Harding in the eye. "You do not want that, Captain."

"Are you threatening me, Lieutenant?"

"If you try to stop me, I assure you, you will be the only one left here."

Harding's neck and ears turned to a furious red and he took a step back. Not waiting for his response, Anthony said, "I am going out there now, and I'm telling everyone you have ordered us to prepare to leave these caves. In two hours, we will begin our move. You will join Lieutenant Dennison and his company to take the wounded back to the hospital. You will officially be bringing the sick back. But let's make one thing clear, Lieutenant Dennison will be in charge."

"You…you can't do that."

"If we succeed, you can have all the credit. You are officially in command. But tonight, we are going to do exactly what I said."

"And if your plan fails? You want me to take the fall for you if the Krauts destroy us out there?"

"If we don't leave, they'll destroy us in here," Anthony said. "If we get out, we'll at least have a fighting chance."

"You are in serious violation of military codes, Lieutenant." Harding squinted his eyes. "I will not let you get away with this."

"Court martial me then when we're back at base. I don't care." With that, Anthony walked away. He was done letting Harding gamble with their lives.

# # #

When night came, Jonesy led the company out of the caves. At an entrance farthest from where the Germans had congregated, they formed a defense line for the rest of the troops to escape. Shielded by darkness, the infantry units slipped out segment by segment. Company H was the first to leave. Leading his men, Dennison directed his troops to carry the wounded soldiers. They had to carry them on litters by foot. It was the only way to move those who were hurt through the narrow ravines. If they could get them through without drawing the Germans' attention before daybreak, they could reach their motor convoy on the other side of the ravines and rush the wounded back to the beachhead.

While Jesse packed the remainder of the medical supplies into his bag, Anthony said to him, "You remember what I told you, right?" Still worried that Harding might interfere with Dennison, he had arranged for Jesse to leave with Company H.

"Sure."

Anthony glanced at Company H's departing troops. Harding had now joined them. Before he left the caves, he gave Anthony a bitter, resentful stare.

"If Harding makes trouble for Dennison," Anthony said, watching Harding, "you will declare him mentally unfit and relieve him of duty. I've talked to Dennison. He knows you'll be backing him."

Jesse whistled. "Wouldn't want to cross you." He winked at Anthony and jokingly saluted in deference. Anthony smiled and walked away.

There was only one last piece of unfinished business. While the troops lifted their wounded out of the caves, the family of the boy burned by the grenade huddled around him. Claudina was with them.

"You can all come with us," Anthony said to Claudina. "These caves aren't safe anymore. If you and your people want to come with us..."

"We won't be any safer with you. Maybe the Germans will leave us alone if you're all gone."

"We have a good chance of making it out."

"No. We'll take our chances here."

Anthony looked at the civilians. There were close to a hundred of them. He wished he could tell her they could guarantee their safety if they came, but he couldn't. In truth, traveling with a large group of civilians who did not speak the same language would only add more risks and endanger everyone even more. He looked over to the boy and his family kneeling around him.

"Your cousin should come with us." He could at least offer that. "He needs medical attention. If we can get him to our hospital, we can help him."

Claudina hesitated.

"It's the right thing to do. He might not survive if he stays here."

Unsure, she looked at the boy. The poor kid was moaning in delirium from pain and morphine.

"You can come with him."

She considered his offer. "I will ask." Returning to the boy's family, she spoke to them. The mother of the boy turned around and stared at him. She looked uncertain and anxious. He nodded at her. She pulled on Claudina's sleeve and questioned her. The other family members threw in their questions too. After a heated exchange of words that left him confused, Claudina came back to him with the boy's mother. The mother stared at him, her face full of hope.

"We would like for my cousin to go with you." She put her arm around the older woman's arm and drew her closer. "His mother wants to come as well. She can't speak English, so I will go too."

Relieved, he gave the older woman a reassuring smile. "That's good. I'm glad. You can go with our company that's returning to the hospital. I'll arrange for someone to carry your cousin."

"Thank you," she said. "Good luck to you."

"And to you."

As she walked away, he looked at the group of villagers. Weak and vulnerable, they would have no way to defend themselves if the Germans came into these caves. And yet, the Allies were not their saviors. The American army's arrival had only brought them more destruction. His own battalion's presence had brought them more danger.

If they did win this war, he would always remember Claudina's bitter face. He would never forget the wounds on the boy's small body. He would remember, there were no heroes.

# # #

Their evacuation continued through the night. When the Germans discovered they were on the move, they waged another assault, trying to stop their escape. Anthony stayed with the troops guarding the ravine through which Dennison and his troops were moving the sick and wounded soldiers. Aided by the darkness and the confusion of gunfire, Company H succeeded. They got out and reached the vehicles waiting beyond the gullies.

As their troops continued their escape, Anthony remained behind, staying as long as he could until most of their men had gotten out. From his experience with Harding, he had come to understand one thing. It was not enough to hold the rank. It was not enough even if he could devise smart strategies and sound battle plans. For them to succeed and survive, he needed to have the troops on his side. The only way they would be on his side was if they believed he cared about them. For them to believe that he cared about them, he must put his own interests aside. He must think of their well-being first and foremost, always.

At daybreak, most of their troops were already gone. The first unit that escaped had reached the reinforcement battalion and made contact. It was time for him and the last unit to retreat and join them.

He had just started to run when a bullet swooshed past within an inch of his head and scratched the side of his helmet. His heart flipped up to his throat. He turned around. A sniper was aiming at him from behind the bushes. For a split second, he thought it was all over, but Fox was quicker. A shot hit the sniper in the shoulder and he yelped. Fox jumped into the bushes, subdued him, and captured him.

His heart still pounding, Anthony watched Fox lead the sniper away. The bullet was so close. His helmet might have protected him, but if Fox hadn't come to his aid, the next shot might have killed him. He was within inches of losing his life.

As they continued on their way, it all made sense to him. He finally grasped the answer to how they would all make it through to the end. He had to put himself out front. He had to take the same risks as the rest of the troops and even more. He must show them he would risk his own life to protect them. In return, they would give him their loyalty. They would give their all to protect him and keep him alive.

This was the key. To lead them meant he must expose himself to more risks than anyone else, but it was the only way to get everyone through this. It was a dangerous burden, one which Wesley had borne, and one which he now must bear.

Joining up with the reinforcement battalion, they were finally able to hold the Germans at bay. The dominating booms of American gunfire reverberated across the fields. The enemy would not advance any further. Not here. They would not break through this point and drive them back to the beach.

That night, all the soldiers in his company who had escaped the caves gathered for an impromptu celebration. Even away from them, Garland had come through for them again. Somebody from the medical unit had sent up a dozen bottles of liquor.

Sitting by his own pup tent, Anthony watched them pass the bottles around.

It's up to you and me now to get everyone through this, he could almost hear Wesley say to him.

Did it, Wesley. Got everyone through this.

Chapter 19

When the German soldiers first appeared at the field hospital, neither Tessa nor Gracie could take their eyes off them. Even though the medical staff were rushing all about them, and the ambulance sirens and military traffic police whistles were alerting everyone that injured troops were arriving and needed immediate attention, the two of them could not help but stop to watch the German prisoners. They had both heard plenty of rumors about the Wehrmacht from their patients and the nurses who had treated German POWs in Africa and Sicily, but seeing the enemy soldiers in person was something else.

Curious, Tessa watched as Jonesy marched the six German men over to the aid station. With heavy footsteps, the prisoners plodded forward. Two of them were carrying a litter that held their wounded comrade who could not walk. The other three had bandages wrapped around various parts of their bodies. Their injuries did not seem life-threatening. A look of defeat hung on their glum, weary faces, but none of them appeared frightened. The Americans were known to comply with the Geneva Conventions, and having been brought here to the hospital instead of the American base camp gave them another level of relief.

"Are we really expected to treat them?" Gracie wrinkled her nose and whispered to Tessa. "They look scary."

Tessa observed the enemy soldiers more closely. They didn't scare her, but they did intrigue her. These were the people who had been shooting bombs and firing at them day in and day out? After seeing all the deaths and horrific injuries inflicted on their own soldiers, she had imagined the enemy to look more evil, more sinister. Now that the enemy was before her eyes, they did not appear like what she had imagined. The style of their grey uniforms did look menacing, but marred with stains of mud and blood, the posh design had lost its intended effect. With their worn-out faces and disheveled hair, the prisoners did not look intimidating to her at all. Under the guard of the healthier American soldiers, they looked to her like pathetic, insipid weaklings.

She supposed that being a nurse, she should feel sympathy for them, but she didn't. What she felt was a mixture of pity and repulsion. These were the people who had started everything that took her away from her home and parents? The ones who hauled her and Anthony into this horrific mess? The ones who made their every night in Anzio a living hell?

She almost found it hard to believe. The evil that was the German empire, shouldn't it be more grand and majestic in its own nefarious way? How did these banal-looking men bring forth a sea of terror across the entire continent?

Are we really expected to treat them? Tessa asked herself the same question.

The prisoners came closer with Jonesy and the American guards. Gracie's eyes remained fixed on them, and so were Tessa's. While they both stood bewildered, Ellie rushed out with her aides to greet Jonesy. Since Captain Milton left for Naples two days ago, Ellie had been working nonstop. She had more than proven herself capable of managing the nursing staff and the hospital's operations.

"Quick," Ellie ordered, pointing to the German soldier on the litter. "Get him to surgery." Her aides immediately took him away.

"Thank you, Lieutenant Swanson," Jonesy said. "We'll take these two." He pushed the two uninjured prisoners who were carrying the litter. "Take them back to base for questioning." He told the army guards and two of them marched the uninjured prisoners away. "What do you want done with these ones?" he asked Ellie about the remaining three German soldiers.

Ellie turned to Tessa and Gracie. "Can you two please take them to Ward 6 and see what needs to be done for them?"

Too overwhelmed to respond, Gracie stood speechless, but Tessa answered, "Yes, Ellie."

"We'll go with Lieutenant Graham and Lieutenant Hall," Jonesy said to Ellie.

"Thank you." Ellie walked away.

Tessa eyed the prisoners again. "Come with me," she said to Jonesy and his men, then led them toward Ward 6.

"Go on," Jonesy said. "Walk, you stinking sonsofbitches." He poked one of the three remaining prisoners with the butt of his rifle. "*Weitergehen, Arschloch.*" The prisoners moved, following Tessa and Gracie, with Jonesy and the army guards behind them.

A small aid station with several adjoining tents, Ward 6 was designated for treatment of POWs. When there were no prisoners, it was used for treatment of patients who did not require emergency care. Inside, Tessa found several medical corpsmen goofing off, passing around a copy of the *Yank* magazine with Ann Savage in fishnet stockings on the cover.

"What are you all doing here?" Tessa scolded them. "We have a lot of patients arriving. Would you please go out and lend everyone a hand?"

The corpsmen quickly cleared out of the tent. Tessa pointed to the beds and motioned for the three Germans to sit down. Warily, she and Gracie prepared scissors and equipment for undressing their bandages while Jonesy and the other American soldiers stood guard.

"That one with the scar over his eyebrow scares me," Gracie whispered to Tessa. Tessa looked at the man. He hadn't shaved in a while, and his stubble covered the cheeks of his long face. His scar, stubble, and calloused skin made him look rugged and rough. With a devil-may-care attitude and a cigarette hanging from his mouth, he stared blankly into space. The bandages could not conceal his muscular shoulders.

"Isn't he scary?" Half joking, Jonesy came up behind Gracie, startling her. "That bastard shot at Lieutenant Ardley. The sniper bullet came this close to Lieutenant Ardley's head and almost killed him." Jonesy held up his thumb and index finger to show how close the bullet was. "But Lieutenant Ardley was swift as a stallion and got out of the way quick. Then Fox fired at the bastard and shot him. The bastard got lucky. The bullet only grazed his shoulder. You should've seen how quick and brave Lieutenant Ardley was, Lieutenant Graham. You would've swooned if you were there."

Tessa didn't hear a word Jonesy had said in praise of Anthony. All she heard was "shot at Lieutenant Ardley" and "almost killed him." She spun around and glared at the sniper. Unsure why Tessa was looking at him this way, the man straightened up on his bed. As they stared at each other, Tessa felt anger rising inside her. She felt an uncontrollable urge to confront him for what he had done.

"Gracie," Tessa interrupted Jonesy's babbling and walked over to the man. "You said this man scares you. Why don't you take the other two prisoners to the next tent? The guards can go with you and keep watch for you. Leave this one to me."

"Are… are you sure, Tessa?" Gracie asked, uncertain.

"I'm sure." She broke the stare and looked at Jonesy. "Sergeant Jones, will you stay with me?"

Oblivious to Tessa's odd tone of voice, Jonesy said, "Sure. I'll stay."

Tessa stared down at the sniper. "Go on, Gracie. Leave this one to me. I'll take care of him."

"I… okay. As long as you're sure." Gracie was still hesitant, but Tessa was as firm as Gracie was indecisive. Gracie motioned the other two prisoners to get up and, together with the American guards, led them away. The man with the scarred eyebrow started to get up from his bed to follow, but Tessa pushed his uninjured shoulder down and signaled him to stay. He looked at Tessa, confused.

Her eyes still on the sniper, Tessa said, "Jonesy, you speak German, correct? Would you please tell this man who I am?"

"Excuse me?" Jonesy asked.

"Go on," she said. "Tell him. Tell him I'm the girlfriend of the man he shot at. Tell him I'm the girlfriend of the man he tried to kill."

"Uh… okay." Befuddled by Tessa's request, Jonesy nonetheless acquiesced. "*Die Schwester will, dass Sie wissen. Sie ist die Freundin des Offiziers Sie versucht haben, zu töten.*"

The sniper raised his eyebrows slightly and sized Tessa up, but then lost interest and looked away from her. He inhaled a drag of his cigarette and ignored her.

Irritated by his indifference, she moved closer to him. Refusing to meet her eyes, he frowned and turned his head. "I've got nothing to say to you."

"You speak English!" She waited for him to answer, but he remained unmoved, offering not even a word of regret or apology. She felt her anger turning into rage.

Outside, the ambulance sirens screamed louder and louder. People shouted and yelled orders everywhere. The chaotic noises of a massive descent of patients had reached a fevered pitch. A private pulled open the tent flap. "Sergeant Jones! Captain Harding wants to see you. We have more German prisoners arriving."

Jonesy looked at the private, then at Tessa.

"It's okay, Jonesy. You can leave him to me. Looks like I don't need a translator after all. You can go."

Sensing the tension between Tessa and the sniper, Jonesy made a wry face. "I don't think I should."

"I can handle him."

"But…"

"I'll be fine. He's injured. He needs me to treat him. He's unarmed. This whole place is guarded. He's got nowhere to go."

Jonesy hesitated.

"The captain's waiting, Sergeant," the private reminded him.

"Go on, Sergeant Jones," Tessa said.

Conflicted, Jonesy said, "Uh… all right, but only if you let me take some precautions." He walked over to the prisoner, tapped his arm, and told him to lie down. The prisoner threw his cigarette butt on the ground and grudgingly lay down on the bed. Jonesy strapped the restraints on the side of the bed around the prisoner's wrists and ankles. "If anything happens to you, Lieutenant Ardley will kill me. Kill me!"

Tessa didn't answer. Her entire attention was focused on the prisoner.

Jonesy followed the private to the exit. "I'll be back as soon as I can. Come find me if you need anything." In a hurry, they left.

Alone in the tent with the prisoner, Tessa asked, "Are you not sorry at all?"

The sniper grunted and would not answer.

Infuriated by his silence, she raised her voice. "You're not going to say anything? You realize you're at my mercy now, do you?"

The man squinted and leaned away from her. "What are you going to do? You can't harm me. I'm a prisoner of war. I'm injured. You have to follow Geneva Conventions."

"You people don't follow the Geneva Conventions. You target and kill our medics on the front line. I saw a German plane bomb a medical ship with my own eyes."

The sniper's face twitched, but he exhibited no other response. He still refused to look at her. His apathy and continued disregard of her made her feel powerless. She tightened her fists. No. She would not let him get off so easily. "How about I treat you the exact same way you people treat us?"

Struck by the chilling tone of her voice, he glanced at her. She hovered over him while he lay tied down on the bed. Her cold eyes made him shudder and he gripped the metal bars on the side of the bed.

"Wait… I… I didn't know… I didn't know he was your boyfriend."

She didn't answer, but stared down at him. The look of rage on her face at the mention of her boyfriend sent him into a state of panic. He tried to get up from the bed, but the restraints held him down. His earlier air of nonchalance vanished.

"I don't want you to treat me. Leave me alone."

This time, it was her turn to ignore him. Without saying another word, she walked away from the bed to prepare a tray of medical items. The sniper's eyes followed her.

"I didn't know, and… see… I wasn't trying to kill him. I swear to God. It wasn't my intent to kill him..."

"Shut your mouth! Liar!"

The sniper stopped talking. Tessa carried the metal tray over and set it on the cart next to the bed. She picked up a pair of scissors from the tray and held the sharp blades in front of him. He cowered away in the bed.

Swallowing hard, Tessa cut open the dirty bandages wrapped around his shoulder. The bullet had sliced his muscles. She looked at his wound, then at him. This man would've inflicted the same wound on Anthony without a second thought. The same wound on Anthony's head would be an entirely different matter. That thought made her lightheaded. She scowled to steady herself, then examined his wound again. It crossed her mind that if she pressed her fingers hard on his wound, she could make him squeal in pain.

She took a deep breath and put down the scissors.

"You and I are the only ones here," she said to the man, her voice flat and emotionless. "I can do anything I want to you. No one will ever know."

The man cringed. "Please. I'm sorry. I am sorry I shot at him."

Her rage rose again when she heard him say "I shot at him." A vision of Anthony lying on the field, dead, came to her mind. Why wouldn't these Germans stop? Why wouldn't they stop waging this war so Anthony wouldn't be subjected to the risk of death?

She glared at the sniper. The sight of him enraged her. "I can hurt you too. I can make you feel a lot of pain." She held up the bottle of antiseptic solution. "You see this? This hurts a lot." Without explaining what it was, she opened the bottle and poured the antiseptic solution onto a handful of cotton wipes. Her words must have spooked him. When the cotton wipes touched his bullet-torn flesh, he howled.

All she was doing was cleaning his wound. Although the antiseptic stung, the prisoner was unharmed. His pain was necessary and normal, but he did not know that. He did not know what she was doing to him.

Normally, she would warn the patients that the antiseptic would hurt. If she was in a good mood, she would even say something soothing to distract them from the pain. But this time, she meant for him to feel the pain. She hated what this man and what his people were doing. She wanted him to feel every bit of the pain he and his people had caused. She wanted him to feel fear and think the worst of what might happen to him, just like the American soldiers in Anzio had to do every day.

When she finished, she picked up a syringe from the tray and filled it with morphine. The man watched her in terror, fearing what she would do next.

She thought of Anthony again. She could almost sense what it would feel like if Anthony were really dead. Anthony, gone, forever, and she, abandoned, left behind. If she reached out her hand, she would not be able to touch him. It all felt so real, she felt herself screaming inside.

She held up the syringe with the needle attached and, taking another deep breath, steadied her shaking hand. She wished she could make the entire world of madness stop with the syringe and needle in her hand.

"I can put poison in you, you know that?" she said. "Or an overdose of anesthesia and put you to sleep forever. I can put everything to an end once and for all." She grabbed his arm. "We're very busy here. No one will have time to question why a German prisoner of war has died."

The man struggled in the bed, but was unable to free himself from the restraints tying him down. Tessa ran the end of the needle over the skin of his arm. He shook his head violently left and right. She ignored him and inserted the needle into his vein. Helpless, he gave up. He turned his head away from her. Her vision blurred by the rage and bitterness mounting inside her, she did not notice the tears falling slowly from his eyes.

"Or maybe a quick death is too good for you." She withdrew the needle. "Maybe I should dress you with contaminated bandages and let germs infect your wound. We can watch the gangrene grow, turn green, and eat your flesh alive. We can let you die a slow and miserable death. Let's see how you like what you all are doing to us."

Still facing away from her, the man said nothing more. He lay motionless on the bed, crying silent tears. His crying annoyed her. Anthony almost died because of him. And here she was, treating him and helping him heal. How dare he lay there and cry like he was the victim? "Stop crying and look at me!" she cried out. She wanted him to yell back at her, threaten her or fight back to try to harm her. She wanted him to be the evil killer that he was so she could lash out at him and tell him he was a monster.

He turned his head toward her. For a moment, they stared at each other. A teardrop fell from the corner of each of his eyes. All the things that she wanted to say choked in her throat. She wanted to see the eyes of the devil, but what she saw were human eyes. Eyes that reflected pain, fear, hopelessness, even regret.

Taken aback, she looked away from him. Methodically, she cut up the bandages and dressed his wounds. When she finished, she said to him, "I'll get the guards to come and take you." Unable to look at him again, she walked away.

Behind her, he whimpered, "I'm sorry."

She didn't answer. Clenching her fists, she exited the tent as fast as she could. Once outside, tears swelled in her eyes and she sobbed uncontrollably, holding her hand over her mouth. The thought of Anthony almost getting shot and killed horrified her. Worse, she hated herself for what she had just done. The evil of this war had brought out the darkest, most vindictive side of her. It made her do something heinous out of love. That love, so pure and beautiful before, was now tainted by her own actions. Disgusted with herself, she walked faster and faster, wanting to run away. If she ran fast enough, maybe she could run away from everything that occurred in the tent like it had never happened.

PART SEVEN

Catastrophe at 33rd

Chapter 20

Pink clouds stretched across the sky as the sun's golden rays beamed from the horizon. On the beach, Jesse watched the ship sail away from the port. It was only five o'clock. He could indulge a while longer in this magnificent scenery before darkness emerged and the Luftwaffe returned to turn this place into a theater of terror.

Beside him, Gracie leaned against his arm. She was talking about moving to New York again. In a matter of weeks, she had told him everything there was to know about herself and was already dreaming of their wedding. As always, the hardest part for him was to appear genuinely interested. It was always the same with girls like her, the good girls who never crossed any lines or asked any hard questions. They had no interests beyond what the world told them their interests should be. Their lives culminated in a fairy-tale wedding. Their stories numbed his brain even the first time he had to seduce someone like this. To pretend to be enthralled all over again each time thereafter was a special form of torture.

But if there was even a tinge of boredom on his part, they would never know it. He might be a cad, but he was professional. Always, he gave them the time of their lives, especially if they had something he wanted. He let them live out a fantasy love story that existed only in their limited minds. In his own way, he played fair. It was what set him apart from the rest of the world's scoundrels. It was not unusual for women he had betrayed to still think fondly of him afterward. With him, women always got what they bargained for. Only the ones like Gracie didn't see or understand that and always wanted more.

He looked out to the sea. How he wished it were Tessa watching the sunset with him instead. Tessa should be returning from her shift any time now. Gracie didn't know that, but he did. He had spoken to Tessa an hour earlier at the hospital. He wanted to see her one more time before he returned to base. Gracie was the perfect excuse.

"I wrote my friends back home and told them all about you," Gracie said. "They're very excited to meet you. There's Ingrid, Beatrice, and Margaret. I told you about them, remember? And Lois. Lois always thinks she's better than me, ever since we were in grade school. Then she met this guy in the navy, and she acted like she's superior to all of us. Especially to me because I didn't have a boyfriend. I can't wait to introduce you to everyone. Wait till Lois sees you. I've met her boyfriend and, well, let's just say, he's nothing compared to you. He was only a clerk before he went off to the navy. She'll be so surprised when she finds out my boyfriend is an investment banker from New York."

She turned her face up toward him, expecting a kiss. He gave her what she wanted. She was a clumsy kisser. She had a tendency to smash her nose and lips too hard against his face and everything got too wet. Gently, he held her shoulders to push her back, then guided her and eased her into the act with his own soft kisses. He tempted her with warm breaths and tender caresses that made her lose all her inhibitions.

"I want to be with you forever, Jesse." She took his hand and led him to stand up. He knew she wanted him, and she assumed that, like all men, this was what he wanted too. No doubt, she believed this would close their bargain. She lowered her eyes with an embarrassed smile and led him toward her tent.

He hesitated. He never cared for breaking in a virgin. They didn't know how to do anything, let alone do things right. The entire act was a miserable chore. But on the ground of principle, he never held back on efforts and he never shortchanged them. During the act, he would take his time to make them feel like the most beautiful girl in the world. He gratified them while he introduced them to the gateway of carnal pleasure. He wouldn't be there forever as they hoped, but for as long as he was there, he would give them an experience they might never have again.

It was a lot of work on his part, not to mention the aftermath. With virgins, there was always an aftermath. They would expect a commitment, generally in the form of nothing less than a marriage proposal. If he couldn't disappear soon after the act, he would need to have a plan for dealing with that. Otherwise, everything was more trouble than it was worth. For him to make all these efforts, the prize he got in return had to be worth it. With Gracie, he wasn't sure. Was it worth it? Could he go through all this trouble for nothing more than to see Tessa more often?

She was taking him inside her tent, but it was not too late to stop. It would be easy enough. Excuses were abundant. He could tell her he honored her and wanted to wait. He could pretend to be upright and refuse to take advantage of her. He was about to pull her back from entering the tent, but Tessa returned.

Seeing Tessa, he almost halted. But then, he saw the expression on her face. If shock or indignation was her reaction, he would have quit right that minute. He could still dispel everything as a misunderstanding and salvage her opinion of him. But she didn't look shocked. She looked disappointed.

Could this really be? Was Tessa really disappointed to see him dallying with another girl? This was the first time she had shown any reaction to anything he did, and her reaction was disappointment at seeing him be intimate with another girl? It was more than he could hope for. He wanted more. More of her disappointment. More of her resentment. Even her anger.

He smiled at her in defiance and followed Gracie into the tent. The entire time, his eyes and Tessa's never left each other's. They held each other's gaze. A voice in the back of his mind warned him that he would regret this later. He ignored it. He couldn't help being reckless. He wanted Tessa to know what it was like to have the tables turned, to have her on the outside looking in.

Already halfway inside the tent, Gracie didn't realize Tessa had returned. With one last brazen smile, Jesse disappeared with Gracie into the tent.

# # #

Jesse's heart was still pumping when he entered the tent. The way Tessa looked at him when she saw what he and Gracie were about to do made him think that Tessa might feel something for him after all. The expression on her face was unmistakable. She looked disappointed. It was the only evidence he had ever seen that she cared. He wished he could grasp it, hold on to it, and keep it.

What a strange moment this was. Between himself and Gracie, he didn't expect to be the one entering the tent spellbound.

He had never been inside their tent before. Gracie led him to her cot and they sat down. Tessa's cot was only a few feet away. She had folded her blanket neatly at the foot of the cot and placed her army-issued duffle bag at the other end to use as a pillow.

At first glance, it looked no different than any other army personnel's makeshift sleeping space. Yet it was not the same. This was where the girl he loved came back to every day. Being so close to where

Tessa slept drove his imagination wild. He couldn't stop looking at everything that belonged to her.

"I've never done this before," Gracie's voice brought him back out of his thoughts. Too embarrassed to look at him directly, she turned her face away. "You're the only one." She leaned against him. He found it hard to pay attention to her. He was too distracted. Thankfully, he had years of experience and could still function on autopilot while he tried to regain his senses. As if operating on their own, his hand moved her hair away from her neck and his lips caressed her nape. All the while, he couldn't stop glancing at Tessa's cot.

Gracie turned her face to meet his lips. Before he knew it, he was lying on top of her, kissing her and undressing her, undressing himself. He no longer wanted to stop. He was aroused, not by the girl in his arms, but by the one who was not there and yet whose presence was so tantalizingly near.

He glanced at Tessa's cot again, then wrapped his arms around Gracie and rolled her over on top. In playful protest, Gracie laughed. He rolled her over one more time until he was on top of her on Tessa's cot.

He touched Tessa's cot. Was this the closest he would ever come to making love to the girl he loved?

Gracie adjusted her body under him, knocking over Tessa's duffle bag as she shifted. A small pink glass bottle fell onto the ground.

"Tessa's perfume." Gracie sat up and picked up the bottle. Captivated, he stared at the bottle in her hand.

Giggling, Gracie took off the cap of the bottle. "We can make this place more romantic." She kissed his forehead, then squeezed the atomizer and sprayed the perfume into the air. Fragrance of roses spread like magic, transforming the drab interior of the tent into a sphere of dreams. Specks of rose water sprinkled onto his bare skin like soft kisses. Like an aphrodisiac potion, they seeped into his pores, setting his body afire.

"Maybe I'll spray some on myself." Gracie pointed the atomizer at her neck.

He looked at her, alarmed. "No!" He grabbed her hand to stop her. "Let's not mess with Tessa's things." He took the bottle from her and put it back into Tessa's duffle. Tessa's rose fragrance was not to be used on anybody else.

Peeved, Gracie mumbled, "Okay," and slid back down onto the cot. As always, she chose not to be disagreeable. Whether it was because she wanted to please him or whether she didn't know how to ever demur, he did not know. Maybe it was both. Either way, it made everything easier for him and he was glad for that. He rewarded her with caresses that made her moan.

The scent of roses lingered in the air. He closed his eyes and soaked it in. He had never smelled anything more intoxicating in the world. He felt drunk with the fragrance. The sweet smell enveloped him like a lover's embrace. He could almost feel Tessa's own arms around him.

"I lov—" Gracie whispered.

"Shhhhh…" He tapped his fingers over her mouth. He kissed her again to keep her from speaking. He didn't want to hear her say that. He didn't want to hear her voice.

Just once. Just this once. He wanted to imagine that he was making love to the girl he loved. He closed his eyes again and inhaled, drawing in the sweet scent of rose perfume, letting it spread through his every cell and every vein until it became one with him, body and soul.

Chapter 21

In all her life, Fran Milton had only had one goal, to dedicate herself to work. Work gave her existence a purpose, a validation. As long as she did her work well, everything she did was justified. No. More than that. Performing her job well made her superior. Unlike people who received praise for appearances, she didn't get by on mere pretenses. All credit that went to her was justified and deserved.

By that same logic, shouldn't she deserve Aaron Haley's attention too, after all that she had done for him? Every time the army sent them to a new location, she was the one who made sure their hospital was up and running at record speed. Sure, the others had helped, but she was the one who made sure everything happened the right way. With her in charge, he never had to worry about a thing. She handled the lion's share of the hospital's planning and logistics to adapt all of their operation procedures to his preferred work style. She did most of his administrative work too, so he could focus on performing surgeries and treating the patients. She was always there for him, making sure he had everything he needed. She did all this for him. She made everything so convenient for him, he didn't even notice that her efforts were the reason why everything in the hospital accommodated him and his needs. He thought this was how things ordinarily were in military hospitals.

Maybe it was time he noticed.

Lately, when alone in her tent with the solitude of her own thoughts, she had started to feel that her work was no longer enough. Was this all there was to life? The question kept coming to her mind. She used to think that she didn't need more, and perhaps she still didn't. But when she looked at people around her, like Ellie Swanson for example, she wondered why people like Ellie had so much more. Happy family, recognition by her peers, attention from men of substance. What had people like her done to be entitled to so much? If even someone like Ellie Swanson, who had done nothing significant to speak of, could have all that, why shouldn't she have the same and more? She had worked hard all these years, fulfilling all her responsibilities without fail. Didn't she deserve something more for everything she had done?

Yes. She deserved recognition and acknowledgment. Not in the form of medals or awards. No. She wasn't proud and superficial that way. What she deserved was recognition and acknowledgment in the form of appreciation. Aaron Haley should appreciate her. The world should grant her that. He shouldn't disregard her and all that she had done for him anymore. It was time he saw the reality of the situation. She had done so much already. It was only fair. If he couldn't see it, then she would have to take matters into her own hands and show him. Tonight, when they met for their evening tea, she meant to do exactly that.

In Aaron Haley's office, she set a cup of hot lemon-ginger tea on the desk for him. "It's good to wind down the day with a cup of herbal tea." She took a seat across from him. "This tea is very rare. I bought this from someone I know at the army headquarters in Naples. Ginger has a lot of medicinal qualities."

"Thank you," he said without looking at the cup. He was still busy jotting down notes into the patient files.

"Well, wind down for you anyway. My day is only half over."

Aaron looked up from the stack of folders. "I thought you worked the day shift today. You've been here since morning."

"I'm doing a double shift. I noticed last night you had a string of surgeries scheduled for today. I took on an extra shift to make sure you had everything you needed. I wanted to make sure there would be no complications to distract you."

"Oh." He sounded a bit surprised. "In that case, thanks." He made another note in a file.

"You're welcome. I always do everything I can to help you. Not that you ever notice."

He stopped what he was doing and looked at her. She continued sipping her tea. Keeping her eyes downcast and concealed behind her glasses, she gave no hint of anything unusual in her gestures and demeanor, but she was aware that she was making him feel uneasy.

He put down his pen. "Of course I notice, Captain. Everyone notices the exemplary work you do. We all respect you for it. You know that."

"I suppose. You do know I go the extra mile for you, don't you?"

He paused. Choosing his words carefully, he said, "Of course I do. As the hospital's chief superintendent, I appreciate very much the extra attention and help you give me. It makes all the difference in a stressful work environment like ours."

That wasn't the answer she wanted to hear. She was hoping he would honestly acknowledge that what she did for him went beyond professionalism. Nonetheless, she was pleased to see him tense up when he answered her question. At least, she now knew he didn't take her for granted. She lightened her tone and asked, "What do you think is going to happen? Do you think we'll win this war?"

"I certainly hope so," he said, obviously relieved she had changed the subject.

"What will you do when the war's over? If we win."

"I'll go home. Back to Boston, I suppose." Then, seemingly lost in his own thoughts, he said, "Or move to the countryside, somewhere far away like Montana with acres and acres of green meadows and rivers where I can go fishing whenever I want. I can be a country doctor again." His eyes had a faraway look and his lips turned up into a peaceful smile.

"You can't be serious. You're too qualified to be a country doctor. You can contribute so much more doing what you do in a proper city or university hospital."

"I think I will have contributed my fair share by the time this war is over."

"What about your career? You can't give that up. You're way too accomplished. You can still do so much more!"

"My career?" He looked amused. "I've already done more than I ever thought I would. I'm not so young anymore. I guess my ambitions have waned over the years."

His ambivalence alarmed her. Giving up on work was not the life she had imagined after the war. As for Montana, she couldn't even fathom the idea.

"I'm joking about Montana," he said, his voice less dreamy and more earnest, "but I do seriously think about moving to someplace quiet and peaceful. Some place in the countryside where everything is simple would be nice. I can have a small garden and grow some vegetables."

Garden? Grow vegetables? "That's ridiculous." She straightened her glasses. She wouldn't entertain such nonsensical ideas. "You're worn down by the war. We all fantasize about idyllic places to escape what's going on here. You'll come to your senses when you return home."

Rather than contradicting her, he said, "You look different today. I can't quite put my finger on it."

"Oh?" She touched the back of her head. "Must be my hair. I let my hair down."

"Maybe. You've never worn your hair down before."

"It's more comfortable this way when wearing the helmet." She kept her voice indifferent, but she was pleased he noticed. She had bought a bottle of shampoo when she was in Naples. It worked like a wonder compared to the army-issued soaps. It surprised her how much she liked what the shampoo did for her hair. At the same time, she was annoyed with herself for caring about something so trivial like hair.

"What's that?" She pointed to a heart-shaped wooden ornament on his desk.

"This?" He picked it up. "I carved this. A patient was worried his fiancée would be upset if he didn't send her a gift for Valentine's Day. I told him I'd make a wooden heart for him to send to her." He tossed the ornament in his hand. "I chipped this one. I made him another one."

"Wood carving? Is this a hobby?"

"It's something I used to do quite a bit. I picked it back up a few months ago. It's a good way to pass the time here." He tossed the heart back onto his desk.

"I should be going now." She got up from her seat, then glanced at the heart. "Do you mind if I have it?"

"The heart? Sure. Take it."

She picked it up. "Watch out when you carve. Be careful not to cut your hand. You're a surgeon. We can't risk you injuring your hands."

"I'll be careful."

She closed her fist around the heart. Before she left, she asked, "You always address me as Captain. You call everybody else by their names. Why is that?"

He looked puzzled, as if he had never given this a thought. "Everybody calls you Captain. It's what you prefer, isn't it?"

"You can call me Fran."

"Do you prefer we address you that way instead? That would be good. You know I always like it when we keep the hospital environment collegial and casual."

"You misunderstand me, Aaron. I mean, you can call me Fran."

His mouth agape, he stared at her and shifted uncomfortably in his seat, searching for the right words. She could give him a way out by telling him that they could be less formal after working together for such a long time, but she didn't. She stood her ground, waiting for him to respond.

At last, he said, "I think it would be better if I address you the same way as everybody else. We must set an example for the rest of the staff for everything we do. We wouldn't want to look like we make exceptions for each other."

Disappointed, she bowed her head. "You're right. Goodnight, Doctor." She exited the tent, clutching the wooden heart.

Chapter 22

"Unbelievable, those dirty Krauts," said the corpsman delivering medical supplies. "I still can't believe it. Dropping bombs on a hospital. A hospital! I thought I heard wrong when they told us the news back in Naples."

"It wasn't a planned attack, I heard," said the pharmacist while he took inventory of newly arrived medications. "Our fighters were chasing the German plane. Got too close for comfort for the Krauts I guess and their plane tried to lighten its load so it could get away faster. Well, the load landed smack on top of 95th and, boy, what a total disaster."

Tessa gathered the first aid supplies she needed while the two men talked. The bombing of the 95th Evacuation Hospital was all everyone was talking about. It happened only a few days ago. A German plane dropped five antipersonnel bombs on the hospital tents. The bombs killed twenty-six people and wounded sixty-four. Three nurses and two medical officers died. Even the hospital commander was wounded. Twenty-nine ward tents were destroyed and all their X-ray equipment was lost. The bombing put 95th out of operation and reminded them all once again that here in Anzio, nothing was sacred. No one was safe.

She picked up the box of supplies and headed off. Jesse would be coming to pick the box up from her later. She was not looking forward to seeing him.

Back at the patients' ward, she put the two bottles of liquor Jesse had asked for inside the box and placed it on a shelf in a corner. She walked through the aisles eyeing every patient, checking to see if they had enough water and answering the ones who called out to her for help. She passed them one by one until she came close to the German patient with the scar over his brow.

They hadn't talked to each other again since the day he arrived. Each day, she changed his dressing and gave him his medications in silence. A few times, he tried to talk to her, but she ignored him. She had considered asking Ellie to switch him to another ward, but didn't. She regretted the way she had treated him when he first arrived. Attending to his care was one way to make up for it. When he recovered, she would have paid for what she did and would owe him nothing. He would be the one forever indebted to her. In any case, after what happened to 95th, the medical care operation on the beachhead was stressed to the max until a replacement evac hospital arrived. Now was not a good time to ask for unnecessary changes or accommodations.

She passed by the German chatting with an American patient in the next bed. The American soldier, a slim man with messy brown hair and a jolly smile, offered the German a cigarette. The German accepted it and took a deep drag, savoring the smoke. He then pulled out a photo from his shirt pocket and showed it to the American.

"Your daughter? That's your wife and daughter?" the American asked.

"Heidi. Seven years old."

The American soldier pulled out a photo of his own. "My son. Michael. Three years old."

The German took the photo. "Handsome boy. Like his father," he said, and both men laughed.

Tessa looked on at the bizarre sight. On the field, these two men would be doing everything they could to kill each other. But here, in the army hospital, they were exchanging family photos.

The German noticed Tessa watching him and lost his smile. Tessa turned and walked away. Her thoughts were still on the German prisoner when Jesse showed up.

"There you are." Jesse's eyes brightened as soon as he saw her. "Hi. I came to pick up supplies."

She walked over to the box of supplies and pointed to it.

"I have more booze I need you to stash away for me." He showed her several bottles hidden in a small leather bag he used to carry liquor. Without answering, she walked toward the tent's exit to take him to the underground medical supplies storage room.

"What? You're not talking to me? Are you mad at me?"

"I had to sleep in Ellie's tent because of you." She refused to look at him.

"Is that all you're upset about?" he snuck up to her ear and asked in a low, seductive voice.

"No." She turned to face him. "No, that's not all I'm upset about. I expected better of you. All the girls here think you're a callous womanizer. I thought they were wrong. I thought better of you. Much better."

He slowed down. So eager to see her disappointment at him cavorting with another girl, he had come to the hospital today filled with anticipation, hoping to see that some part of her deep down had feelings for him after all. It hadn't occurred to him she could be disappointed in him. No one ever had any expectations of him to be someone better.

"You shouldn't have taken advantage of Gracie." She kept on walking.

"Is that all you care about? Whether what I did was right or wrong?"

"You'll hurt her."

He stopped and dropped his bag to the ground. When she realized that he wasn't following her, she stopped too. The letdown look on his face confused her.

"You know something, Tessa? I thought better of you, too. I thought you of all people would see past all that. I guess I was wrong."

Unsure of what he meant, she didn't answer.

"Maybe in your perfect world with you and Ardley in love, you can't see how things are for everyone else. So let me tell you, why don't you? Gracie. Look at her. Look how happy she is. Do you know why? It's because of me. Yeah! Me. We're in this Godforsaken hellhole and still she's the happiest she's ever been in her entire boring little life, and it's all because of me. I'm not saying this to brag either. I'm saying this because it is true."

Taken aback, Tessa dropped her shoulders.

"You're right. I don't love her. But how's her life any better without me? Treating maimed and broken bodies with ghastly wounds, seeing deaths every day, always in fear of dying from bomb attacks. So I'll admit, I have no intention of being with her forever, but right now, I am the one thing that makes her forget about everything miserable around her. She's not strong like you. She tells me she cries herself to sleep at night and you never say a word to console her. I am what's getting her through all this. When she's with me, she thinks she's in love. So if you ask me, she's getting a hell of a better deal than I am."

"Jesse…"

"You say I'll hurt her. What do you know about that? You're not her. How do you know she wouldn't mind being hurt as long as she has me for however long she can? You don't know what will happen today, tomorrow, or the day after. Being with me may be the happiest memory she'll ever have. Who are you to decide what's best for her? She's a big girl. She knows what everyone says about me. If she's still stupid enough to fall for me anyway, what is it to you?"

"Jesse… She's my friend… I don't want to see her get hurt."

"I'm not your friend? Why don't you think about how I feel? I'll tell you how I feel. If I can be with the person I love for just one night, I don't care if she hurts me. She can break my heart a thousand times after that and I still won't regret that one night I have with her."

His outburst left her speechless. He spoke with so much emotion, it almost sounded to her as if he, not Gracie, was the one who would be wounded. She wondered if someone he loved once had hurt him and if he was still remembering that person. She wanted to say something to comfort him, but as usual, she was lost for words to console others.

Even if she could think of the right words, she would not have the chance to tell him. Down from the sky came the skin-crawling sound of metal-on-metal brakes that she now knew well. It was the sound of a shell dropping. By reflex, her body tensed. She held her breath, waiting for the bombs to explode. Her mind could not register why bombs were dropping in their midst in broad daylight.

While she tried to process her thoughts, a thunderous explosion behind them shook the ground. The deafening sound blasted her ears. Chunks of shrapnel and pieces of debris flew in all directions. They turned around. A German anti-aircraft shell had blown up the ward from which they had just come. The tent was no more than sixty or seventy yards behind them.

"That's us!" Tessa screamed. "That's our hospital! That's our hospital! They bombed our hospital!" She ran toward the ward which had now caught on fire. Jesse grabbed her wrist and pulled her back.

"We have to go help them. We've got to go help them." Hysterical, she pointed to the disaster and tried to pull him that way with her.

"Come back here!" he shouted and pulled her to him. She resisted and tried to fling his hand off her arm. He grabbed her by the waist, threw her over his shoulder and ran in the opposite direction toward the underground medical supplies storage room.

Thinking of all the people still in the tent, she tried to wriggle herself off him. "Let me down!" She pushed on his shoulders and shouted. "Let go of me." But he would not release her. Determined to free herself, she grabbed his shoulder to push again. A sticky wetness under her fingers made her pause. She held up her hand and gazed at her fingers. They were covered red in blood. A piece of shrapnel had hit Jesse and sliced the back of his shoulder. She stopped struggling and put her hand over his wound. The impact of what was happening hit her, and she didn't know what else to do but to cling onto him. As he ran and carried her to safety, she watched the fire grow and the flames burn. She thought she heard voices crying and screaming for help, but she couldn't be sure. So many people were running, screaming, and yelling. Sirens broke out everywhere. The noises all around were drowning her and the clouds of smoke in the air were smothering her. Her mind faded out.

# # #

At the entrance to the underground storage room, Jesse let Tessa down. In the heat of chaos and confusion, he had only one thought. He had to protect her. Tessa was now in a daze. He took her hand and led her to run down the steps. While running down the stairs, another bomb exploded outside. The ground shook and chunks of earth and sand fell from above. He swung his right arm around her and forced her to get down.

When the shaking stopped, he found himself sitting on the stairs with her in his arms. He looked at her leaning against his chest, her hands covering her ears and her eyes squeezed shut. Dirt had soiled her helmet and uniform. A loose lock of her hair dangled in front of her face.

He knew they had narrowly escaped death and a catastrophe was unfolding outside. But sitting here with her, he felt happy. He felt as if they were in a place secluded from the rest of the world. He wished time would stop and he could sit with her in his arms like this, just the two of them, in here where no one could intrude upon this precious moment.

Smiling, he pushed the lock of her hair away from her face with his finger. "You can open your eyes now, Tessa. It's over."

Slowly, she opened her eyes and raised her head to look at him. He smiled to reassure her she was safe. She lowered her hands from her ears and looked about her as though she was coming out of a trance.

"I think it's over," he said. "Let's go back up and see if we can help."

Silently, she got up and followed him up the stairs.

Chapter 23

Outside, the fire trucks had put the fire under control but firefighters were still rushing to put out the flames. Joining the rescue efforts, Tessa and Jesse scoured the wreckage and searched for surviving victims and dead bodies. As she lifted a fallen tent pole, Tessa drew in a deep breath. The stench of smoke choked her throat and muffled her lungs. Unwittingly, she flipped up a torn piece of canvas and caught a nauseating whiff of burnt human flesh from the dead body lying underneath. She dropped the canvas and covered her nose and her mouth.

"Are you all right?" Jesse shouted.

Trying not to throw up, she yelled, "Yes."

Fueled by adrenaline, they pulled out victim after victim, sending them off to the 56th Evac, which was now the only hospital on the beachhead that still hadn't been bombed. Hours later, when the rescue was nearly over, Tessa looked around and took in the scene. The damage was massive. Nearly half of the hospital was destroyed.

Looking from left to right, she noticed something moving beneath a broken bed covered by fallen tent poles and a pile of sand and debris. A head of brown hair jutted out from the heap of ruins. The head, though, showed no movement at all.

Pointing to the pile, she said, "Jesse."

Dropping the broken litter he was holding, Jesse looked at the pile. Something moved again under the bed at the bottom of the pile. Quickly, they ran over. Before they reached the pile, Tessa already knew who was buried underneath. The brown hair belonged to the American soldier who was showing photos of his son to the German prisoner earlier today. She came to him first. Pushing the pile off his head and chest, she found him unconscious with his eyes closed. She checked his neck for a pulse. It was useless. He was dead. She looked up at Jesse and shook her head.

Beneath the pile, someone moaned. Tessa felt goosebumps rising on her arms. It was the German prisoner. He was buried. She jumped up. Frantic, she pushed the pile off him, but the mangled metal bed frame was too heavy and was stuck. Desperate, she tried to lift it.

"Tessa! Tessa!" Jesse yelled.

Almost in tears, she looked at him. He picked the metal bed frame up and pushed it further to the side. "Go find a litter," he said. She ran away, searching everywhere for an empty litter. She couldn't lose another minute. A corpsman and a nurse were unloading a victim into a truck. She ran toward them, grabbed their litter, and ran back to the pile. Jesse was still removing the heap of debris. She dropped the litter to help. They found the German prisoner at the bottom with blood dripping down his forehead and from his nose as he struggled to breathe.

"Hold on," she said to him while they cleared away the debris on top of him. Carefully, they pulled him out, laid him on the litter, and carried him to an ambulance with Jesse leading the way.

In pain but conscious, the German looked at her. "Hold on, okay? We're getting you help," she said to him. He let out a whiff of breath and rolled back his eyes. "No!" she cried out, almost ordering him. He strained to open his eyes and look at her. "Hold on," she said to him again. Unable to speak, he blinked his eyes.

They came to one of the last ambulances. Before they loaded him into the vehicle, she grabbed his arm. "Hold on, okay? You're going to be fine. Just hold on."

The German tried to move his lips to say something, but his lips quivered and no words came out. She squeezed his arm, then let go for the others to take him away.

They watched the ambulance drive off. When it was gone, Tessa felt her entire body aching. She took her helmet off and ran her hand over her head to try to clear her mind. Dirt and ashes had smeared her uniform black. She felt like a mess. She glanced over at Jesse standing a few steps in front of her. A large brown stain had marked the right side of the top part of his uniform. Fresh red blood was still seeping through it. It reminded her, shrapnel had struck him earlier when the bomb went off. She walked up to him and touched the stained spot. "Jesse, you're hurt. Your shoulder's bleeding."

He put his hand over his shoulder and touched his wound. The blood on his fingers surprised him.

"You were hit when the bomb dropped," she said. "Why don't I take a look and fix it up for you?"

"Okay." He smiled.

His smile comforted her. It was the only thing that kept her feeling steady at the moment. "Come on." She started walking toward an aid station nearby and he followed.

# # #

Jesse followed Tessa into the aid station where she led him past the people receiving treatments for minor injuries to an empty bed. He sat down and watched her gather cotton and disinfectant from the first aid cabinet.

"Take off your shirt," she said.

He dipped his chin and suppressed a smile. "I always knew you wanted to see me with my clothes off." He couldn't help teasing her.

She didn't answer him. As usual, she didn't take his flirting remarks seriously. He unbuttoned his shirt, took it off, and tossed it aside. Torn and soiled in ashes, sweat, and blood, it was ruined and he needed a new one anyway.

She came next to him and dabbed medicated cotton wipes on his wound. Then, very lightly, she ran her fingers around where he was cut. At her touch on his skin, a flush of warmth poured out from his heart like water bursting out of a floodgate. He closed his eyes and took a deep breath as his heartbeat quickened.

"I'm sorry. Does it hurt?"

"No," he said, almost talking over her. "No it doesn't hurt at all."

"It's a deep cut." Her voice sounded wrenched. "You need stitches."

He glanced at her, surprised to see the pained look on her face. She was staring at his wound as if she couldn't bear to see him injured. She brushed her fingers over his shoulder, trying to make his pain go away.

Seeing that she cared about him sent his heart racing. He looked away from her to stop himself from taking her into his arms this very moment. With every ounce of self-control he could muster, he forced himself to sit still.

"I'm starting the suture. I'll apply topical anesthesia." She gathered the needle and thread.

"No. No anesthesia."

"What?"

"Don't use anesthesia. I don't want it." He didn't want to be numbed to her touch.

"It'll hurt."

"I'll be fine."

Although doubtful, she did as he asked. Without using anesthesia, she stitched his wound together. Each prick of the needle gave a spike of piercing pain as the needle punctured his flesh. He clenched his teeth and squeezed his eyes shut, bearing the pain so he could feel every sensation of her hands on his body. The pain didn't matter, as long as he could deluge himself in the sweetness of feeling her fingers on his skin. The traces of her touch ignited him and set his heart on fire. He grasped at his knee to resist reaching out to her.

When she finished, she spread medication on his wound and covered it with bandages. Then, as she always did with all her patients, she placed her hand on his hand. "You'll be all right now."

Her hand on his own set his entire body aflame. Staring at the ground, he dug his fingertips against his knee. It was all he could do to hold himself together.

"I'll go find you a clean change of uniform," she said.

He couldn't control himself anymore. He raised his hand to grasp hers, just as she took her hand off his and turned to leave him. His hand missed hers and all he caught was air.

"I'll be right back," she said and disappeared, leaving him sitting on the bed alone, lost in the agony of his own private torment.

# # #

Standing with the soldiers on the field, Anthony watched Colonel Callahan arrive with his lieutenant attaché. Today was a rare day of recognition for the soldiers of their company. For holding their position and defeating the German troops after their last mission, the entire company would receive the Army Meritorious Unit Commendation. Captain Harding would be awarded a bronze star for his gallantry against the enemy and his exceptional leadership in guiding the battalion out of the hedgerows and the caves under fierce German attack.

The Colonel called out the name of each of the unit's members. One by one, they accepted the red ribbon symbolizing the award. When the ceremony came to its end with the award of the bronze star to the captain, Jonesy passed Ollie a sneering look and Ollie smirked. Anthony glared at them to stop and maintain their decorum.

"Congratulations, Captain Harding. Well done." Colonel Callahan shook the captain's hand.

"Thank you, sir." Harding accepted the award without a hint of irony.

When the ceremony was over, the officers took turns congratulating the captain. Anthony did the same. "Congratulations, sir."

"Thank you, Lieutenant," Harding said hastily and passed him over to talk to the next soldier in line. Since the attack, neither of them had said anything to each other or anyone else about the escape from the caves and the company's successful advance to link up with the reinforcement battalion.

A jeep sped up the road and came to a grinding halt. The driver, a private, dashed out of the vehicle. "Colonel! Colonel!"

"What is it?" the Colonel asked.

"The 33rd Field Hospital has been attacked."

"Attacked? How?"

"Shells, sir. It's been bombed."

Alarmed, Anthony asked the driver, "Did you say 33rd?"

"Yes."

Anthony felt his heart plunging to the ground and even further down under.

"Status report?" Callahan asked the private.

"Ward C. Half of Ward C's been blown apart."

"Jesus Christ," Callahan muttered. He turned to the lieutenant who had come with him. "Let's go." He hurried to his jeep as everyone began speaking at once.

"Colonel Callahan, sir. Colonel!" Anthony chased after him. "Can I please come with you?"

"No." The colonel closed the vehicle's door. "You can't help. You'll just add to the chaos." The colonel gave him a grave look. "Stay here. I'll send back news as soon as I can when the situation's under control. You can come then."

The colonel and his men drove away, leaving Anthony behind. Images of all the things that might have happened to Tessa terrorized his mind as the colonel's jeep vanished down the road.

Chapter 24

There was much to do in the aftermath of the bombing, and Tessa was thankful for that. Inundated with work, she had no time to stay traumatized or think about the horrifying event that had just occurred. There was follow-up paperwork for the patients transferred to the 56th Evac Hospital, and there were still patients in their own hospital who needed treatment and attention. New X-ray stations, pharmaceutical units, and patient examination areas all needed to be set up. The army engineers were already hard at work building new tents and cleaning up the massive piles of debris.

With so much work to do, she couldn't think about anything else. Her mind was singularly focused on reorganizing a new storage area for bedsheets, blankets, and clean uniforms. Together with Irene, she stocked pile after pile of linen onto the shelves.

"Well just look at her." Irene stared out the opening of the tent. "She's milking all the attention she can get, isn't she?"

Tessa looked at the direction where Irene was looking. Outside the tent, Gracie cowered in Jesse's arms. She had just arrived for her shift. With her shoulders hunched and her head down, she looked small and helpless.

Anthony. The thought struck Tessa. Seeing Jesse and Gracie together reminded her that she still had to find a way to send word to Anthony to let him know she was safe. The news of the bombing must have reached him by now. He must be so worried, but there was no way she could contact him. Jesse was still here helping out. Everyone else was busy attending to more urgent matters at hand. No one had time to help her take a personal message to a member of an army unit unrelated to the bombing.

They watched Jesse console Gracie. To Tessa, he looked like he was trying to soothe a child. He talked to her until she stopped sobbing and looked at him with adoring, docile eyes. He took his arms off her, gave her a light kiss on her head and walked away.

"Makes me sick." Irene dumped a pile of towels onto the shelf.

Unaware they had been watching her, Gracie came over to them. She looked much calmer than when she was outside with Jesse. "I'll help with that." She picked up a stack of clean bedsheets from the bin and handed them to Tessa. Irene eyed her up and down. Gracie looked back at Irene, confused.

"You know it's not going to last," Irene said. "He's just playing with you. Don't say I didn't warn you. Jesse Garland is not the type of man who would stay with one woman."

Defiant, Gracie frowned and held up her chin. "You're wrong about him. Jesse and I love each other."

Irene snorted. "Jesse doesn't love anybody."

"He loves me. He's changed because he loves me. When the war's over, we're going to get married."

"Ha!" Irene laughed. "Good luck with that, girl." She dumped the pile of towels she was holding into the bin and walked away. Tessa lowered her head and looked to the ground.

"She's wrong about him. He's the nicest guy I've ever met, and he loves me."

"Let's put these away," Tessa said. She bent down and picked up another stack of linen. They worked in silence until Aaron Haley walked in.

"Tessa, Gracie, have either of you seen Ellie?"

"No, I haven't," Tessa said. Gracie too shook her head.

"Is she missing?" Tessa asked. As far as she knew, Ellie wasn't among the injured or deceased. The hospital was still recovering from chaos. No one could keep track of where everyone else was. She assumed Ellie was helping out someplace where she was needed.

"No one has seen her. Everyone else has been accounted for," Aaron said, his face visibly distressed.

"Do you want us to look for her?"

He thought for a moment, then said, "No. You have your work to do. I'll check with others on staff first. But keep an eye out for her, will you?"

"Of course, Doctor."

"Yes, Doctor Haley," Gracie said at the same time.

Before he left, Fran Milton entered. "Doctor, I've been looking all over for you. We need to discuss how to alter our operations and logistics in light of the bombing. This is urgent. The staffing schedule needs to be changed too. Can we please talk about this now?"

Looking conflicted, he nonetheless said, "You're right. Let's do that. Let's go to my office." He followed Fran Milton away and left.

When they were gone, Tessa laid down the pile of bedsheets in her arms and said to Gracie, "I'm going to look for Ellie."

She went through several rows of tents that were still intact, scouring the area for her friend, and found Ellie returning with a convoy carrying supplies from the 56th. Ellie had gone to the 56th Evac to help transfer several patients injured by the bombing.

"I'm so glad you're all right too, Tessa," she said as soon as they found each other.

"Dr. Haley was looking everywhere for you."

"Why? Does he need my help with something?"

"Ellie! Don't you understand? He's worried about you. You need to go let him know you're okay."

Ellie hesitated. "You're teasing me."

"I am not. I swear. Go find him. He's in his office. He'll be happy to see you."

With Tessa's encouragement, Ellie took a deep breath, smiled, and headed toward Aaron's tent office.

# # #

Near Aaron's office, Ellie slowed down her steps. She wondered if it would be too forward of her to go to him without an official reason. But then, it was not so strange for her to report to the hospital superintendent and let him know that she was safe. On the other hand, she was not sure if that made sense either because the person she ought to report her safety to should be Captain Milton, the Chief Nurse. She almost wished she hadn't let Tessa talk her into coming here.

While she hesitated, Fran Milton exited the tent with Aaron following behind her. Ellie stopped and went no further. Captain Milton didn't like seeing young nurses around Dr. Haley. It would not be good if Captain Milton thought she was behaving improperly toward Dr. Haley. She decided to wait until the captain left.

The captain and the doctor remained there for a while, talking to each other. Deep in conversation, Captain Milton moved closer to him. Too close. It almost appeared they were more than simply colleagues. Captain Milton picked up his hand. For a moment, they stood there, holding hands.

Crushed by the sight of them holding hands, Ellie turned back and walked away. Thankfully, she hadn't gone in and interrupted them. Why hadn't it occurred to her before that Dr. Haley and Captain Milton might be more to each other than they let on? Now she understood why Captain Milton didn't like having young nurses around Dr. Haley. She felt foolish for having thought that her feelings for the doctor might be mutual. It must have all been her imagination. She hoped her feelings were not obvious to him or the captain. If they were, it would be so embarrassing.

# # #

For more than an hour, Aaron listened to Fran drone on. He was coming off his shift when the bombs dropped. After the shelling, he stayed and worked for hours directing the emergency reorganization of the hospital. He had just caught a break when Fran found him. All he wanted was to make sure that Ellie Swanson was safe and unharmed. He needed a few hours of shut-eye before he could think clearly about operations, staffing, and logistics. In his exhausted state, this meeting was not at all productive.

Lately, all their meetings felt suffocating to him. Since that time when she suggested that he call her by her first name, he had been feeling awkward around her. He was not so insensitive as to not understand what she had implied. He had hoped that when he declined, it would be enough to put the matter to rest. But rather than backing away, Fran Milton had doubled her efforts to impose herself upon him. She was trying to achieve her desired end by trying even harder. It was the same tenacious approach she took toward her work. She didn't understand that human relationships were not merit-based pursuits.

Things were getting worse. Last week, she had taken it upon herself to organize his office daily while he was on duty. She did this under the auspices of helping him. He must admit too that she did a fine job. His files were now always in order and easy to find and there was never a shortage of office items or supplies, but he could not appreciate the improvements. He didn't like her forcing her systems and methods upon him. And although nothing in the army territory was ever truly private, it bothered him that she now knew every detail about what he did in his office.

Her intrusion extended beyond the office. Several times, she had left him personal items on his desk. Bartering went on among the military personnel. When soldiers received goods from home, sometimes they would trade or sell items they received. Fran had somehow procured items she found useful for him. She would leave on his desk shaving cream, toothpaste, socks. The quality of the items she gave him was much better than those issued by the government, but her actions were becoming too personal. He did not want her to choose for him the things he would use for himself.

She left him magazines and journals too. She thought he should quit wood carving. She said there was too much risk of injury to his hands. For leisure, she wanted him to read the magazines and journals she had picked for him instead. Two copies of *National Geographic* she had brought now sat on his desk. He glanced at the magazines, feeling slightly annoyed. The only time he had ever injured himself wood carving was two days ago when she barged into his tent office to bring these magazines to him.

To be fair, she didn't know he was there. He was supposed to be meeting with Colonel Callahan at Callahan's office, but the colonel had a last minute change of plan. As a result, he had an hour of free time. An inspiration came to him to carve Easter bunnies for the hospital's corpsmen who had small children back home. He was in the middle of carving when she entered unannounced. Her unexpected arrival startled him and his fingers slipped. Since then, she had been even more insistent that he should stop with his hobby.

He knew he had to put a stop to her meddling. The problem was, nothing she did was overtly out of line. Everything she did was done under the guise of helping him. He could not fault a nurse for making her best effort to ease the life of the doctors she served. Moreover, turning someone down was not an easy task. If he made himself clear, they still had to work together. If he didn't handle the matter carefully, their fallout might affect the running of the hospital. He could not let that happen under any circumstances. So for now, it seemed the best thing to do was to do nothing.

When their meeting was over, he walked her out, anxious for her to leave so he could continue to look for Ellie. Fran, though, was in no hurry. She reminded him to get his rest, asked if he would like to have the army chef prepare a meal for him, and gave him consoling words that he did not need about the bombing. Everything she said could pass for concern by a well-intentioned colleague, but he knew her words meant more than that. They were an unwanted intrusion into his private life.

"How's your hand? Has it healed yet?" She picked up his hand and examined the place where he had cut himself while wood carving. So surprised at what she did, he froze without withdrawing his hand from hers.

"You need to change the bandages," she went on as if she was doing nothing unusual. "We don't want you to get an infection. It won't be good if you can't perform surgeries or if you pass on germs to patients."

"Yes." He pulled his hand away from her. "You're right. I'll do that."

"Good. I'll see you later." Although this was the second time she had taken her leave, she was still standing there and showing no intention of moving.

"I'll go to the aid station now and change my bandage," he said. His own words annoyed him. He said it as an excuse to get away from her, but he sounded like he was doing what she wanted.

Finally, she walked away. He rushed back to the main hospital area to search for Ellie. To his relief, Ellie was unharmed. She was helping to set up the new X-ray station.

"Ellie!" He called out to her as soon as he saw her. He shouted so loud, everyone in the ward turned to stare at him.

"Yes, Doctor Haley?" Ellie asked with a cordial smile.

"You're all right!"

"Yes, Doctor Haley. I'm fine."

"You were the only nurse unaccounted for after the bombing. I was worried."

"I'm sorry about that, Doctor." She kept her distance. "I didn't mean to worry you or anyone. It was my fault. I took some of the patients in critical care to the 56th. I should have let someone know. The scene was so chaotic, I neglected to think of it."

"Don't be sorry. I'm so glad you're safe."

"Thank you for your concern, Doctor. Is there something I can help you with?" Her impersonal tone puzzled him. She had never spoken to him this way before. He didn't know what to make of it. Maybe he was being too brash.

"No." He checked himself. "No, I just came to make sure you're okay."

"Thank you. I apologize again for making you worry." She looked around at everyone who was staring at them to remind him that there were people around them. Realizing that they were not alone, he held himself back from saying more.

"I must get back to work," she said.

"Of course."

She stepped away and returned to her tasks. He watched her for a little while longer. She paid him no attention. Dejected, he lowered his eyes, slid his hands into his scrubs pockets, and walked out.

Chapter 25

Sitting on a mound halfway up the hill, Anthony could not see what was happening in the area of the 33rd Field Hospital. He peered into his binoculars. It was useless. All he could see were streaks of smoke rising from the ground. He could not see what people there were doing.

It had been hours since the bombing occurred. No word about Tessa had come yet from Colonel Callahan. As the sky darkened, he felt even more restless and helpless.

Why was this happening? Their future together held so many promises. A little over a year ago on New Year's Day, the day after he had confessed to her he loved her, she had sat with him in his room. In the late afternoon while she was reading in his arms, he had gazed out the window and thought he was the happiest person in the world.

As if she had read his mind, she turned around and smiled at him. He knew he would do anything for her when he saw that smile. Before she came into his life, he thought he knew what love was. And then, the moment they kissed, he realized that everything he thought he knew about love was wrong. Love was instinctual, not intellectual. It was wild and daring, not premeditated and controlled. Only she could make him feel this way. Only she could set him free and fulfill his entire world.

He knew she felt the same way. She loved him, so much so that she had come halfway across the world, braving a war to find him. What would he do if something happened to her? How could he ever go on?

Why couldn't things be the way they were back in that afternoon? He wished they could leave everything here behind and go back to that day. He wanted to be with her, only her, in the quietness of their own home without all the conflicts and burdens of the world.

He hoped she was alive. He prayed she was not hurt. He felt like this was all his fault. If anything bad happened to her, he would never forgive himself. If he could, he would go to the hospital at once and be by her side.

She had to be alive. How could this be the end? Their time together before he was drafted was so short. He still had so many things he wanted to do with her. They had so much more ahead of them.

His heart and stomach twisted in knots. The knots pulled tighter and tighter as the sun disappeared.

Warren walked up to the mound and sat down next to him. "Want some?" He handed Anthony a flask of whiskey.

Anthony glanced at the flask. "No, thank you." He turned his attention back to the direction of the hospital far away.

Warren opened the flask and drank a mouthful. "You should eat." He took a pack of C-ration out of his bag and tossed it onto the ground next to Anthony. Paying no attention to the food, Anthony continued to stare at the beach.

From far away, the rumbles of the night raid had begun.

Please be alive. He looked helplessly into his binoculars again.

Please be alive so I can tell you again how much I love you. He turned the cross around his neck.

Please God, let her be alive.

# # #

When Tessa returned to her tent, she had worked for twenty hours without stop. She still hadn't managed to find someone to help her send a message to Anthony. Thoughts of contacting Anthony weighed heavily on her mind, but her aching body felt even heavier. She couldn't stand up anymore. Her feet were sore and her back was stiff. Anthony would have to wait a little while longer.

She crawled into her tent and flopped down. For once, the thin cot felt heavenly. She lay on her stomach and listened to the white noises surrounding her tent. The night raid had ended. She could hear only the whooshes of wind beating against the canvas.

"Hi, can I come in?" The flap on her tent lifted open an inch. It was Jesse.

Tired, she sat up. "Yeah." Her voice dragged. "Gracie's not here. She's still at work."

He came inside. "I'm looking for you." She stared at him, puzzled. He held up a bottle of scotch. "I thought we should celebrate."

"Celebrate what?"

"That we survived. You and I came to the edge of annihilation and survived. Shouldn't we celebrate?"

"Shouldn't you be getting back to your unit? People must be worried about you."

"Nah. Nobody ever worries about me. My ride doesn't leave for another hour. Let's have a drink." He sat down and leaned back against the large metal container at the end of her cot. She and Gracie had taken this metal container left behind by a naval vessel. They used it to lay out their kerosene lamp, mess kits, and hair brushes.

He opened the bottle, took the two cups on top of the container, and poured the liquor into each cup. "Consider yourself lucky. This one's my favorite, Talisker. Aged eighteen years." He held up the bottle to show her. "They are impossible to get. There's only one bottle where this came from. I'm sharing it only with you." He handed her a cup.

"You are unbelievable. It's six o'clock in the morning." Nevertheless, the whiff of maple and butterscotch intrigued her. She took a small sip. The pleasant oaky taste warmed and calmed her.

"Don't you know by now?" he asked. "Time ceased to matter to us a long time ago."

She took another sip. The sharp, spicy finish gave her a much-needed release. "Don't you want to wait for Gracie to come back and share it with her too?"

He frowned at the mention of Gracie. "Gracie can't drink. She has no tolerance for alcohol." He paused. "Not like you." He looked at her with a smile that seemed to convey too many meanings all at once. His eyes, warm and unreadable, looked to her like dark, bottomless wells.

"So," he relaxed against the container, "I always wanted to ask you. You're an American nurse. How come you don't speak American? Why do you have a British accent?"

"I grew up in London. My mother is American and my father is British."

"Is that why you're always so reserved?"

"I'm reserved? I don't know. Maybe. I don't think I'm reserved."

"Where are they now? Your parents. In Chicago?"

"No. They're in London. They sent me to live with Anthony's family in America before the Blitz. I haven't seen them in years. I really miss them." She finished her drink and held out her cup. He poured her some more. The alcohol loosened her muscles and even her guard against talking about herself. "I can't wait to go back and see them again. It's the only thing I ever wanted since I left London." As soon as she said this, the thought of Anthony sprang into her mind. She had always thought of America as a temporary interlude in her life. Even the war was temporary. It had to end sometime, didn't it? But if that was the case, was Anthony temporary? She did not want to think about this. "What about you?" she asked Jesse. "Where are your parents? Back in New York?"

His smile disappeared. His eyes, warm and intense just a moment ago, turned emotionless and detached. "I don't know where my father is. I've never met him. My mother's in New York." He looked down at the ground. "She's a prostitute."

Surprised, she held her cup in midair. From the tone of his voice and the look in his eyes, she knew he was telling the truth.

He stole a nervous glance at her. "I've never told anyone this before." He didn't know what kind of response he expected from her by telling her this. She raised her eyebrows slightly, but showed no reaction otherwise. She lowered her cup and let silence linger between them. It was a soft, comforting silence. Without saying a word, she had let him know that what he had just told her was not important to her.

"She's not like how most people think of prostitutes." He swallowed a big gulp of his drink. "She services only the wealthiest and most powerful men. I lived very well growing up until I left home when I was fifteen."

"She must be beautiful."

"How would you know? Because rich and powerful men patronize her?"

"Because you are very handsome. Extraordinarily handsome."

"You think that?" He couldn't believe his ears.

"It is a fact. It's why all the girls like you. And yes, I think so too." She took another sip of her drink as if she had said nothing unusual. Silence flowed between them again, masking the stream of emotions simmering in his heart.

"What happened afterwards? When you left home?" she asked.

"I became an apprentice to a master con man. He showed me how to make my way in the world. I learned to run all sorts of schemes to steal people's money away from them. That's how my life was until I joined the army." He avoided looking at her as he spoke. He didn't know why he was telling her all this. Alone in the tent with her, her quiet acceptance of him disarmed him. He felt he could confide in her everything he thought he would never say to anyone.

He mustered the nerve to look at her reaction. Her expression showed no prejudice or distrust. Neither did she show any irritating magnanimous sympathy. There was only understanding and acceptance. Her eyes brightened and she smiled at him. He felt a wave of relief and smiled back. She moved closer to him and sat back against the side of the container adjacent to him.

"What was that all about with you and that German?" he asked, referring to the German patient they found in the ruins of the hospital. "You went berserk when you found him. You weren't even that worried when you were saving our own. I couldn't believe you tried to lift that bed frame."

Ashamed, she lowered her head. "I threatened to kill him when he first arrived. Jonesy told me, that German soldier shot at Anthony and almost killed him. When I was treating his wound, I told him I would shoot poison in him or wrap his wound in contaminated bandages to kill him." She rounded her shoulders. "I shouldn't have done that."

"So you felt guilty and you worried he might really die." He laughed. "Don't feel bad. If it was me, I would've killed him for real."

She looked at him, skeptical.

"What? You don't believe me?"

Still smiling, she shook her head.

"Why?"

"Because you can't kill."

"Sure I can."

"No, you can't. It's not in your nature to kill. You can't even kill a dying dog."

He thought about what she said. He had never considered whether he could kill or not. He only knew that every time he saw a soldier killed, he felt a rottenness eating him from the inside. It was why he tried so hard to save them on the field, and why he didn't give up on any of them until they breathed their last breath.

"Is that why you became a medic? So you don't have to kill anyone?" she asked.

He thought back to his last day at training camp. A call came for volunteers to join the medics unit. He could either do that or be assigned to a rifle company. He signed up for the medics unit at once, even though he didn't know the first thing about medicine or trauma treatments. It felt like the best choice at the time. He could shoot as well as his fellow recruits, but the guns never felt right in his hands during shooting practices. "I don't know," he said. "Never gave it much thought. The army said they needed medics. Being a medic suits me fine. I don't like seeing our soldiers killed. I don't like watching life go out of them."

"I know what you mean."

Talking about death dampened their spirits. He took a pack of cigarettes out of his pocket, lit one up, and took a deep drag. "Do you ever wonder, what are the last thoughts of a dying soldier? Does he think of his family? Or could he maybe see angels in the sky?"

"I don't know. Maybe everything happens so fast he doesn't even have time to think anything."

"It might not be a bad thing to die quickly. In that case, they won't feel any pain."

"I wish we didn't have to think about these things. I don't know what I would do if anything ever happened to Anthony. Sometimes, I feel like, in a split second, he would be gone?"

Anthony. Jesse took another drag of his cigarette. That was the piece of the puzzle he couldn't solve. As long as Tessa was in love with Anthony, he could never find a way into her heart.

"I took him for granted for so long," she said, still talking about Anthony. "I guess he took me for granted too, at first. But then later, he tried so hard to win me over. He's so optimistic. It's infectious. He makes me think that everything will always turn out all right in the end. And he's so sincere. He always tries to do the right thing. It's adorable."

There was nothing Jesse wanted to say to that. He stared at Gracie's bag directly in his line of vision and finished the rest of his drink. Hearing Tessa talk about Anthony this way irritated him.

Unaware that his mood had shifted, Tessa's smile widened. "He has such a positive outlook. His whole world is beautiful." She was talking to herself now. Jesse was sure it wouldn't have mattered if he was listening or not. "I love being in his world," she said, her voice barely audible to anyone except herself. Then, she choked up. "I'm so afraid something terrible will happen to him. I don't want to imagine life without him."

He glanced at her and saw her wipe a tear from her eye. Although his heart felt hollow, he didn't like seeing her distraught. He refilled her cup. "Let's not think about it then. Let's hope he'll have all the luck in the world and nothing bad will ever happen to him."

Mistaking the sorrowful look on his face as sympathy, she gave him a grateful, tender smile.

"You know, my world is beautiful too," he said.

"I can imagine." She glanced over at him.

"New York is a wonderful place."

"I've heard."

"The entire city is filled with life. The Lower East Side, there's no other place in the world like it. Immigrants from all parts of the world live there and you'll see the wildest mix of people. Chinatown is there, next to the Jewish blocks. There are tons of pushcart markets and street foods. Some days, there are mass discount sales down in that area and all these people line up for deals. The Fulton Fish Market is not too far away from there. You will never see such an amazing variety of seafood in one place. The market is right by the piers where a lot of ships come in. From the piers, you can see the Brooklyn Bridge. At night, all the giant billboards on Forty-Second Street light up. The bars and restaurants stay open until very late."

"Sounds exciting."

"It is. I live in a neighborhood called Greenwich Village. A lot of artists live there. Washington Square Park is two blocks away from my place. Folksingers and street musicians perform there. Sometimes I go sit in the park and listen to them."

"I like folk music."

"You should come visit. I'll take you to the top of the Empire State Building. You can see the view of the entire city from sky high up top."

"Okay. After the war, I'll come."

"You will?" His mind shot in all different directions thinking of the places where he wanted to take her.

"Yes. Anthony too. What do you say we do our own victory tour?"

"Right, Anthony too. Of course." Silently, he mocked himself for thinking even for a moment that she would come to see him in New York alone.

"Jesse?"

"What?"

"I'm sorry for all the things I said to you yesterday about you and Gracie."

"It's all right. You were being a good friend to Gracie."

"No. I'm not that. Of course I don't want her to be hurt, but that wasn't the main reason why I was upset. I think the real reason I was upset was because I felt bad for you after I saw you and her together. You always say you're a cad. I know you're not. But you think of yourself as one, and then you purposely do deceitful things to prove it, like you want to convince yourself you really are a bad person. The more you do to prove it, the more you think badly of yourself. I wish you wouldn't do that."

He looked away from her and said nothing, but she continued. "And you are right. Gracie is a lot happier because of you. You give her what nobody else can. So I was wrong. I shouldn't have assumed the worst of you."

"You're not entirely wrong. But if she truly loves me as much as she thinks, she would be hurt whether I return her feelings or not." He picked up a small stick and scribbled on the ground. "It doesn't hurt any less when the person you love doesn't love you."

"You sound like you've been there."

"I have." *I'm there now.* He drew a large circle. "It can hurt so bad, you feel like your heart will never stop bleeding. The way I see it, if it's going to hurt this much anyway, then you might as well be with that person somehow no matter what happens in the end."

"I never thought of it that way." She held her cup close to her chest. "You're right. I would rather I had been with Anthony than never at all, no matter how much it might hurt later if something terrible were to happen."

He dug the stick into the ground. "If I can have even one night with the person I love, I would not regret it if she hurts me a thousand times afterwards." He said that with such intense conviction, she looked him once over. But as usual, she didn't pry deeper. She only stayed with him, sharing with him not consoling words but her silent presence. He drew in another breath of smoke and blew it out.

"I understand what you said about Gracie being happier because you are with her." She picked up their conversation again. "There's just one thing I don't understand."

"What's that?"

"Why do you care whether Gracie is happy or not? You have so many girls worshipping at your feet. Why choose Gracie? It can't be because you feel charitable."

Why choose Gracie? He wondered how he should answer that. He had run out of lies. He was tired of pretending it was another womanizing conquest. He felt an overwhelming urge to tell Tessa the truth, to let her know how he really felt. It had been so hard, keeping it all bottled up and burning inside. He knew telling her would be reckless. She would not want to hear it. She was too loyal to Ardley. Most likely, she would stop seeing him altogether if she knew, but his emotions were overtaking his rational thoughts.

"I'm with Gracie…" His voice trembled and trailed off. He swallowed and took a deep breath. "I'm with Gracie because all I want to do is to see you." The words tumbled out of his mouth. A vision of Pandora's box opening appeared before his eyes. He might have just made the biggest mistake of his life. Not daring to look at her, he waited for her to respond, but she said nothing.

He didn't think she would suddenly give up on Ardley and tell him she felt the same way about him. But still, her silence hurt. He waited, giving her time to let his words sink into her mind. When she remained silent, he wondered if she didn't understand clearly what he meant. Since he couldn't take back what he had already said, he decided to tell the whole truth. "I'm using Gracie to get closer to you."

He waited for her answer. Rejection. Disapproval. Anger. Whatever might be. But minutes passed, and still she said nothing. Warily, he raised his eyes and looked at her. She had slid down onto her cot, fast asleep and curled up on her side. Her empty cup had tipped over on the ground. She had passed out from the liquor and hadn't heard anything he said. He let out a cry of relief and disbelief.

He looked at her again. Asleep, her face was flushed and her lips were red from the alcohol's effects. Watching her, his heart softened.

He bent down toward her ear and whispered, "I'm crazy, madly in love with you."

Unable to hear him in her sleep, her eyes remained closed. He sat back against the container and took a big gulp from the bottle.

"Ardley. Bastard." He drank another gulp, then turned toward Tessa, who was deep asleep. "Why do you have to love him so much?" He smoked the last drag of his cigarette and exhaled. The cloud of smoke gave him no answer. He stubbed out the cigarette on the ground and leaned over her. Her chest heaved lightly up and down as she breathed, contrasting with his own quickening breaths. He wanted to kiss her cheek. Just one kiss. She would never know.

He gazed at her this way for a long time, debating to himself while his heart thumped in his chest. Then, instead of kissing her, he pulled her blanket over her, picked up the half-empty bottle, and left. Holding the flap of the tent open, he turned and looked at her one more time. Seeing her asleep in peace, he smiled and headed outside.

Chapter 26

The day was almost over when Tessa woke up. She looked at her watch. She had slept for ten hours straight. It was almost five o'clock. Gracie had returned and was asleep in her cot.

Tessa pushed her blanket off and sat up. The last thing she remembered was drinking with Jesse. He was no longer there. Two empty cups lay on the ground near the container against which they had sat.

Still groggy, she grabbed her canteen and poured water down her throat to quench her thirst.

More awake now, she hastily tied her hair into a ponytail and got up out of her cot. Grabbing her helmet, she went outside to the barrel that held their supply of water. She scooped some up with her helmet and splashed the water on her face with her palms. The cold, refreshing feeling cleared her mind. She continued to wash up and get herself ready to return to the hospital. Behind her, she heard a familiar set of footsteps.

"Tessa?" The voice came to her like a warm breeze.

"Anthony!" She dropped her towel and ran into his arms. Tears flooded her eyes and her vision blurred.

"I came as soon as I could. I wanted to come right away but the army wouldn't let me." He closed his arms around her and lifted her feet up off the ground.

"I was so scared," she cried out. "You almost died! Thank God, I'm so glad nothing happened to you." She held onto him as tightly as she could, wanting with all her heart to keep him in one piece.

"Me? I was worried sick about you."

"Jonesy told me all about how that German sniper nearly shot you in the head and killed you."

"What! Jonesy, that big mouth. I'm going to give him hell for scaring you like that."

"I'm so glad you're safe."

"Let me look at you." He wiped away her tears. "I thought I might have lost you." Overwhelmed with relief to see her alive, he kissed her hard on her lips. She let her herself fall into his embrace, thankful for the feeling of his breath on her face.

When he released her, she took his hand and led him to sit down with her on a tree trunk lying on the ground.

"I almost lost my mind when I didn't know if you were okay or not," he said. "Warren got the early reports, so I knew there were several deaths and a lot of people were injured. Good thing Garland finally came back this morning and told me you were safe. I came as soon as the hospital was back in operation. I looked everywhere for you until some of the nurses told me you were here." He put his arm around her shoulders and pulled her closer. Leaning against him, she felt infinitely thankful that he was alive next to her and she could hear his heart beat.

"I wanted to let you know I was okay, but it was chaos here and I couldn't find any way to send a message to you." She looked down at her hands. "Jesse probably saved my life. We had just left the ward when the shell dropped. I was in shock and my first instinct was to run back to save everyone. I would have too, if he hadn't held me back and made me go into the underground storage room with him. The bombs were still dropping when we went in there. I might have been killed if it weren't for him."

Alarmed, he tightened his arm around her. "He didn't tell me anything about that."

"He never tells anyone when he does anything good. He keeps a lot to himself. He's very lonely."

"Jesse? Lonely? Are you kidding me? If he's lonely, dozens of women would line up to keep him company."

She thought of Jesse sitting in her tent before she fell asleep. "No. People don't understand him. We might be the only real friends he has."

Still looking doubtful, Anthony nonetheless said, "Of course then. Anyone who saves my girl is my friend for life. I'll do anything for him, any time."

Pleased, she reached up and touched his face. He looked down and kissed her. She closed her eyes to feel the full sensation of the touch of his lips. They were older now, older than when they had first admitted their feelings to each other. With all that they had seen and gone through with the war, she had long ago left behind the girl she once was back in Chicago. But even with the passage of time and everything that had happened, the touch of his lips still paralyzed her heart. That hadn't changed.

She opened her eyes and saw his smile. She loved his smile. It brightened her life like a ray of sunshine and pushed her heart wide open.

"I had a lot of time to think while I was waiting to find out if you were safe," he said. "I think I haven't told you nearly enough how much I love you. If I have neglected to let you know, then I want to tell you now." He raised her hand and kissed it. "I love you, Tessa, more than anything in the world."

"I love you too," she said. "But… I did something terrible because of it."

"What did you do?"

She dropped her shoulders, trying to find the right words.

"Tell me. Whatever you did, it can't be that bad."

"The German sniper who tried to kill you, he came to my hospital. When I was treating him, I threatened to kill him."

He listened with his arm still firmly around her.

"Jonesy put him in restraints, so he was helpless and at my mercy. I told him I would do all these horrible things to hurt him and kill him. I didn't do any of the things I said, but I wanted to. I was so angry at him. He could've killed you."

When she finished, he stroked her arm to comfort her. "You wanted to kill an enemy soldier, and that makes you feel bad. Well, I've killed enemy soldiers. I killed them for real. I've killed more of them than I can count. What does that make me?"

"That's different. You did it because you had to."

"No. I don't have to. I could've tried to join the conscientious objectors back home. I could've dodged and gone to South America. Uncle Leon would've arranged that. I can desert now and escape or go to prison. Those aren't good choices, but they're still choices. But I am here. I kill people."

Not wanting to hear this, she threw her arms around him and shook her head against his chest. "Don't say that. You're doing what you do to protect us."

"And you did what you did because you wanted to protect me." He tightened his arm around her again. But even with all his support, she still felt their love had been damaged. It was not only what she had done to the German soldier. It was both of them. She and Anthony were both irrevocably scarred by the ugliness of this war. Neither of them was innocent anymore. They would never be able to look back and see only pure and untainted memories. There were burdens that they would have to carry with them as they went on. They would both know that the person they loved had the capacity to kill.

"Look at the sea, Tessa," Anthony said. She looked out at the direction where he was looking. "Look how vast and beautiful it is. The Germans come every day, but they always have to go away when the night ends no matter how ugly they've made this place. Everything they bring with them is temporary, but this view we're seeing now, it never goes away. It outlasts the Germans, every day. It will outlast this war. It will last forever."

She watched the sea expanding out to the horizon. The sea didn't end there. It continued on. It moved with the tide to a place beyond and faraway into the unknown.

"We have so much ahead of us, Tessa. The war is like those German planes that come every night. It won't last. One day, it will all end. What we have ahead is this sea. It'll be the same sea we're looking at now, vast and beautiful. It's already here, waiting for us. It won't change. The war can't take it away. We have to be like the sea. We have to try our best and hold on to who we are. Everything that happens in this war, everything that's not really us, it'll all go away. The sea, the things that are beautiful, those are what we have waiting for us."

She gazed into the far distance. As the waves rolled, she repeated his every word in her heart, hoping that soon, they would be able to ride the waves to the vast beyond, to a place where a better, beautiful world awaited them.

PART EIGHT

The Mercy of Time

Chapter 27

The winter morning sun shone through the window, warming Jesse's face and bare shoulders as he woke. Lying face down on his bed, he opened his eyes. The pillow felt so soft. He was back in New York City in his brownstone apartment, sleeping under his goose-down duvet in his own room. The smooth, clean white linen smelled freshly washed. He hadn't felt this comfortable in a long, long time. He closed his eyes, almost falling again into a deep sleep.

The rich aroma of coffee prompted him to open his eyes a second time. He lifted the duvet off his body, got up, and hastily washed up in the adjoining bathroom. When he finished, he put on his Turkish bathrobe and followed the smell of coffee through the living room into the kitchen. A plate filled with freshly baked croissants sat on the dining table. Over by the stove, the girl he loved was busy cooking breakfast. She had her back toward him and didn't realize he had come in. She wore a simple yellow blouse. Her ponytail swung and her skirt swayed as she moved around the kitchen. She was the most beautiful girl in the world.

He watched her crack the eggs over the frying pan, turn them, and serve them onto the plates.

"Good morning, Jesse." Her eyes lit up when she saw him standing by the kitchen doorway. She gave him a bright, cheerful smile. "I went to the French bakery downstairs earlier and brought back those croissants you love." She put the eggs down on the table.

He walked up to her, took her into his arms, and planted a long but gentle kiss on her lips. The sweet scent of her rose perfume aroused all his senses. They looked into each other's eyes. He took her hands and led her back into the bedroom, where he pulled her toward him and kissed her again. She returned his kisses as they fell onto the bed. Slowly, he unbuttoned her blouse and undressed her. They continued to kiss as he caressed her. Her skin felt so soft.

He wiggled out of his robe. Lying on top of her, he gazed at her face. She gazed back at him with her sharp, clear eyes. So clear, they looked almost translucent. They could see into the deepest depths of his soul.

"I love you, Jesse," she said.

A cascade of emotions washed over him like a waterfall. He held her body against him and found his way into her. She accepted him with her gentle, tender embrace. His breath quickened as he reached deeper and deeper inside her. "Be with me… Please… Say you'll be mine," he whispered and kissed her lips. "Say you are mine," he pleaded with kisses all over her cheeks and her lips. Hungering for more of her, he pushed until he drove all obstacles between them aside and she opened all of herself to him and they soared and became one. He let out a long breath of air and collapsed onto her.

She lifted his face with her palms and looked him in the eye. Her eyes were full of sorrow.

"What's wrong?" he asked her. She didn't answer. "What's wrong?" he asked again, but she only stared back at him. Her eyes looked distant and far away.

The crack of a rifle shot woke him. Sitting in the foxhole, Jesse glanced at his watch with his half-opened eyes. Three o'clock in the morning. Another medic who was in the foxhole beside him stirred, mumbled a few incomprehensible words and fell back asleep.

Three more shots came from beyond the woods. Warning shots, or noise intended to keep them from a full night's rest. The enemy liked to release shots in the middle of the night to remind them that the Wehrmacht had not gone away. More shots might go off before the night was over.

He raised his head and looked up at the leaves and branches they had used to cover the foxhole. The forest debris made an imperfect shield for protecting them against rough mountain weather. He could see the ground above through the gaps between the branches. Outside, it was pitch black. There was not a star in the sky.

Drafts of night wind cut through the gaps between the branches and chilled him to the core. He bent his toes. Frozen numb, they felt painful inside his boots. The government-issued blanket, smeared with dried dirt, had slipped from his body while he slept. Shivering, he pulled it up and covered his neck and shoulders. The rough fabric scratched against his chin and did little to keep him warm.

He leaned back against the foxhole's wall. Closing his eyes, he tried to forget the cold by remembering the dream he just had. He was in Tessa's embrace. He longed for her embrace now. If only dream and reality were reversed and he could wake up from the torment of this foxhole to find himself in her arms. If only he could wake up from this nightmare.

Chapter 28

"Captain Milton." Aaron walked up to Fran at one of the long tables in the mess hall.

Fran looked up from her food. As usual, she was dining alone. At two-thirty in the afternoon, the lunch rush was over and the mess hall tent was almost empty. She preferred to dine late when the crowd was gone. She didn't like eating in front of her staff. Eating was a need. Having needs made her feel vulnerable. To be seen eating by her staff annoyed her.

"Mind if I sit down?" he asked.

"No." Surprised to see him, she picked up a napkin and wiped her mouth. "Please."

He took a seat across the table from her. She pushed her mess kit to the side.

"Sorry we had to miss our breakfast meeting this morning," he said.

"It's okay. I know you had a surgery scheduled."

"I saw the seed cake you left on my desk," he said, his tone friendly as always. "Thank you. You must've gone through some trouble to get it."

"It was no trouble at all." She let slip a smile. "I asked the army cook to bake it. You've been working very hard. I thought it would be a nice treat." A group of medical corpsmen shouted to each other as they passed by outside the entrance, hauling several dead bodies. "This month has been atrocious. It's as bad a blood bath as I have ever seen."

"Yes. It's horrendous what our boys are going through. That's why I gave the cake to the ones we discharged back to the front line today. You should've seen them devouring it."

"You gave the cake away?" Her face turned white as a sheet.

"I thought it'd be a good send off, knowing they'll be eating nothing but C- and K- rations for God knows how long after they leave the hospital. The shaving cream and socks you for left me, I gave those to them too."

"Why'd you do that?"

"It's the least we can do to give them a bit of luxury. It's so little that we can do for them."

"But I got those for you."

"And I in turn was able to give them to the people who deserve them most. So what you did was a wonderful thing. Nothing's too good for our boys on the front," he said with his usual kind, benevolent smile.

She tried to smile back in agreement, but she couldn't. Keeping stoned-faced was the best she could do.

"I appreciate what you do for me, Captain," Aaron continued. "It was very thoughtful of you to give me so many useful gifts. It means a lot to me that we all look out for each other as colleagues, but the boys need those things more than I do."

A large lump rose in her throat. She couldn't say anything.

"You know, what you did gave me an idea. Instead of us on the staff giving gifts to each other, we can do it for our soldiers instead. I want to start a fun project to garner gifts for our boys who have to return to the front line. We can get our whole staff in on it. When the patients leave, we'll give them a 33rd Field Hospital care packet."

Fran stiffened. This was not the outcome she wanted at all. She had never taken the initiative to ingratiate herself to another person the way she did with Aaron Haley. Those gifts were carefully chosen and meticulously packed. He didn't cherish them. He gave them away. The thought of loud, callous soldiers touching and using those gifts made her ill. All those gifts and her feelings were now exposed. Passed around. Trashed. A gnawing pain festered and boiled in her chest. She felt like crying. She couldn't remember the last time she cried. She swallowed to clear the lump in her throat, glad that her glasses concealed her eyes. She blinked and rolled her eyes to suppress her tears.

"I don't agree with your plans, Doctor," she said plainly. "I've been a nurse for more than twenty years. I don't make it a practice to become personal with my patients. It is my strong, personal belief that we should not become emotionally attached to the people we treat. It would cloud our judgment. We treat them. We tend to them. They get better. We let them go. It's the best policy."

"I see what you're saying. I'm not suggesting that you or any of our staff should become personal with our patients. We're talking about giving them send-off gifts. Our judgment won't be clouded by doing something nice for soldiers who have already recovered and are leaving the hospital."

She stared at him through her glasses as he spoke. He radiated warmth when he talked about the soldiers and what he wanted to do for them, but none of his warmth touched her. The more he talked, the icier she felt. She hardened her face and looked away.

He took her silence as acceptance. "I'll get the project started then," he said. "From now on, I'll donate all the gifts I receive from anyone to the recovered soldiers when they return to the front. I'll suggest that everyone on the staff should consider doing the same and pass along some of the gifts they receive from home or from here."

"If that's what you wish to do, Doctor, it's your choice, but I won't be a part of it. I advise against it. Frankly, it's a waste of our time. We have too much work to do already. We're here to treat the patients, not babysit them or be their friends."

Rather than argue with her, Aaron softened his expression and let the tension between them subside. "Captain, we've been working together for a long time."

"Yes."

"You know I value our work relationship very much. Your work is exemplary. Our hospital is fortunate to have you."

"Thank you."

"We work well together." He looked directly at her. "I hope that won't change."

"No. Of course not," she said, nonchalant. "Why would it?"

He waited, giving her a chance to say more if she wanted to, but she said nothing.

"I will see you later then? We'll go over Colonel Callahan's new directives when we have tea this evening?

"Sure. See you later."

He got up from the table and gave her one last look, a look of sympathy. She did not want that. She did not want sympathy.

After Aaron left, she sat alone with her leftover tin can of food. The gravy on the morsels of meat had dried up into a layer of brown crust. The little dinner roll, which tasted as good as a paper towel even at the time it was served, had hardened to the point of being inedible. Everyone who had come to dine had left. Only the cook and the kitchen staff remained. They carried on with their jokes and horseplay as they cleaned the place. Their jolly bantering and the clinks and clanks of pots and pans had overtaken the tent. None of them paid any attention to the woman sitting alone at the long table, frozen in her shell.

Chapter 29

On his way back to his office after checking on his patients, Aaron thought of his earlier conversation with Fran Milton. He hoped she did not take everything too hard. He knew her life here was not easy. Her reputation among the staff for being steely, hard, and demanding, sometimes even verging on unreasonable, made the 33rd a very lonely place for her. The staff revered her. Some were afraid of her. Many outright disliked her. Unlike them though, what he saw was a reclusive person who had very little in life besides her work. In that way, she and he were a lot alike, and he could sympathize with that. He led a lonely life too.

Lately, though, things had gotten out of hand. Perhaps her loneliness had reached a breaking point. In that case, he would feel sorry for her. He could not, however, be the answer to her loneliness. Whatever burden she was carrying, it had tainted her outlook on life. She was not a happy person. This was obvious to everyone. Whatever she may think of him, he was not the answer to her problems. He was not a young man anymore. He harbored no youthful illusion that he could be the key to any woman's happiness. At his age, that was beyond his abilities. Beyond any man's abilities, actually, to rescue a woman who was unhappy with her own life.

Of course, Fran Milton was not seeking to be rescued. A woman of practical mind with years of life experience herself, she did not give him the impression that she wanted someone to save her. What she wanted, it felt to him, was validation. Somehow, she had gotten it into her head that she could justify herself through him. He wished she could see that she didn't need anyone to justify her worth. As a nurse, she had done so many worthwhile things already. He would tell her that too, if he could, but things being the way they were now between them, it would probably be best if they left certain things unsaid. He didn't want any awkwardness when they had to work together. As long as she understood he did not wish to receive special treatment from her, he saw no reason to further upset her. She was his colleague. In that respect, he did care about her.

Arriving at his tent office, he found Tessa Graham, the young nurse who had joined them shortly before Anzio, waiting for him outside. Earlier at the ward, he had sent her a request to stop by to see him. He wanted her help with his new gift packets project. Tessa was one of his favorite nurses on the staff. She was audacious and could work under pressure better than most people. Nothing scared her. Not the soldiers' ghastly wounds, and not the enemy bombshells and guns. Military nurses needed fortitude, and she had that in spades. On a more personal level, he felt protective of her. He suspected that she was younger than she claimed. He felt compelled to look out for her. "Tessa."

"Hello, Doctor. You wanted to see me?"

"Yes. Thank you for waiting. Please, come in and have a seat."

They entered the tent and she sat down in one of the empty chairs. He walked around behind his desk and took a seat himself. "I have an idea that I need your help with. I want to start a project for our hospital to give send-off gifts to recovered patients returning to the front line."

"That's very thoughtful of you, Doctor. How can I help?"

"Primarily, I want you to help me gather gifts. I don't know where you all get everything that's not rationed. I never have time to look into that sort of thing. I know some corpsmen trade and barter with the locals and with each other. I've noticed too that you often pass things on to the soldiers in Lieutenant Ardley's company. And you're good friends with Lieutenant Garland, aren't you? Isn't he the one who everybody goes to when they need things?"

A mischievous smile came to Tessa's face, which she tried to hide. "I see. You think I have sources from where I can get things. I don't. I pass on gifts I receive from my parents and Anthony's family to his troops. But you are right about Lieutenant Garland. He does have sources. I can ask him to help. Our laundry staff can help too. They know all the local women who wash our clothes. Sometimes they can buy things from the locals. What kind of gifts do you have in mind?"

"Small things the soldiers can carry with them. Nothing too costly. Anything they can use to make their lives easier. Pencils and notebooks, shaving cream, toothpaste, chocolates, cigarettes. Food is always good."

"I have another idea. I can ask my father to send us autographed pin-up photos of actresses."

"Pin-up photos of actresses?"

"Yes. My father's an actor. He's very well known in England. He knows a lot of actresses, even famous ones. I'll ask him to send me pin-up photos signed and autographed by beautiful actresses. This will be an exclusive benefit for patients of the 33rd Field Hospital."

Aaron laughed. "Okay, fine, but don't mention it to Captain Milton. I'm not sure how she would like that."

Tessa feigned an innocent face.

"Good. Now, do you think you can help with soliciting our staff to donate the money to buy the gifts?"

At this request, Tessa hesitated. "Doctor, I am not very good when it comes to talking to a lot of people. Why don't we ask Ellie to help instead? Everybody likes her. If she asks people to donate and contribute, I am sure they'll help."

"Ellie..." Aaron said, distressed. "Tessa, do you know if I've done anything to offend Ellie recently? Has she said anything to you?"

"No. She hasn't said anything to me. Why would you think that?"

"She seems to be avoiding me. She doesn't seem at ease when I talk to her lately. Maybe she's upset with me."

"That doesn't sound like her. Ellie's never upset with anybody."

Aaron wasn't convinced. Ellie Swanson no longer came by his office anymore unless she had no other choice. He hoped it wasn't because he had been too forward the way he went around looking for her everywhere the day the hospital was bombed. That was imprudent of him, but he had been so worried.

"I assure you, Doctor," Tessa said. "She wouldn't avoid you. She's very fond of you." Hearing that Ellie was fond of him made him smile, even though he wasn't sure this was the case.

"She cares a great deal about you," Tessa said in a low, serious voice and gave him a meaningful look.

"I know what you're suggesting, Tessa, but, like I told you before, I'm an old man. Look at me. You've even said yourself I look the same age as your father. Ellie's only a little older than you. She has a long future ahead of her. You shouldn't think these kind of thoughts about me and Ellie."

"All right, if you think you could be my father, then I'll speak frankly to you like a daughter. You're not old. You have a long future ahead of you too. Why should your age matter?"

Aaron considered what Tessa said. There was genuine concern in her eyes, but how could a young girl like Tessa Graham understand?

He tried again to explain. "It matters because I want what's best for Ellie. You're young. The world for you is full of dreams and promises. I've already lived half my life. All I have is work and more work. If I've had dreams before, they have already come true, or they didn't. Either way, I don't have dreams anymore. There aren't many more surprises ahead for me. Ellie… she's young like you. She's bright and vivacious. She should be with someone closer to her age. They can live out their dreams and future and spend an entire lifetime together. I don't want to be in the way of that." He sighed. "If I was younger…" He picked up a small hourglass on his desk. "Time has no mercy. It passes. Next thing you know, half your life is over."

Tessa watched him turn the hourglass ornament over and over in his hand. "I don't agree with that. I think time has been exceedingly merciful to you. Have you ever considered that maybe time passed for you, kept you in waiting so that you can finally meet the person who you deserve?"

Intrigued, Aaron halted the hourglass in his hand and pondered that thought.

"You and Ellie wouldn't be possible before now. If you were younger, she would be a child, and you would indeed be too old."

Aaron chuckled. There was irony in that thought.

"Besides, you're not being fair to her. You said you want what's best for her, but shouldn't she be the one to decide what's best for her? You worry you can't be with her for her entire lifetime. But maybe for her, it would be enough if she can have even a moment in time with you? Maybe for her it would be worth it even if it is not forever and there might be pain in the end?"

He still felt conflicted, but her words gave him a new rush of hope.

"You do have a long way to go in your life, so we're talking about more than a moment. Anyway, the point is, what matters is the time you will have with the other person. Otherwise, you're not giving yourself a chance."

Surprised that someone as young as Tessa would think this way, he asked, "Where did you get these ideas?"

Tessa smiled to herself. "I learned these wise words from a good friend recently." For an instant, she looked as if her thoughts had wandered elsewhere.

He looked at the hourglass in his hand. For the first time, he began to think that maybe he should put his worries away.

"At least you should ask her to help with your project. I am sure she would want to help you." She rose from her seat. "In fact, I'll go find her right now and ask her to come and talk to you."

Before he could respond, Tessa was already gone. Left alone, he thought of Ellie. No matter what Tessa said, he was sure Ellie had been oddly cool and formal toward him in the last few days. When they talked, he felt an awkwardness between them. Could he be wrong? Was he only imagining it?

He pulled the top file from the stack of reports on his desk and tried to turn his mind toward something else, but he couldn't. Tessa would be bringing Ellie here soon. He felt nervous. He felt anxious to see her too. He felt like an eighteen-year-old boy, about to ask a girl out for his first date.

Stop it! You old fool. He made a wry face to himself.

He wondered if Tessa might be right. Was he meant to be waiting all these years so that he would meet Ellie in the present day? It had been so many years since he had seriously entertained the thought of himself and a woman. He didn't know what to think anymore.

About half an hour later, Tessa returned with Ellie. He could hear them talking outside. "Go on in," Tessa said. Ellie mumbled something inaudible. Tessa entered his tent, pulling Ellie's arm.

"I'm back, Dr. Haley," Tessa said.

Hopeful, Aaron got up from his desk. Ellie gave him a quick smile and looked away.

"I told Ellie all about your plan for the gifts project. She will help us. Won't you, Ellie?"

Ellie did not refuse outright, but looked reluctant.

Disappointed to see her hesitation, he said, "You don't have to do this, Ellie. I don't want to impose..."

"No. I'll help," Ellie said. "It's a very good idea. I'd like to do more for our soldiers too."

"Okay, then…" Aaron said, still wondering if inviting Ellie was a mistake. "We'll need to procure small gifts. I have some I can contribute myself." He opened his desk drawer and took out a dozen little carved wood bunnies. "Easter's coming up. I made these for our doctors and medical corpsmen with small children back home. I can make more. I can make other things besides bunnies too."

Ellie picked up one of the bunnies. "You made these?"

Aaron admitted it with a modest smile.

"They're adorable!" Ellie examined the bunny. "You made these for our men with children back home? That's so kind and thoughtful of you."

"They are very cute," Tessa leaned over his desk, admiring them.

"Thank you," Aaron said. "I got into trouble with Captain Milton for making them."

Ellie's face dimmed when he mentioned Fran.

"How?" Tessa asked. "What kind of trouble?"

"I cut myself carving the bunnies, and she scolded me for it." He held out his hand to show them. A bandage covered the side of his palm. "She thinks I should stop because it might affect my work if I injure my hand."

"You hurt your hand?" Ellie asked.

"Yes, but this is the only time I've ever hurt myself carving. It was a fluke. That reminds me, I better change the bandage again, or else she'll complain like she did a couple of days ago that I might infect the patients."

Ignoring what he was saying about his bandage, Ellie said, "You mean, she… your hand…" She grabbed Aaron's hand and looked at it. "It was about your hand?"

Aaron and Tessa stared at her, puzzled. Realizing she was holding Aaron's hand, Ellie dropped it. "I'm sorry, Doctor." She took a step back away from him, but she couldn't stop smiling. "I…I hope you're not hurt too badly."

"It's only a small cut. Not a big deal." Ellie's overreaction confounded him.

"It's all settled then," Tessa said. "Ellie and I will help get your project started."

When Ellie and Tessa left the tent, Ellie gave him a warm smile. The awkwardness between them was gone. He was not sure what had happened in the last few days, or why things were now back to normal. All he knew was, whatever the problem was, it had gone away. Ellie was not distancing herself from him anymore.

He thought of what Tessa had said again. All those years that passed didn't feel like lost time anymore. Tessa was right. Time had been merciful to him. He didn't know it before, but all those years, he had been waiting for Ellie. The woman he wanted in his life had finally appeared. The wait was over.

He only had to find the right opportunity.

Chapter 30

From the canteen, Tessa picked up three C-rations to bring to the ward for the Italian boy and his family. The poor boy had been hurt so badly by the grenade. If only she could give him something to make up even a little for what he had suffered. She wished she could at least bring him better food, something children might like, but C-rations were all they had at the hospital. She was more than sick of it herself, but what could one do?

She took a bar of chocolate out of her jacket pocket and placed it on the tray. At least she could give the boy this. Jesse had somehow procured this for her to give to the boy. Where Jesse had gotten it from, she hadn't a clue, and she knew better than to ask. The fewer questions there were, the better he would be able to continue to do favors for her and everyone else.

In the ward, the boy's mother sat by his side holding his hand. His cousin, the Italian girl named Claudina, was teaching several soldiers near them how to speak Italian. Claudina's presence had had a wonderful effect on the soldiers. Oddly enough, even though she was a foreigner, talking to her gave them a sense of normalcy. They peppered her with questions about her village, about Italy, how the Italians lived, what kind of food they ate. They yearned for a return to civilian life.

Tessa came to the boy's bed and set down the packets of C-rations. She then showed the boy the bar of chocolate. "Grazie." The boy gave her a shy smile and reached out to take it. Tessa's heart broke to see the visible signs of burns on his arms. His wounds would eventually heal, but the scars would remain with him for the rest of his life.

This war. It scarred everybody in its path. It spared no one.

While the boy and his mother ate, Tessa checked on the other patients who needed their temperature taken, jotting down notes. Her attention on her work was broken when the boy's mother began to sing. Tessa looked up from the clipboard she was holding. The boy's mother was singing to him while he fell asleep. The sight brought forth a spate of nostalgia for Tessa. Her own mother used to sing her to sleep too when she was little.

What was her mother doing now? She wondered. And her father. Where was he performing now? Was he doing Shakespeare again? It had been so long since she had seen them.

"Tessa." Gracie passed by her. "Better finish up here soon. We have to get to the staff meeting. Captain Milton will scold us if we're late."

Tessa checked her watch.

Remember, darling, it'll only be a matter of time before we see each other again. Her father had said this to her at the Southampton Port the morning she left for America. He and her mother had given her a beautiful Bulova ladies watch to remind her of that.

It'll only be a matter of time...

The matter of time.

She looked at her watch again. The watch she wore now was a utilitarian one issued by the army. She had to leave the Bulova behind in Chicago. When she was deployed, she had to conform to the military's dress code.

She reached up to her neck for her rose pendant. She no longer wore the Bulova watch. She wore Anthony's rose pendant now.

London. It felt so far in the past.

It would only be a matter of time before she and her parents would see each other again. When they did, what then?

Could she turn back? She was no longer fourteen. Her life had changed. It had changed long before she fully realized it. It changed forever the moment Anthony entered her life.

She turned the rose pendant in her fingers. The matter of time was exceedingly complicated.

PART NINE

Spring, 1944

Chapter 31

The arrival of April coincided with the opening of the beach in Nettuno that the army had reserved for the troops' private use. Coming to this beach was one thing that Anthony had been looking forward to on his return from the front line. He had wanted to bring Tessa here as soon as the temperature allowed.

In a secluded spot, he helped Tessa spread out the torn piece of canvas they had brought with them. After weeks of holing up in dugouts, he was ready for a good afternoon of rest.

The warmer weather had brought both relief and trepidation. Gone were the snowstorms on the mountains and the blistering cold that made the lives of their troops hell beyond hell. At the same time, the turn of the weather also meant that the inevitable confrontation with the Germans was drawing near. Without the impediment of ice and snow, the troops on both sides would pick up their battles in full force again to try to claim Anzio. He wanted to take as much advantage as he could of the time he had before then to be with Tessa.

Seize the day. That was what he must do. Few people could understand the idea better than those who do not know whether each day might be their last.

The beach today was nearly empty. For most people, the mid-April temperature was still too cool for water sports. About sixty yards in front of them, three men huddled together, joking with each other while drinking their beers. Two women, probably nurses or Red Cross aides, strolled along the shoreline. Tessa sat down on the canvas and took a drink of water from her canteen. Kneeling on the sand, Anthony leaned toward her and gave her a loud, smacking kiss on her cheek before he stripped off his uniform for a swim.

"You're really going in?" Tessa asked.

"Yes, I'm going in.

"It's too cold. You'll freeze."

"It's seventy degrees. I won't freeze." He started to walk toward the water.

"Anthony!" Tessa called out to him, still worried.

He turned around, happy to see the look of disbelief on her face. To be able to impress his girlfriend, and one as hard to impress as Tessa, was especially satisfying.

"Don't worry," he yelled back. "I did the polar plunge in Chicago for three years. This is nothing." He headed toward the ocean as she looked on, stunned.

He waded into the water on the edge of the beach. White foam covered his feet as wave after wave of seawater broke onto the sand. The water felt chilly, but the cold did not faze him. It had been too long. The last time he had had a good swim was in Los Angeles when he took one of his weekend passes from training camp before his deployment, and this might be his only chance for a swim for a long time to come. The warm temperature today was an anomaly. The climate here was not suitable for swimming until May. By then, his division might be on the move toward Cisterna again. He had to seize this one day while he could. It was too rare a treat to be able to do something he loved, and with the girl he loved near him.

He turned around and waved at Tessa. He hadn't seen her in weeks. The day couldn't be any better with the reassuring sight of her being there.

He waded in deeper. When half his body was immersed, he dove in and swam out to the open sea. The biting cold water shocked his body at first but he soon acclimatized. In the water, his spirit started to revive. He felt his body awakening as if it was coming out of a forced hibernation. He hadn't felt this free in ages. With each stroke, the power in his arms strengthened and the blood in his veins pumped faster. He felt alive again.

How he missed the old days of swimming in the lake back in Chicago. He missed the swim team and the competitions. In another month, the swimming pool back home would be filled again. He wondered if Alexander and Katherine would be using it. It would be a shame if no one used it. His father didn't swim much, and his mother used it more for sunbathing.

The tide rolled him back and forth as he swam along the beach. The undercurrent beneath the water reminded him of a painting that Tessa had once made. He never told anyone, not even her, that the waves she had painted aroused him. The undercurrent in the painting looked to him like a deep potent force of desire. Hidden below the sea surface, its pull was quiet and slow, but powerful. Its breadth was wide and overwhelming. The first time he saw the painting, he felt her arms encircling him. He felt her essence enveloping his body, the same way that the water now swept and whirled around him. Whenever he thought of that painting, he could almost feel the smoothness of her skin and the feel of her naked body against him.

These thoughts about her only intensified since she had arrived in Italy. Before, when they were separated, he had loved and adored her. There were times when he had occasional thoughts about her that weren't so innocent, but she was far away. Sometimes she was more like a dream than a real person. Whatever he could have with her was a promised reward to come in a future that was too far removed. Now, things were different. She was here. His feelings toward her were no longer contained in a dream. They were real. They were real for her too. Those feelings manifested themselves every time they looked at each other and every time they touched. Those feelings could only take them to an inevitable end.

If things were normal, if he was back home and the times were normal, there would be rules to guide them and boundaries to keep. But times were not normal. With all that they saw and experienced every day, the rules of decorum back home felt so trivial. What would happen tomorrow, or the day after? They didn't talk about it. They didn't know what each day would bring, and nothing was guaranteed. What he really wanted was to seize every moment with her. Every time he saw her, he felt an irrepressible desire to let her know how much he wanted her. All of her.

He wondered what she thought. Tessa was unlike any other girl. Rules had no meaning to her even when times were normal. She never put on airs and pretensions when she was with him. When they were together, everything she did was out of instinct and feelings of the moment. She trusted in their love, wherever it took them. In these unusual times, without lines and boundaries, when every time they saw each other might be the last, he didn't know anymore where he should let his feelings take them.

Waves of water swarmed his body. The undercurrent rolled back and forth on the ocean floor, pulling at him and refusing to let him ignore the seed of desire that had been growing ever since he and Tessa reunited. Even the cold water of the sea could not quench the heat rising inside him. He swung his arms harder and harder with each stroke and sped up his kicks, exhaling lungfuls of air with each move to release the pent-up energy trapped within him. He kept on going until his arms and legs gave out.

Returning to shore, he rose out of the ocean. Water dripped down his chest and shoulders. Sunlight shone around him, glistening on the ocean surface as he walked back onto the beach.

He returned to Tessa and she handed him a large towel. He dried himself and sat down next to her to catch his breath.

"How'd that feel?" she asked, still in awe.

"Fantastic. You should've come in with me."

"I don't have a bathing suit."

Leaning closer to her ear, he lowered his voice and whispered, "That didn't stop you last time."

Last time. She glanced at him. He looked intently back in her eyes.

Last time was the night at the lake after they left the Biograph cinema. That night meant so much more to them now. Embarrassed, she broke away from his gaze and stared down at the sand. "You still remember that? That was so long ago."

"I remember everything," he said, his voice firm and unwavering.

She kept her eyes lowered, looking away from him, but his eyes remained fixed on her. "I remember the way your body looked when you were under the moonlight." He stroked her gently on the cheek. "I remember when you stood naked next to me, daring me to touch you." He ran his finger down her neck along her uniform's collar above her chest. Her breathing became faster and deeper as he traced his finger on her skin.

"I tried to look away from you but I couldn't. You were so beautiful."

She broke into a smile. The excitement in her eyes prompted him to go on.

"For days afterwards, every time I saw you, all I could think of was the way you looked under the moonlight. I couldn't even talk to you."

All the while he was talking, he continued tracing her collar along her skin until he reached the first button of her uniform. She gasped and looked up. In her eyes, he could see the same longing that he felt. She put her hand on top of his and held it close against her chest.

A gust of wind blew by them, carrying with it the scent of rose perfume on her body. The fragrance inflamed him like a splash of fuel across fire. He took her hand and put it against his lips, leaving small, deep kisses on her fingers. "I'm having some very improper thoughts about you right now that I shouldn't be having."

"Is that right?" she asked with her own suggestive smile and, leaning into his embrace, teased his lips with light kisses.

He pulled her into his arms and kissed her deeper, wanting more. He slid his hand down her arm and her leg, feeling her body through her clothes. The rising and falling sounds of waves crashing on the beach spurred him on. He wanted to know what her body felt like. He wanted to feel her body moving against his like the rolling undercurrents. He wanted her. He wanted all of her. He reached up to the top of her uniform again and loosened the button.

Chattering voices and laughter broke the private ambiance around them. The two women who were strolling on the beach had come to the area of the shoreline directly in front of them. They stopped at the spot and continued chatting while looking out at the sea.

He released her from his embrace. "I wish we could be some place alone."

Tenderly, she put her hand on his arm.

"I can't wait till all this is over. Everything will be so much better when we go back to America."

She looked away and stared out into the waves. A note of sadness fleeted past her eyes.

"What's the matter? Don't you want all this to be over too?"

"Of course I do. It's just... when I left London, all I wanted was to go back. I never thought I was leaving my parents for good."

His heart sank. "You want to go back to London when the war's over?"

"No. I mean, I don't know. I don't want to be away from you."

"So you'll come back with me, right? Back to Chicago?"

She could not bring herself to answer. He put his arms around her again, holding on to her as if he was afraid he might lose her.

"I miss London and my parents, that's all." She forced a sad smile.

"Come back to Chicago." He kissed her hair, not letting go of her. "I want you with me." He leaned in close to her again, seeking her lips.

She gave him the kiss he wanted, but he worried that part of her mind was still in London, with her parents, her home, and everything she had left behind. He loved her. He wanted a future with her. What would winning this war mean to him if they couldn't begin a new life together when the war ended?

Chapter 32

In the small bar at the recreational center, a group of officers grumbled and cursed as Jesse pushed piles of coins and cash into his corner of the table. He was on his usual winning streak when Tessa and Anthony walked in. He didn't expect to see them here. He rarely saw them together. His heart pinched at the sight of them walking with their arms around each other. When they saw him on their way to the bar, they waved at him. He acknowledged them without betraying a hint of his pain.

At the bar, Tessa and Anthony each ordered a drink. They were there for only a short while, and were soon gone. Still, their presence distracted him. He lost all interest in the poker game and could not resist looking their way whenever it was not his turn. His spirits darkened every time he glanced over and saw the way Tessa looked at Anthony.

"Ha!" The officer sitting across from him grinned. "Two pairs. Aces over Jacks."

Jesse looked down at his cards and folded them onto the table. The other two officers at the table followed suit.

"And the pot is mine," said the officer who had won. A cigarette dangled from his mouth. He swiped all the cash in the center toward him while the other two officers hurled curses at him. Laughing, he ignored them and said to Jesse, "What's the matter, Garland? Lost your magic touch?"

Jesse didn't answer. He picked up his shot of whiskey and downed the entire glass. "Sorry, gentlemen. I'm done for the day." He put down the empty shot glass and got up from the table.

"Oh, come on," said the officer. "You can't be done. Don't be a sore loser."

"I'm done," Jesse said. He walked to the bar and ordered another shot. The empty glasses that Tessa and Anthony had left behind were still on the bar. He looked at their glasses. The ache in his heart bore deeper and deeper. The server gave him his drink. He downed it and ordered two more. He drank both shots one after another. It was all he could do to numb the pain.

# # #

After she finished her morning rounds, Tessa took the bag of gifts she had gathered to Dr. Haley's office. Stuffing gift packets every Wednesday during their mid-morning break had now become their weekly routine.

"Hello, Dr. Haley," Tessa greeted Aaron in his tent office.

"Good morning, Tessa."

"Look at these." She put the bag on his desk. "My mother sent a dozen pairs of new socks. The boys can always use more socks. Ellie collected cigarettes from everyone who doesn't smoke. We have an assortment of chocolates and snacks." She looked through the items in the bag. "We have beef jerky, dried fruit someone received from home, three decks of playing cards, handkerchiefs, and some books and magazines. And look! My father came through. The pin-up photos arrived. They're all autographed." She placed a stack of color photos of actresses in bathing suits and lingerie on his desk.

He looked away but laughed. "That's great. You can sort those out. You don't have to show them to me." He put down his pen. "Is Ellie coming?"

"She's on her way."

"I'm right here." Ellie entered with Jesse. "I ran into Lieutenant Garland. He's got something for us too."

Jesse put a small bag on Aaron's desk. "Lighters. And a few flasks full of fine liquor."

"Thank you." Tessa opened the bag.

"Really?" He winked at her and whispered in her ear. "Can I get a thank you kiss then?"

"Will you stop flirting for one moment?"

"No. Never. Especially not when it's you."

"Tessa," Ellie said. "I have good news. Sarah's coming."

"Sarah?" Tessa put down the lighters in her hand. "Sarah Brinkman?"

"Yep," Ellie said with a huge smile on her face. "I got a letter from her today. It's written to both of us. Look." She took a letter out of her pocket.

"Let me see!" Tessa took the letter from Ellie and skimmed it. "She's coming with the 11th Evac Hospital."

"The 11th will be replacing 93rd."

"What wonderful news," Tessa said. She was surprised at how happy she was to hear that Sarah was coming.

"Who's Sarah?" Aaron asked.

"Sarah worked with us at the Veterans Hospital back in Chicago." Tessa gave the letter back to Ellie. "She's a real talker. She could go on and on, but who knows? Her stories might actually be good diversions here."

"She's all ready to bake you a birthday cake too, Tessa," Ellie said. "Did you see that in the letter?"

"Oh yes." Tessa turned to Aaron and Jesse. "That's another thing about her. She loves to bake. Even with sugar being rationed, she always found ways to make batches of pies. It would be wonderful to have some of those pies now, especially after what we've been eating every day." She looked at Ellie again. "It's nice of her to want to make me a birthday cake, but I don't think she knows what it's like here. I don't know how she could talk the kitchen into letting her bake a cake."

"Don't be so sure," Ellie said. "She's very committed when it comes to baking."

Interrupting them, Jesse asked, "It's going to be your birthday?"

"Her birthday is the sixth of May," Ellie answered before Tessa could.

"Maybe we should celebrate," Aaron said.

The sixth of May, Jesse thought to himself. That would be the last day of his five-day rest pass to Naples. He wouldn't be back in Anzio until May 7th. Disappointed, he looked down at the floor. He wondered if he should return early. He looked up at her.

"I think Tessa would rather spend whatever little time she has that day with Lieutenant Ardley," Ellie said. "Wouldn't you, Tessa?"

Tessa smiled and didn't deny it.

"But if Sarah bakes a cake, then you must make a small sacrifice and celebrate with all of us because we'll all want some of that cake."

"Must be some delicious cake this woman makes," Aaron said. "You're all making me hungry."

"It will be a treat for sure, Doctor."

"All right," Tessa said. "If Sarah can find a way to convince the cook to let her mess around in the kitchen, I will bring Anthony along and share the cake with all of you." She and Ellie continued their animated talk about Sarah and their old times back in Chicago while Aaron listened and sorted the gifts. Only Jesse remained quiet, alone in his own thoughts.

PART TEN

The Guardian Angel

Chapter 33

Sitting on the ground near the woods by the nurses' tents with Anthony lying beside her, Tessa pulled out the letters she had received from home. Today was the last day they could spend together before his company would be taken off reserve and sent back to the front line.

"Sophie and Leon are volunteering at the Veterans Hospital where you used to work." Tessa read a letter from Uncle William out loud. "Twice a week, they visit veterans and bring them books, magazines, and treats. Katherine is finishing her first year at Wellesley. She has decided to remain in Boston for the summer to intern for the *Boston Herald*." She stopped reading. "Interesting. Katherine's not returning to Chicago for the summer. Maybe she really has found her calling. Can you imagine her leaving behind Chicago society life?"

"I always had faith in her." With adoring eyes, he watched Tessa read. Her every move and expression brought a joyful smile to his face. The time they had together was so limited, he would much rather spend it looking at her. He could always read the letters again later. Being here, in Anzio, he had learned not to take anything they had for granted.

"You don't ever say anything critical about anyone, do you?" she said. "You make me look bad."

He stroked her back gently and changed the subject. "Go on. What else did Father say?"

She continued. "Leon finally agreed to take Alexander camping when summer begins. Alexander, of course, is overjoyed. I will be going with them. I want to make sure Leon will survive the trip. It turns out, Leon's idea of camping is very different from mine. To begin, he bought himself and Alexander a load of camping outfits, complete with matching hats, socks, hiking boots, and shoes. As far as the actual camping part goes, he is so worried about staying outdoors in the mountains, he practically bought out the entire camping goods store. He bought cookware, canteens, walking sticks, compasses, visors, and a load of other accessories. We will have way too much gear. I tried to tell him it will be a burden to carry so many things. Rather than listening to me, he bought a camp trailer to haul everything. But because auto manufacturers are not producing trailers now due to the war, he had to settle for buying a used one." She handed Anthony a photo of Uncle Leon and Alexander standing in front of the trailer. Leon was all decked out in a camping outfit and looked entirely too suave and dandy to be an outdoorsman. Alexander looked embarrassed.

"As for me, everything is as usual. Some days, I would really like to retire and spend more time with Sophie. Anthony, I cannot wait until you return. When you finish school, you can take over the business. Anyway, this is all for now. You both take care of yourselves. Let us know if you need anything. Love, Father/William."

Tessa looked at the letter for another moment, then folded it and gave it to Anthony.

He sat up and put his arms around her. "I wish I didn't have to go back. I could loaf around here all day."

"Me too." She glanced at her watch, sad to see the hour was almost over. He would have to leave soon.

He nuzzled his face in her hair. "Unless things are really bad and I'm held up, I'll get a special pass and come visit you on your birthday. I'll try to get away, even if just for a little while." He kissed the back of her hand.

"It's okay. You have to do what you have to. My birthday is not a big deal."

"It is a big deal. It's your eighteenth birthday."

"Shhhhh." She hushed him. "It's supposed to be my twenty-second birthday."

Smiling, he tapped her on her nose. "Our secret."

"Speaking of my birthday, did I tell you my old co-worker Sarah Brinkman is coming?"

"Sarah… she worked with you in Chicago, right?"

"Right. She wrote me and Ellie and told us she'll be coming with the 11th Evac. She should arrive any day now. Remember I told you she's an excellent baker? She said she wants to bake me a birthday cake when she gets here."

"In that case, I'll definitely have to come visit. Even if not for you, I got to come for the cake."

She punched him lightly on the arm. While they were laughing, someone shouted her name from afar. "Tessa! Tessa!"

She looked up and saw a small, faraway figure of someone in a nurse's fatigues running across the field toward her. As the figure came closer, she recognized the person. Sarah.

"Sarah!" Tessa got up from the ground. "She's here," she said to Anthony. "Sarah's here! When did she get here?" She started to run toward Sarah. He got up to follow.

She had run barely a few steps when out of nowhere, the flacking sound of anti-aircraft guns assailed the sky. A trail of black smoke led by a falling plane dropped from the aerial space above. What happened next turned to a blur. She felt Anthony's arms wrapping around her from behind, and they both fell onto the ground just as the airplane crashed. The plane exploded into fire. A gigantic cloud of dust and debris blasted out from behind the figure that was Sarah.

Down on the ground, Tessa felt Anthony's body on top of her back, covering her and shielding her. Her heart pounded so hard, she felt it might burst out of her chest. The acrid smell of burning metal singed her nostrils. She lifted her head to look at the crash site. Before her very eyes, a large scrap of flying metal torn from the plane hit Sarah. It sliced all the way across her neck and detached her head from the rest of her body. Another blast of explosion followed and blew her decapitated head and her body into shreds. In an instant, Sarah's entire body dematerialized and disappeared.

Tessa felt the world around her began to spin and everything before her went dark. With Anthony still holding her down on the ground, she blacked out.

# # #

In a strange hospital, Tessa found herself walking down a long white corridor. She had never been here before. An eerie white light beamed down from the ceiling above. Under it, everything looked haunted. The place was empty. Between the cold, sterile white walls, the only sounds she heard were the echoes of her own footsteps.

She walked to the room at the end of the hallway. The door to the room was ajar. Low sounds of music emitted from within. She knew the music well. It was the familiar tune of the song "Happy Birthday."

She pushed the door open and went inside. The room reminded her of the commons room where the nurses used to take their breaks back at the Chicago Veterans Hospital. There was no one in there. The music came from a phonograph set on top of a cabinet. The record album spun around and around as the music played. The music's tone was off. The uneven tempo disquieted her nerves and the pitch grated her ears. It sounded like the creaking voice of a witch. It sent chills up her spine and made her skin crawl.

On the small table in the middle of the room, a single candle burned on top of a white birthday cake. She walked closer. The cake had crimson-red frosting around its rim. The words "Happy Birthday" were written on top of with bright, scarlet-red icing.

The scarlet-red icing began to melt and the words "Happy Birthday" started to bleed. The words smeared into a thick, illegible red patch of liquid like a patch of blood. The crimson frosting, too, started to spill. It dripped like blood down around the side of the cake until the entire cake was covered in red. She gasped and took an involuntary step backward. The candle on the cake was no longer there. A stick of dynamite had taken its place. The flickering fire of the candle had changed into sparks. The sparks burned through the fuse and the dynamite blew up, blasting the cake into flying pieces with blood splattering everywhere.

# # #

Jolted awake, Tessa found herself on a hospital bed sectioned off by curtains from the rest of the military patients. Discombobulated, she looked around. At the foot of her bed, Ellie was reviewing her charts.

"You're awake." Ellie put down the chart when she saw her stirring.

"What happened? Why am I here?" Tessa sat up.

Ellie came to the side of her bed. "Our anti-aircraft unit struck down a German plane. It crashed near our camp site. Do you remember?"

Tessa tried to recall, but her mind was blank.

"You passed out. Lieutenant Ardley brought you here. You've been out for more than twelve hours."

"I don't remember," Tessa mumbled. Her head was throbbing. "Anthony. Where is he?"

"He had to return to base. His company's probably gone now. They went back to the front."

Tessa fell back against the headboard. Her mouth was dry as paper and her mind was thick as a fog. The image of a bleeding cake appeared to her, followed by an explosion. She gasped. She couldn't breathe. "Sarah! Where is she? Is she okay?"

Ellie's face dimmed. "Let's talk about it after you get some rest."

"Where is she?" Tessa demanded to know.

Ellie touched her on the shoulder. "Tessa, Sarah's dead. She was killed instantly during the plane crash." Choking back tears, she turned her face away.

Tessa's body froze. She felt like someone had punched a giant hole through her core. She wanted to cry but no tears would come out.

A minute later, Aaron came in. "How's she doing?" he asked Ellie.

Neither Ellie nor Tessa answered. Ellie looked at him with tearful eyes while Tessa stared blankly into space. Aaron nodded at Ellie, then came next to Tessa.

"How're you feeling?" he asked.

She felt numb. Memories of the plane crash and explosion slowly returned to her. The vision of Sarah being decapitated came back. It should shock her but she only felt frozen.

"She was going to bake my birthday cake."

Chapter 34

On the hillside where their company was holding their position, Anthony walked through their camp to get the pulse of the troops. They had ended three days of heavy fighting to move forward into this area. It was important that all the men still had enough fight within them to move ahead. The tide was turning. Unable to withstand the Americans' vast arsenal of military resources, the German defense was slowly disintegrating. Cisterna was finally within their grasp.

While the Germans might be losing, the weather remained an unyielding enemy. The rain earlier in the afternoon had soaked the grounds again. In their muddy dugouts, everything was soaked and the troops could get no rest.

Anthony continued to inspect the grounds. A German airborne propaganda leaflet lay in his path. These stupid things were all over the place. This one showed an illustration of a dead American soldier on the field and a drawing of a girl's face above him. Beside the illustration, the word "WAITING" in large bold print screamed out from the page, followed by the enemy's warning:

> How many American women are waiting in vain for their husbands? How many girls for their sweethearts?

What about the girl you love?
Will she also be one of those
WAITING IN VAIN?

Annoyed, he stepped on the leaflet as he passed.

He wondered how Tessa was doing. After she fainted and he took her to the hospital, he had to leave her and return to his troops. She still hadn't awakened when his company took off, so he wasn't able to see her again when she regained consciousness. Garland had brought back a note from her, but the note was too short. She only wrote two sentences saying that she was fine and telling him not to worry. The terse tone of the note worried him. He had sent several messages to her after that, asking her to write again, but she hadn't.

Her birthday was coming up in another week. If they were in a holding position then, he would take a few hours and return to the hospital to check on her. He had already cleared it with Harding.

Not that Harding would have refused his request. After the battle of the caves, he and Harding had come to an unspoken understanding. As long as he never spoke of how they came about leaving the caves, Harding would not impose upon him again. And needless to say, he was never to speak in any way but praise for Harding's receipt of his bronze star.

The arrangement suited Anthony just fine.

He passed by Jonesy's dugout. Jonesy's radio was on and the broadcast could be heard by everyone nearby.

"Hi fellas, how are you all doing this evening?" Axis Sally's sultry voice emitted from the radio. The treacherous American woman's show came on every night, broadcasting propaganda for the German radio station. She spread her propaganda messages in between popular American music that homesick U.S. soldiers were desperate to hear. She taunted Americans craving war news and reports by giving them precise and accurate updates commingled with bad news on the American front. "I'm afraid you're yearning plenty for your sweetheart back home instead of me, but I just wonder if she isn't running around with the 4-Fs way back home," she mocked them. "Just think. Your girls with those lucky 4-Fs. Men who your government has excused from service for one reason or another, while you're all out here, hurting, dying."

"Hey bastard!" Ollie yelled from his dugout not too far away. "Turn that off. Stop listening to that bitch."

"I can't," Jonesy yelled back. "She's the only one playing Glen Miller."

Ollie shouted back a string of curse words.

"Speaking of hurting and dying," the vile woman continued, "I'm so sad to tell you that on the Monte Cassino front today, forty-six American men were killed, one hundred thirty-eight were wounded, and twenty-two were captured. Some of the captured ones are injured. The doctor said… well, I'm just not sure if they'll make it."

"Turn it off!" Ollie shouted again and threw an empty can into Jonesy's dugout.

Jonesy threw it right back and turned the volume louder. "So sad. Our boys, losing their lives. At best, coming back home crippled, useless for the rest of their lives. For whom? Roosevelt, Churchill and their Jewish cohorts. But let's take a break here and listen to some Glen Miller."

The song "In the Mood" came on, a jarring contrast to the reports of the dead and wounded they had just heard. The jubilant big band dance music rolled on as if the men who died were nothing but an afterthought.

Anthony walked on until he reached Beck's dugout. Beck had returned from the hospital and rejoined the company that morning. When Anthony approached, he dropped his cigarette at once.

"Good afternoon, Lieutenant." Anthony crouched down. Beck started to get up out of his foxhole but slipped. "You can stay there," Anthony said. "No need to come out."

"Yes, Lieutenant." Beck said. In his dugout with his back hunched, he looked small. His uncertain voice showed no trace of his usual cocky attitude.

"Glad you're joining us again."

"Yes, thank you."

"Now that you're back, I want to make one thing clear." Anthony stared straight at him. He thought of the moment when Jim Darnell fell to his horrific death. "If you ever pull any stunt like you did back in Carano again, I swear I'll make your life hell and the Germans will be the least of your problems. You report to me. You answer to me. You don't do anything unless I say okay. You understand me?"

Cleary uncomfortable, Beck dug his boots into the muddy ground. "Yes, Lieutenant."

"Good." Anthony stood up to leave.

"Lieutenant, wait," Beck called out.

Anthony stopped.

"Thank you for saving my ass in the forest."

Without acknowledging the incident one way or another, Anthony glanced at him one more time and walked back to his own foxhole. On his way, he passed by Jonesy again. Axis Sally was still speaking. "To Sylvia Edinger of Santa Monica, your brother got his left leg crushed. To the family of pilot George Jones, your boy didn't survive a fatal parachute jump..."

He picked up his pace and walked on without looking back.

Chapter 35

In the hospital ward, Tessa checked on the patients down the rows of beds and cots. As she came near, each patient would hush, stop whatever they were doing, and look away from her. Being near her gave them the creeps. They knew she was not the friendliest or most talkative nurse at the 33rd, but lately, they could not even bear her presence. Her eyes looked emotionless and empty, almost dead. The fatalistic look on her face made them depressed.

"Your arm," she said to the lanky soldier sitting on the bed with a cigarette in his mouth and legs wrapped in bandages. He had arrived yesterday and hadn't yet noticed the darkness she carried with her.

"Sure, sweetheart." Eagerly, he held out his arm. While she methodically wrapped the cuff of the blood pressure gauge around his arm, he took a closer look at her profile. She was the first pretty nurse he had seen since coming to this hospital. "How are you today, sweetheart?"

Tessa ignored him and pumped the bulb.

Unabashed, the soldier continued. "I didn't expect to find a pretty nurse like you here. Got here yesterday and all I saw were doctors and nurses who look like they could be my mother. Where are you from? I'm from Phoenix. Phoenix, Arizona. Wish I was back there now. Got hit yesterday and I thought to myself, damn! Finally got my ticket home. Honorable discharge, Purple Heart, all that good stuff. But no such luck, is there? The doctors said I'll heal in a few weeks, so I guess I'm still stuck here. Well. At least Uncle Sam's got a little mercy in him, sending a pretty girl like you to fix me up. Say, I've been lying and sitting here all morning. My ass hurts. You think you can turn me around and give me a little backside massage after you're done with whatever you're doing there?"

Keeping her head down, Tessa unwrapped the cuff from his arm.

"What's the matter, sweetheart? Don't like to talk?"

Tessa looked up. The dead, hollow look in her eyes startled him. Her eyes were like the windows to Death, the gateway to the Grim Reaper himself. The soldier fell speechless.

She handed him a cup of medicine. He took the cup and swallowed it without saying another word. He wanted to be done and for her to go away. He had always been superstitious. The girl carried with her an aura of death. He didn't want any of it to rub off on him.

The bitter taste of the medicine remained in his mouth long after she moved on to the next bed.

From several aisles away, Ellie looked up from time to time to check on Tessa. A week had passed since Sarah had died. It still pained her to think about it. Tessa was having an even harder time. She had withdrawn into herself. All day long, she moved around like a walking shadow of death.

When their rounds were finished, Ellie caught up to Tessa outside. "Tessa." She took hold of Tessa's arm. "Let's take a break."

Tessa neither agreed nor declined. Her spiritless face showed no interest or will of her own.

"Come on." Ellie wrapped her arm around Tessa's and led her to a quiet spot in the rest area where the staff took their coffee and cigarette breaks. She left Tessa seated at a small table while she went to get some refreshments, and returned with two cups of coffee. Tessa stared blankly at the coffee in front of her without touching it.

"Are you holding up okay?" Ellie asked.

Tessa nodded.

"Do you need more time off? We can ask Captain Milton."

She shook her head.

"I'm writing a letter to Sarah's parents to give them my condolences and to let them know how much Sarah meant to us. Do you want to write it together with me?"

Sarah's parents… Tessa remembered Mr. Brinkman. He was the nice man who arranged to film Ron Castile, the patient suffering from battle fatigue back in Chicago. They had needed proof to convince General Castile that Ron really was afflicted with a serious condition and required medical treatment. She wondered if the Brinkmans had been notified of the news yet. Mr. Brinkman must be heart-broken. Mrs. Brinkman too. The Brinkmans were nice people. They were the only ones she celebrated with at her graduation ceremony for the cadet nurse training. The Ardleys didn't know about her graduation because she never told them that she had switched to an expedited training program. She did not want them to find out that she was planning to leave Chicago to follow Anthony.

On graduation day, Sarah had insisted that they all take a photo together. Afterward, Sarah gave her a copy. Where was that photo now? Tessa could not remember where she had put it. In fact, she could not remember all that many things about Sarah. She never took Sarah seriously. Back at the Veterans Hospital, she had kept talkative Sarah around only as a convenient excuse to fend off small talk with her other co-workers.

How many times did Sarah tell her something and she didn't listen or pay attention? Did Sarah ever notice when she tuned her out? If she did notice, was she ever upset about it? Tessa grimaced at the thought of her own callousness.

"I'm thinking of writing to her brothers too," Ellie said. "I can't decide if it would be a good idea or not. They're all in the military. It's so hard to bring bad news to soldiers who are already fighting the war themselves."

Sarah's brothers… Sarah often talked about her brothers back at the Veterans Hospital. Tessa had never truly listened or paid attention. She couldn't even remember the brothers' names.

But Sarah paid attention. Sarah noticed when she was desperately trying to get assigned to join the 33rd to be closer to Anthony. Sarah was the one who suggested she should ask General Castile for help. If it weren't for Sarah, maybe she would never have gotten here.

And Sarah remembered. In her letter to them, she wrote an entire page about baking a birthday cake for her when she arrived at Anzio. Sarah remembered her birthday.

"What do you say?" Ellie asked again. "We'll write a letter of condolence to Sarah's parents together? Maybe you'll feel better after that too."

Write a letter to Sarah's parents… How could she? How could she even face the Brinkmans? How hypocritical would it be of her to write sad words and caring thoughts now? She had never truly treated Sarah the way a real friend should. She only used Sarah as a convenient chatterbox. She didn't deserve to be Sarah's friend. Sarah deserved better.

"Sarah didn't deserve to die that way," Tessa finally spoke. "When I looked up, I saw the scrap of metal cut through her neck. I saw her head fall off her body. And then, there was an explosion, and she evaporated." She closed her hands around her cup of coffee and tightened her fingers.

"Evaporated out of existence. Not a trace of her was left. It was like the world didn't care if she was ever here."

...Like how I didn't care if she was ever there, she thought but didn't say out loud.

Ellie's eyes turned red and tears rolled down her face.

"I'm sorry, Ellie. I don't think I should be the one to write a condolence letter." Tessa got up and walked back to the hospital. Her coffee remained untouched.

Alone at the table, Ellie could not stop crying.

# # #

Not too far away from the small table where Ellie sat after Tessa left, Aaron and Fran passed by on their way to meet with Colonel Callahan for an administrative briefing. When he saw Ellie crying by herself, Aaron stopped. "Captain, would you go ahead first? I'll catch up."

Fran glanced in Ellie's direction. "No, Doctor." She put her hand on his arm to stop him from heading toward Ellie. "Let me. It's my job, not yours. She's still upset about her friend who was killed last week. I'll give her the rest of the day off. You go ahead and meet with Colonel Callahan first. I'll join you both in a bit."

Reluctantly, Aaron agreed. Fran watched him look back at Ellie several times as he walked away. A lump of bitterness rose up in her throat.

She had thought about Ellie Swanson a lot since Aaron Haley turned down all the gifts she had given him. She wished Ellie had never come to the 33rd. For two years, she was Aaron's only female friend and confidant. Given more time, they could have had a chance to become more. She was sure of it. He would have grown accustomed to having her around. He would have come to depend on her. Need her even. They had a chance until Ellie Swanson arrived.

She came up behind Ellie. Ellie, hunched over in her seat crying, was too absorbed in her own thoughts to realize someone was standing behind her. She eyed Ellie from head to toe and studied her. What was it about Ellie Swanson that interested Aaron so much anyway? Ellie was a competent nurse. She would give her that. Maybe even more than competent, but certainly not exceptional or experienced like herself. Ellie was young, but there were plenty of other young nurses. What was so special about Ellie Swanson? As for her looks, there were at least several other nurses in the 33rd prettier than her. She did not understand. What was Ellie's appeal?

Fran wrinkled her nose as she looked at Ellie sobbing like a water bag. Right now, Ellie looked downright pathetic. Fran herself would never be caught bawling in public like this. She would never even bawl in private. If nothing else, she was made of much tougher stuff than Ellie Swanson. Too bad Aaron didn't appreciate that.

"Lieutenant Swanson," she said in her usual, commanding voice.

Caught by surprise, Ellie quickly got up from her seat. "Yes, Captain." Fran frowned in disgust while Ellie wiped the tears off her face and tried to compose herself.

"Take the rest of the day off. I can't have you going around the hospital blubbering like this. You'll upset the patients."

"You're right, Captain."

"If you can't handle what goes on here then you shouldn't be here," Fran scowled. "What an embarrassment, breaking down like this in front of everyone."

"I'm sorry, Captain. It won't happen again."

"Go. Take the day off. Stay in your tent. Don't come out till you get a hold of yourself."

Ellie wiped the back of her hand against her eyes and tried to hold back her tears.

"I said go."

"Yes, ma'am." Ellie hurried away.

After Ellie left, Fran resumed her way to the meeting. She hoped Ellie would stay in her tent for the rest of the day and would not come out.

"Out of sight, out of mind," she muttered to herself.

The thought turned in her head.

Out of sight, out of mind.

She needed to find a way to get Ellie Swanson out of Aaron's sight and out of his mind.

Chapter 36

In a tavern crowded with servicemen, Jesse sat alone at the bar, nursing a glass of bourbon. The liquor had no appeal and failed to numb his senses. Lively piano tunes and accordion music continued to roll in the background, but merry voices and drunken laughter could not fill the empty void he felt.

It had been three days since he had come to Naples for his rest leave. He should make better use of his five-day pass. It would be months before he would get another break like this. Everyone else who had come with him to Naples had gone off. They had been partying for days now, getting their fill of normal food, attending shows, or simply drinking themselves into oblivion. In Naples, it felt like the music never stopped and the people never slept. He had meant to join them, but once he arrived, his interest vanished. Within hours of arriving, Naples had lost all its appeal for him. Tessa was not here.

All he had done in the last three days was hole himself up in this inn. During the day, he took long walks on the streets, walking without purpose and going nowhere in particular. The only times he stopped anywhere were when he passed a store or a street vendor selling gifts. Consciously or subconsciously, he had been looking for a gift for Tessa, either for her birthday or something to cheer her up from the recent death of her friend, the nurse from Chicago who had met her untimely demise soon after arriving in Anzio.

In the evenings, he would come downstairs to this tavern and drink by himself, hoping the seedy scene would help him find his way back to his old self.

He didn't want to stay in his room alone. At night, alone in his room, his mind was occupied with only one thought: Could he forget Tessa?

He had hoped that being away from Anzio would clear his head and he could leave his thoughts of her behind. If he could ignore her on her birthday, treat her like an afterthought the way he used to do with other women and continue to have the time of his life, he might still be able to get through this. Instead, without having anything to do, she was all he could think about. His mind switched back and forth, alternately rationalizing to himself why he should forget about her and wishing she were here with him.

His mood darkened. He felt worse than ever today. Today was her birthday.

If she were his girlfriend, he would do everything he could to make her happy on this special day. If he were home in New York and she were with him, he would take her on a private evening cruise on the Hudson River and show her the night view of the Manhattan skyline. He would make it the most romantic evening ever for her. He would buy her the biggest, most beautiful diamond ring he could find and give it to her under the magical city lights.

He had considered returning to Anzio a day early, at least to wish her happy birthday. He could've been a part of her day and her life in whatever small, insignificant way possible. Even that would be something.

The rational part of his mind told him to stay in Naples. Maybe he could still save himself. Maybe he could forget about her. Maybe he could try.

The day passed. Nothing changed. It was now evening and he was sitting at the bar, more alone than ever. His feelings for her were not something he could reason himself out of.

He picked up the bourbon and drank the entire glass in one gulp. Maybe the alcohol could numb his feelings.

"Jesse." A low, sensuous voice called out his name. A woman's figure appeared next to him. He glanced at the body, then the face. Irene.

She leaned her back against the bar. The way she stood accentuated every curve and line of her body. "Fancy seeing you alone," she smiled. "What a coincidence. I'm on leave too." She took out a cigarette, held it up to her lips and raised her eyebrows at him. He picked up his lighter on the bar and lit the cigarette for her.

She inhaled a deep drag and blew out a whiff of smoke. "You don't come around to see the rest of us girls anymore. It's not fair, you know."

He signaled the bartender for another drink. "One for the lady too, please."

The bartender brought them two glasses of bourbon with ice.

Irene took the drink into her hand and stared into his eyes. "I miss you. We used to have so much fun together."

He sipped his bourbon without looking at her.

"Why her, Jesse? What's so great about Gracie?"

She waited, but he did not answer.

"Why her and not me? If it was Alice or someone else, I could maybe at least understand. But Gracie? She's a dumb small town girl. You gave up all of us for her? I don't get it. Tell me. In what way is she better than me? What does she have that I don't have?"

With a straight face, he turned toward her and looked her over from top to bottom. By any standard, Irene was a beauty. Seductive eyes, full lips, and a body to die for. She moved closer to him, positioning herself so he could have a close-up view of her chest. She had left the top of her shirt unbuttoned. From the way she was leaning, he could see a full view of her cleavage. While he looked at her, she ran her fingers up his leg.

"Nothing," he said. "She's not better than you." He took out his wallet, pulled out several bills and laid them on the bar. "You're better than her in every way." He got up, grabbed her hand, and led her out of the tavern up the stairs to his room. She followed him with a victorious smile.

Inside his room, he took her to his bed and undressed her while she unbuttoned his uniform.

He closed his eyes and kissed her, hoping she could make him forget Tessa, hoping he could return to the way he used to be.

It was useless. The minute he closed his eyes, images of Tessa were all he could see. In his mind, Tessa was the woman in his arms.

To rid himself of his thoughts of her, he opened his eyes. Irene's face appeared before him. At the sight of a different woman, the fire within him fizzled. His heart felt like deadwood. He turned his face away from Irene and closed his eyes again.

Images of Tessa returned. He could smell her rose perfume in his imagination. He kissed the lips of the woman in his bed the way he wanted to kiss Tessa.

Irene moaned. The sound of her voice jerked him out of his fantasy. He opened his eyes and saw Irene's face again. He didn't want to see her. He didn't want to make love to anyone else. This whole thing was a mistake. There was only one girl he wanted. Why couldn't he have her? Why couldn't he forget about her? Frustrations rose inside him. He quickened his pace and pushed harder, in part to get the whole business over with, and in part to expel the desperate frustration he felt.

When Irene cried out in pleasure and the regretful ordeal was over, he felt even worse than before. He felt like he was sinking into a deep hole.

The next morning, while Irene got ready to leave, he sat motionless on the bed, waiting for her to be gone. When she was fully dressed, she came back to him.

"Thank you for last night." She kneeled on the bed and gave him a light kiss on his lips. His lips remained cool and still. He lowered his eyes to avoid looking at her.

She pulled back and put on a brave face. "It's okay. I understand. I know not to expect more and I won't cause you trouble. I'm not that kind of girl." She stood up. "I just wanted to find out if you were really serious about Gracie. Now I know." She took her bag, opened the door, and gazed at him again. He didn't look up and didn't say goodbye. She walked out and shut the door behind her.

The room turned dead silent after she left. There was no sound except for the ticking of the second hand of the clock on the nightstand next to his bed.

There is no such thing as love, sweetheart.

He gripped the sheets on the bed.

No, Mother. You're wrong. You're wrong because I love her.

He looked up and stared into space. He thought of the way his life was, and the way he used to be. He couldn't go back. He didn't want to have all those girls and women anymore. Maybe he never did. Maybe he only convinced himself that he did. Either way, it didn't matter. After last night, he knew his career as a womanizer was over. That side of him had fallen apart.

He spent his last afternoon in Naples wandering aimlessly around the streets. He was almost relieved that his time off was coming to an end. In the past, he would have amassed a small fortune by now. He would have made a killing at the poker table. For the remainder of the time, he would've sniffed out whatever opportunities there were to fleece someone and lined everything up for future bargains. This time, he did none of these things. His heart wasn't in it. It occurred to him that he never liked gambling. He merely became good at it out of necessity, and he learned all the tricks to cheat. As for looking for opportunities to swindle, even the thought of it tired him.

You're not a cad. You're just pretending to be one.

Tessa's voice chimed in his mind. He smiled at the memory of what she had said. He wondered how he had ever been able to live the way he used to in all the time before he had met her. It amazed him that he was able to live a life so empty and devoid of meaning.

You're doing something good now. You save lives.

He smiled again. How ironic. It was because of this wretched war that he finally did something worthwhile. He had to come to hell to find a modicum of honor and decency.

"You carry a lot on your mind, young man." The voice of a local street vendor brought him out of his thoughts. She looked to be in her late forties or early fifties and she dressed like a gypsy. A young teenage girl about thirteen or fourteen who looked to be her daughter stood by her side. He had come upon their wooden cart displaying handcrafted souvenirs and jewelry. He smiled at the woman and her daughter and, out of courtesy, examined her goods. They were all junk jewelry, trinkets, charms, and bracelets.

"You won't find your answer among those," the woman said to him. "Here. This is what you want." She pulled out a small wooden box from under her cart, opened it, and picked out an amulet tied to a short string. The amulet was an angel made of a stone of a very pretty clear blue color. "It's hand carved. It's made out of celestite. Do you know what celestite is?"

He shook his head.

"Celestite is the gemstone of angels. According to folklore, celestite can help a person connect with his guardian angel."

"You think I need a guardian angel?"

"No. Not for you. Give it to the girl."

"What girl?"

"The girl on your mind. You know who I'm talking about." She held up the string and dangled the amulet before him. "You are her guardian angel. Give this to her, and you'll always be in her heart."

He gave the gypsy woman a skeptical look. "Signora, I'm from New York. Street artists and their tricks don't work on me." He smiled. "I don't get taken in easily."

The woman didn't take offense. "Of course you don't. It takes one to know one." She looked him in the eye, as if challenging him. "You're a street artist. If I'm lying, you would know. Am I lying?"

His doubt shaken, he stared back at her.

"It's okay. I'm not offended. I'm not a fortuneteller. I can't see into the future and I don't know magic. But sometimes, I know things." She placed the amulet in his hand. "Three thousand lira."

He held up the amulet and took a closer look. He was sure the woman was gouging him. At the same time, he believed her. He had a gut feeling that the amulet was important to him. He took out his wallet and gave her the money.

She took the cash. "She'll know how important you are to her, in time." She put away the wooden box that held the amulet. "Stay a while. Let me play a song for you." She picked up an old violin lying on her cart. As if on cue, her daughter grabbed the mandolin next to the violin.

"You heart is hurt, and your mind is burdened," the woman said. "No one can help you, but maybe this music will ease your mind for a little while until you figure things out."

The woman nodded at her daughter. The girl plucked at the strings of the mandolin, starting a gypsy song with a series of pleasant, inviting beats. The older woman joined in with her violin, infusing the beats with mysterious, mesmerizing tunes. Soon, a crowd gathered around them. He stayed and listened until the song ended. By then, the woman had gained herself a small group of new customers and was busy pushing her goods onto them. Quietly, he walked away.

He decided to head back to the inn. On the way, he pulled the angel amulet out of his pocket and looked at it again.

Give this to her, and you'll always be in her heart.

He smiled to himself and continued on his way.

Chapter 37

Next to Tessa's tent, Anthony sat on the ground, waiting for her with a small bouquet of wild flowers in his hands. Gracie had been there when he arrived. Before she left for the hospital, she had told him Tessa would be returning soon from her shift. Rather than going to the hospital to look for Tessa, he decided to wait for her. He wanted to begin their time celebrating her birthday away from all the wounded soldiers.

Although he had told her weeks ago he would try to come visit her on her birthday, she probably wasn't expecting to see him. He was on an away mission, and Garland had gone on leave to Naples. He had no good way to send a private message to tell her he was coming. He couldn't wait to see the surprised look on her face.

Part of him was worried about her. Since the plane crash, she hadn't written to him at all except that one, short note telling him she was okay. He wished he could've come earlier to check on her.

Finally, he saw her, a small figure far ahead walking up the field. His eyes brightened up as she came closer and closer. In her white dress uniform, she looked like a fairy. He hadn't seen her wear that since she had come to Italy.

Not knowing he was here, she stopped momentarily when she passed the area where the plane had crashed and stared at the spot where her friend was killed. That troubled him. She hadn't gotten over what had happened.

When she reached the tent and saw him waiting for her, the look she gave him was not the one of happy surprise that he had expected. Rather, she looked confused. She looked disoriented. The confusion lasted only a few seconds and was replaced by a hollow emptiness. He had never seen her look so despondent.

"Tessa." He put on a big smile despite his worries. "How've you been? I've been worried sick about you."

"I'm fine." She stood without energy. Her voice sounded flat and lifeless.

"You look very pretty in your dress uniform." He came closer to her. "I haven't seen you wear that in ages."

Rather than being flattered, she simply said, "It's all I have left to wear. My fatigue uniforms need to be washed. I don't feel like going to the laundry."

Her tone of disinterest alarmed him. "You're not mad at me for leaving you after the plane crash, are you?"

"No."

He could see she was not angry, but he wished anger was all there was. If she was simply angry at him, he could apologize and try to make it up to her. What he saw instead was a blank look on her face. She showed no interest in anything. She hadn't even asked how he came to be there. He touched her shoulder to comfort her. Her body was as stiff as wood. It pained him to see her like this. "I wish I could've come back to see you sooner. I'm glad I was able to get away today though. The captain gave me the afternoon off to come visit you."

Rather than being excited that he had come, she said, "You didn't have to. I'm fine."

"Of course I have to. It's your birthday."

The reminder seemed to stir her mind. A flicker of emotions returned to her face, although the emotions seemed like anguish and distress.

Seeing her like this, he felt lost at what to do. "I wish I could get you a better present, but this is all I could do." He held up the bouquet of flowers, still hoping to make the best of the situation. "When I was on reserve last time, I asked a local woman working at the laundry station to help me find me something for your birthday present. She picked these flowers this morning. I hope you like them."

Tessa glanced down at the bouquet of wild primroses, pansies, and crocuses adorned with tiny leaves. Her face twisted as if she was in pain.

"I know they don't look like much," he said, "but there are eighteen stems of flowers for your eighteenth birthday." He handed her the bouquet. "Happy eighteenth birthday."

She held the bouquet and stared at it until tears flooded her eyes. "No." She shoved the flowers back to him. "I don't want to celebrate my birthday."

"Tessa," he said, "what's wrong?" He didn't know why the flowers made her cry.

She turned away from him and struggled to breathe through her tears.

"What's wrong, Tessa? Tell me."

"Sarah…" Choking up, she tried to finish the sentence through her crying. She took several deep breaths and started again. "Sarah said she was going to bake me a birthday cake," she said. Then she laughed. Her bleak laughter mixed with her tears. "She came here…she was on her way to being killed, and what she had last thought about was baking me a birthday cake."

Helpless and unsure how to console her, he stood watching her. She was in a state of shock.

Eventually, she calmed down, but she looked even more dead than before. "I'm never celebrating my birthday again."

"Don't say that." He couldn't bear to see her like this. "You don't mean it."

"I do mean it. I don't want to celebrate my birthday again, ever." She met his gaze with a stubborn coldness. "All I'll be able to think of from now on when my birthday comes around is that Sarah was planning to make me a birthday cake, but she didn't because she got her head chopped off and her body was blown to pieces."

He stared at her, bewildered. How could she associate her birthday with such horrible thoughts?

"You should go back," she said. "Let's forget I even have a birthday. It's a death anniversary now is what it is. There's nothing to celebrate." She opened her tent, ready to go inside. "Maybe we should have a memorial instead."

He dropped the bouquet onto the ground. "No." He grabbed her hand and pulled her away in another direction.

"What are you doing?" she asked. "Where are you taking me?" He didn't answer but kept on walking. She tried to stop but he would not let go of her hand. His strides were bigger, and she almost had to run to keep up.

They came to the underground bomb shelter that the army engineers had built for the nurses. He let go of her hand but wrapped his arm around her waist and brought her down to the pit of the entrance.

"What are we doing here?" she asked. He still wouldn't answer, but grabbed her hand again and pulled her inside.

The inside of the shelter was pitch dark. He switched on his flashlight.

"What are you doing?" she asked again.

Instead of answering her, he dropped his flashlight and pushed her against the wall. He embraced her and pressed his lips hard on her lips. She stood frozen, too confused to respond.

"Your birthday will not be a death anniversary," he said. "I won't let it." He kissed her again, so fiercely that she could not breathe.

"Don't remember Sarah on your birthday." He held her face in his hands and gently stroked her cheeks. "There will be time for you to remember her, but not today. Not on your birthday." He lowered his hand. One by one, he loosened the buttons of her uniform.

She stared at him. She could feel the touch of his fingers on the skin of her chest as he unbuttoned her shirt. Her heart palpitated as she tried to grasp what was happening.

"On your birthday, this birthday, and every birthday hereafter, I want you to remember only me. I want you to remember, I love you."

Her shirt now open, he gazed at her body. A look of amazement appeared on his face when he saw the rose pendant hanging around her neck.

"You still have this?" He picked up the pendant.

"Yes," she whispered. Her heart softened at the incredulous look on his face. "I've been wearing it since I sent you my cross on my last birthday." Her voice shaking, she put her own hand over his. "I wanted you close to my heart."

Her words made him want to love her over and over a thousand times. All this time since she had been with him in Italy, he had no idea that she was wearing his pendant. He didn't even think that she had kept it.

He kissed her again, pressing his body against hers as he reached his hand down beneath her skirt. The passion of his kiss and the sensation of his touch beckoned her, pleading with her to come out of the cold, desolate place where she had hidden herself, alone. She wanted to respond to him, if only she could reach out to him. She had wanted this too. She knew it was a matter of time when this moment would come. But could she? Now?

He pulled her tight against his body. "Don't give up, please." He kissed her. "I can't lose you," he said over and over. "I don't want to lose you."

Like a ray of light, his voice drew her from the darkest place of her mind. She closed her eyes and kissed him back. Through their kiss, the emotions she had capped inside her came surging out. The touch of his hand on her body comforted her. It took away the sadness that had grappled her, tormented her, and consumed her. She let go of all the despair and succumbed to the warmth of his touch.

And then, for the first time, he touched her underneath her skirt, stroking the naked parts of her and caressing her in places where he had never touched her before. The shock of this new experience expelled the loss and grief that had overtaken her mind. His touch set off a fire within her. She wanted to forget everything else in the world and lose herself with him. She wanted to let him take them somewhere far away, somewhere in a realm beyond the here and now.

"I want you, so bad," he whispered into her ear. Her body was paralyzed at the sound of his voice. They gazed at each other, feeling for the first time the full, potent power of desire.

She reached down and unbuckled his belt. The top of her uniform slid off her shoulders. There were no more barriers between them, nothing more to separate them and nothing behind which they could reserve their feelings or hold back. He pulled her leg up against his hip, and she felt the force of his passion driving into her. The emotions between them overwhelmed her. She never imagined another person could be this close to her, could invade her and demand for her to accept him so he could enter her and share her feelings from within.

And she wanted him there. To cross this threshold with him brought on a freedom she had never known. Her heart leapt to discover this side of him, to physically feel him wanting her the way a man wanted a woman. She felt her body giving in to his power as he lifted her legs and thrust himself into her again and again. She felt him occupying her completely. His presence was everywhere within and without her, filling her heart and her mind. The force of his desire surged and he pushed faster and deeper. She leaned back against the wall and gave in to it until it found its release.

Remaining inside her, he let her legs slide down. She embraced him and held him close, wanting to prolong the moment of being joined with him. Being one with him made her feel alive. All the terrible things in the outside world couldn't touch them. What they had between them, no one and nothing could take it away, no matter what happened.

"From now on, on your birthday, remember today," he said, his heavy breath reminding her of the force of life. "Remember, I love you." He planted a soft kiss on her cheek.

She clung to him, soaking in the vitality of his warmth. "I love you too."

Chapter 38

The military vessel returning from Naples arrived and docked in the Anzio harbor. Jesse disembarked the ship, relieved that his trip was finally over. His five days in Naples had brought him no peace of mind. He had tried in vain to forget Tessa. All his efforts were futile.

She'll know how important you are to her, in time, the gypsy woman had said. Every time he thought of her words, he told himself it was absurd to take the words of a gypsy woman seriously. The gypsies were good at reading people. She probably knew exactly what to say to anyone from a hunch, but her words were the only thing that helped him make it through the remainder of his stay in Naples. They were the only thing that gave him hope.

One can never know, a voice in the back of his head whispered to him. This was war. Nothing was predictable and everything was random. Nothing was final. Everything was a game of chance. There was always a chance.

Before returning to his unit, he took a detour to the 33rd Field Hospital. He reached his hand into his pocket where he had put both the amulet and his lucky seven dice. He closed his hand around the amulet to make sure that it was there. A sweet feeling filled his heart and brought a smile to his face when he touched it.

He found Tessa in one of the tents cleaning surgical equipment. Standing by the entrance, he noticed something looked different about her. Her eyes were softer, and she couldn't stop smiling. She tried to hide her smile but it could not be concealed. It showed at the corners of her lips. A rosy blush flushed her cheek and a luminous glow glossed her skin. He recognized the look. He wished he didn't have to see this. He himself had been the source of this look too many times.

Ardley… His heart hurt as if it were bleeding.

What did he expect anyway? This was bound to happen sooner or later. He stared down at the ground in defeat.

"Jesse?" Tessa said.

"Hi." He gave her a warm smile.

"You're back. How was Naples?"

"It was fine."

"What are you doing here? Can I help you with something?"

"No," he walked in. "I came by to see you. I missed your birthday, so I thought I'd come and wish you happy belated birthday."

When she heard him say "birthday," a deeper shade of red rose to her cheeks. She smiled ever so sweetly as her eyes shone. Watching her, the pain sharpened in his heart.

"Thank you," she said. "That's very nice of you."

He put on a cheerful face and hoped she did not notice the hurt he felt inside. "I got a birthday present for you." He pulled the amulet out from his pocket. "It's a lucky charm. A guardian angel to protect you, always." He took her hand and put the amulet in her palm. "Happy birthday."

She looked at the amulet. "It's beautiful!" The wondrous look in her eyes consoled him somewhat.

"Look. I have my own lucky charm too." He took the lucky seven dice out of his pocket and showed her. "I got these on my eighteenth birthday. As long as I have these, no evil or bad luck will ever touch me. And now, no evil or bad luck will ever touch you."

She looked at his dice and her angel amulet, and broke into a huge smile. "Thank you, Jesse. I love it." She held the amulet up against her face and caressed it with her cheek. That little gesture was so sweet, he wished he could kiss her.

"I'll carry it with me all the time from now on." She put it into her pocket.

"Well then, I'll be going now. Got to get back," he said. He meant to leave but remained standing before her. There was so much more he wanted to say to her, but couldn't.

It's better this way, he told himself. *Let her be happy.*

He loosened himself and said to her, "I'll see you later."

"See you later," she said. "And thank you again."

He left her and the hospital and made his way back to camp. The entire way, he held onto one single thought.

She'll know how important you are to her, in time.

Chapter 39

Two days had passed since Anthony and his company arrived in this area two miles away from Cisterna. With the arrival of spring weather, the fighting between the Germans and the Allies had escalated tenfold. Still, Anthony was glad the winter was over. It had been four long, wretched months. The troops' will to endure their miserable conditions could not be sustained if they had to go on any longer.

This battle was coming to an end. He could feel it. A sense of finality pervaded. He felt anxious and restless. Whatever happened, they would soon be leaving this place of death and pain.

In his tent, he started to clean his Tommy gun. It needed to be clean and ready.

"Ardley." Warren came inside.

"Hey." Anthony moved over to give him room.

"I've got news. You'll hear about it soon when Colonel Callahan comes. Third Division will be moving ahead to Cisterna again tomorrow. It looks like the Germans are moving to retreat. Our aerial assaults and mortars are smothering them, not to mention our sailors' cannons."

"That's good news." They needed good news. With Rome at stake, the Germans had been fighting with fanatical fervor. Everywhere they went, the Germans would fight to their last man, forcing the Allies to engage in deadly gunfire until the bitter end.

"Yes," Warren said. "Your company will cross Highway 7 with the battalion to move in to Cisterna from the north. We're going to win this time."

Anthony put down his weapon. He hoped so. If their army could take Cisterna and the roads and railway near Highway 7, the German defense along the Gustav Line would be severely weakened, and the Allied troops fighting in Monte Cassino down south would have a great chance of breaking through. When that happened, Italy would be under Allied control.

Outside, new supplies and equipment continued to arrive. Two new companies had been reassigned to join their forces. Captain Harding himself would lead their company when the time came for the attack.

But he reminded himself, it was up to him, the first lieutenant, to see everyone through.

# # #

The attack on Cisterna began early in the morning. Coming closer to the area, Anthony gazed at the demolished remnants of the town. In the last few days, the American planes and mortar divisions had bombarded this place to force a German surrender. The site was now another war-torn ground, razed to ruins.

They were now only two hundred yards away. It had taken them several days to get here. As they marched through the night, Anthony could hear artillery fire going off all around them from places not too far away. Skirmishes had broken out along the way between the German troops and the other regiments also marching toward Cisterna. His company, too, came upon patches of land and houses where they had encountered the slings of bullets. More than once, they had to stop and return fire until they drove the enemy away.

At the outskirts of Cisterna, they joined their battalion and encircled the town. The companies and their squads spread out. Methodically, they began to enter from their designated access points.

Almost immediately, gunfire ensued. The moment the Allies stepped into the town, bullets sprayed from all the windows above. Clustering close to their own companies, the Allied squads dove for cover and diverged according to plan to take over the city.

Behind the broken wall of a house leveled to the ground, Anthony looked up to gauge the positions from where the gunfire had come. To his dismay, the Germans were everywhere. They had entrenched themselves in each and every building. To take Cisterna, their own troops would have to chase the enemy out house by house.

Across the road, Captain Harding led Beck and their squads. The captain waved at the rest of them to move.

With his squad behind him, Anthony exchanged a look with Jonesy, who was leading another squad. In a split moment, each squad charged toward a separate house. Their movements triggered another storm of gunfire. Machine gun bullets splattered from the left and rifle bullets zipped from the right, interspersed with a chorus of pistol shots.

Crouching to avoid being hit, Anthony sprinted forward to the house his squad was targeting to attack. Once inside, they searched room to room. His heart was beating out of his chest. His every sense was heightened in alert. The enemy could shoot to kill at any second from a concealed spot. In stealth, they crept along. One moment, all was quiet. In the next, shouts of men and cracks of gunfire broke out. In the mad exchange of fire, their survival hinged on only luck and speed.

They had the speed, and fortunately today, luck too.

With one house subdued, they moved on to the next one, and the one after, losing some of their own men along the way but still pressing ahead. When they reached the end of the town and the Germans were pushed to the edge, he had lost half of his men. Jonesy's squad, having suffered even worse casualties, joined him. But their battalion was winning. More and more American troops arrived as German soldiers surrendered or fled. Droves of Third Division mortar vehicles were moving in.

At the end of the block, Ollie's squad had raided another house. They exited the door with three German soldiers captured under their guard. The gunfire on the streets behind their company slowed. Only scattered fighting still went on in the few blocks ahead.

"They can't hold much longer," Jonesy said.

"No." Anthony looked at the direction where there was still fighting. "Let's clear them out."

They came to the next street where, from behind a pile of rubble, Harding and his squad were attacking the Germans in a hollow, blown-down building. Positioning themselves at a vantage point, Anthony and his squad joined in, adding their gunfire to support their captain's offense. Outmatched, the Germans began to falter. Harding, however, would not let up. Anthony had never seen the captain fight with such ferocity. The captain fired round after round, chasing the enemy as they dispersed. Impressed, Anthony ran after him. Perhaps the captain did have the spirit to rally and fight like a leader when victory was on the line.

His faith did not last. Among the troops of retreating Germans, a figure appeared and made him gasp. The figure showed himself briefly as he ran from one fallen building to the next, then hid himself again behind an abandoned jeep. Anthony could recognize this man anywhere. Few men could exhibit such calm control while under pursuit.

Klaus.

From behind the jeep, Klaus returned fire as his troops continued their escape. His shots were quick and he never missed. The first shot struck one of Harding's men hiding behind the door of an empty building. The next shot brought down the soldier within inches to Harding's right.

"Bastard!" Harding shouted and unleashed another round, but the onslaught of bullets did nothing to deter Klaus. The captain's shots were as erratic as Klaus' were precise. Between the intervals of gunfire, the German major had slithered away and rejoined his men.

Harding resumed his pursuit. Anthony and the rest of their company followed.

Sprinting along, doubt began to pull Anthony back. This was wrong. The concentration of American gunfire was still behind them. Their company was breaking from formation and weakening their perimeter. They were running away from the town too fast, but their company's troops continued on because Harding was racing ahead. He had no way to stop them. He picked up his speed to catch the captain. He needed to stop him before they got too far and become separated from their own forces.

Klaus and his men slipped inside the last house at the end of the town. Most of the house had been torn down, leaving only four broken walls to serve as the enemy's shield. Harding jumped behind another pile of ruins, trying to locate Klaus. Anthony scooted next to him.

"I've got him cornered." Harding aimed his gun at the building.

While Harding focused on his target, Anthony scanned the area. In the field behind the town, the retreating German soldiers had resumed formation. Their reinforcements had moved up to secure their retreat. From the field, German squads launched multiple series of rockets, creating a fog of smoke as the speeding weapons shot across the air. The rockets' menacing whooshes and roars shattered his ears. He looked back at the town. Their own artillery units had not yet caught up.

Behind concealed spots, Jonesy, Beck, and their men fired at the escaping enemy to no avail. More German troops had moved closer to

Klaus and his men to cover them while they proceeded to withdraw from the exit at the back of the house. For a split second, Klaus' face appeared at the corner of a broken window. His expression was as serene as the last time Anthony had seen him.

At the sight of Klaus, Harding fired a rapid succession of bullets at the window. But crouching behind the ruins, he could not get the right angle. He muttered a string of curses and reloaded his gun. When he finished and aimed again, most of the German soldiers in the house had fled through the back. Klaus was the last to depart.

"No!" Harding yelled. "I won't let you get away this time." He rose up and aimed at his nemesis.

"Captain, no!" Anthony shouted, but it was too late. Klaus, as if he had anticipated Harding's move, turned around at just the right moment and fired a single shot. The shot hit Harding, pierced his right shoulder, and knocked him down to the ground.

"Captain!" Anthony rushed toward him. Harding scrunched his face in pain. Anthony slammed his hands over his wound.

"The sonofabitch…" Harding growled. Anthony looked back at the empty house. Klaus and his men were gone. American troops now approached from down the street, but they were too late.

A medic arrived, and Anthony stepped away. On the ground, Harding groaned like a hurt animal while the medic patched him up. The medic stabbed a needle into his arm to inject a dose of morphine. Still, Harding grumbled and grunted. Anthony could not help but feel sorry for him. The medic did not understand. Harding's pain was not the kind that morphine could assuage.

When the medic and another soldier carried Harding away, Jonesy came up to Anthony. "What do we do now, Lieutenant?"

Anthony gazed at the field beyond the town. Their battalion was forging ahead. The American soldiers had driven the Germans out of

Cisterna and were advancing toward the enemy. The thunder of their bazookas answered the German rockets' every roar.

"We go on." He picked up his gun. "We're going all the way to Rome."

To be continued —

Post an Amazon Review

If you enjoyed this book and
would like to post a review,
you can go to this Amazon link:

https://amzn.com/B01F5TMFNK

Thank you!!

Rose of Anzio

Book Four ~ Remembrance

is

Now Available on Amazon!

http://bit.ly/RoseofAnzio4

A sequel to Desire, Remembrance follows the love story of army nurse Tessa Graham and Lieutenant Anthony Ardley after the fiercely fought Battle of Anzio.

With the Allies' victory in Rome, Tessa and Anthony find respite to avow their love in the Eternal City. Their happiness is shattered when Tessa is unexpectedly transferred to Normandy. Now, Anthony must continue on with his troops to Southern France. In pursuit of the cunning Wehrmacht commander standing in the Allies' way of victory, he is caught in a deadly game of chase. How many men will he sacrifice in order to win?

Hopelessly in love with Tessa, Jesse Garland must decide whether to act on his feelings or to lose all possible chances with the only woman he has ever wanted. His unrequited love and his decision will alter their lives forever.

The final book of the Rose of Anzio series, this story concludes in an epic tale of love, loss, and redemption as the U.S. Army Third Division fights two of the toughest battles of WWII, the battles at the Vosges Mountains and the Colmar pocket.

Subscribe to
Alexa Kang's
Email List

Enjoyed my story? Sign up for my email list and receive news, artworks, and updates on the next book release:

http://bit.ly/RoAMailingList

Contact the Author

I would love to hear from you.
Contact me or follow me at:

Website:
www.alexakang.com

Facebook:
https://www.facebook.com/roseofanzio/

Twitter:
http://twitter.com/Alexa_Kang

Email:
alexa@alexakang.com

ABOUT THE AUTHOR

Alexa Kang's writing career began in 2014. She grew up in New York City and is a graduate of the University of Pennsylvania. She has travelled to more than 125 cities, and she loves to explore new places and different cultures. When not at work, she lives a secret second life as a novelist. She loves epic loves stories and hopes to bring you many more.

41742723R00194

Made in the USA
Middletown, DE
21 March 2017